CAST ANGELS
DOWN TO HELL

"A blood-drenched battle of wits and will . . . McMahon's story and prose are fired straight from the hip . . . Slambang!" (*Revolution No. 9*)
Philadelphia Inquirer

"Like John Grisham and James Patterson, McMahon excels at moving his plot along . . . *Blood Double* is all about movement–the only thing stationary is the reader, likely for the entire length of the book."
BookPage

"Intelligent, well-crafted entertainment . . . (with) deft characterizations . . . horrors and more await us in *To The Bone*."
Washington Post Book World

"*Revolution No. 9* spins the thrills and twists like a Tilt-a-Whirl–it's equal parts Stephen King and John Sandford, with a dash of ER thrown in for good measure."
Tim Dorsey

"McMahon . . . delivers his finest achievement to date with this beautifully written stand-alone set in contemporary Montana." (*Lone Creek*)
Publishers Weekly

CAST ANGELS
DOWN TO HELL

Neil McMahon

Quinotaur Press

Missoula, Montana

Almost thirty years ago, an aspiring author who'd had some minor literary success decided to try his hand at a horror novel. He'd never written a full-length book before, he only had a murky idea of how to go about it, and a lot of what he thought he knew turned out to be wrong. There was also another major wrinkle– the pesky need to make a living by some other means, which in his case took the form of swinging a hammer on construction jobs, trading that work for time to write.

As he got into the novel crafting process, he started comparing it to hiking in the mountains. You can stand on a peak and see a clearly marked trail leading down into the forested canyon below, then emerging on the other side and up to the next peak. At first, it looks like a straight shot from here to there. But what you can't see are the hazards hidden in those thick woods between the vista points–a bewildering network of false trails that branch off to nowhere, rockslides and brush-choked gullies, impassable deadfalls and rushing streams.

That labyrinthine trek through the prose wilderness ended up lasting several years and a couple of thousand discarded pages. Along the way, he adopted the pseudonym Daniel Rhodes, for reasons that seemed good at the time and seem better now.

Eventually, in 1987, the book was published as *Next, After Lucifer* (St. Martin's Press). A sequel, *Adversary*, followed in 1988, and a third horror novel, *Cast Angels Down To Hell* (originally titled *Kiss Of Death*) in 1990.

And then, quite suddenly, it was over. Daniel Rhodes was through with publishing (or more accurately, vice versa), those three books faded from print, and he faded with them.

Another decade passed before that writer re-surfaced as Neil McMahon (his/my real name) with a medical thriller titled *Twice Dying* (HarperCollins, 2000). My luck has been much better the second time around, with several more mainstream thrillers published to date. Writing them has kept me busy, and I haven't ventured into horror again (yet, anyway).

But those first three books, and the hope of getting them back in print, were never far from my mind.

The wait turned out to be a long one—roughly one-third of my life—but finally, thanks to a lot of help from terrific people, here they are.

"Look upon them again, I dare not," Sir Walter Scott said of his own earlier works—words that ring so true. As I've gone through mine this time, I've seen countless things I wish I'd done better. (It's a somewhat eerie experience, by the way—like meeting the ghost of who you were many years ago, and getting glimmers, or outright jolts, of how you thought and felt when you were that much younger.) I was sorely tempted to revise, but somehow, it just seemed right to leave them as they were. Except for very minor changes to improve formatting appearance, these are the original texts.

All in all, despite their flaws, I think they still hold up pretty well, and that there's more to them than might meet the eye—elements of religious thought, history, and perhaps most of all, a sense of how the supernatural is tied to human longing, promising the things we all desire but are unreachable to us by ordinary means.

In terms of what these books aim to do and how they go about it, I don't know of anything else quite like them.

I'll close by saying that I believe the story behind all this might be intriguing to readers interested in the writing process. So we've set up a website that's mainly devoted to discussing it in more detail—how the idea for the books first came, the thinking that underlies them (read: method to my madness), how they fared with reviews and the publishing world, my use of a pseudonym, and related issues such as this basic question about the horror genre: Why do so many millions of people love to be scared by stories like these?

Please visit us there at:

EvilAwakens.com

And also on Facebook at:

facebook.com/neilmcmahonbooks

This solemn profession having been publicly made each novice has assigned to him a several demon who is called Magistellus (a familiar). This familiar can assume either a male or a female shape; sometimes he appears as a full-grown man, sometimes as a satyr; and if it is a woman who has been received as a witch he generally assumes the form of a rank buck-goat.

Dr. Montague Summers, citing medieval demonologist Francesco-Maria Guazzo

That there exist such beings as are commonly called incubi or succubi and that they indulge their burning lusts, and that children, as it is freely acknowledged, can be born from them, is attested by the unimpeachable and unshaken witness of many men and women who have been filled with foul imaginings by them, and endured their lecherous assaults and lewdness.

William of Paris

Seeing it is so general a report, and so many aver it either from their own experience or from others, that are of indubitable honesty and credit, that the sylvans and fauns, commonly called incubi, have often injured women, desiring and acting carnally with them: and that certain devils whom the Gauls call Duses, do continually practise this uncleanness, and tempt others to it, which is affirmed by such persons, and with such confidence that it were impudence to deny it.

St. Augustine

PART ONE

June 1966

ONE

The village was like a dozen others they had passed since leaving Toulouse three hours before: a main row of shuttered masonry buildings with a few shops and *brasseries,* and a web of narrow streets fronted by cramped silent houses, branching off toward small farm plots in the distance. Not a living thing was moving in the afternoon sun. Donald Clermont slowed the rented Citröen and glanced at his daughter, thinking she might want to stop for a drink, or just to stretch her legs.

She had fallen asleep; and he realized that it was he who was seeking relief from the heat and the tension of driving. They had combined to give him a sullen headache, compounded perhaps by a second glass of chilled Côtes du Roussillon at lunch.

But the discomfort was minor: certainly not grounds for waking Lisa. He continued through the town, and in another minute reached the outskirts. He was beginning to accelerate onto the highway when he saw the side road angling north and east into the massif of the Cevennes.

The idea of taking the detour came from nowhere; it did not fit at all with their plans. But he hesitated, staring at the distant dark mountain peaks: trying, through the cloudy ache in his head, to assess the situation.

With Lisa, he had arrived in Paris three weeks ago, on a vacation designed to combine his business, wine-making, with the pleasure of introducing her to Europe. But the journey south had become a tug of war; she was bored equally by the vineyards of Bordeaux and by his attempts to impress her with the rich history of France, where his grandfather had made wine before emigrating to California. Only the Côte d'Azur and its beaches inter-ested her, and she had grown increasingly impatient to get there. He, in turn, envisioned with dread the crowds, sweltering climate, and hours of dutifully lying in the sun or lounging in cafés.

He had been reminding himself frequently of what it was like to be sixteen. Reminding himself, too, that the vacation was in truth a sort of buy-off, an attempt to soften the fact that Lisa's mother was no longer living with them. He sensed, with a mixture of gloom and perplexity, that he was not doing a very good job of accustoming either Lisa or himself to the loss.

The side road was unmarked; he lingered, weighing sure and quick progress toward the Côte d'Azur against the longer, slower, and possibly even dead-end route to the left–together with Lisa's displeasure when she dis-covered what he had done. A glance in the rearview mirror showed a small red sports car gaining rapidly. This day, like every other since he had taken the Citröen's wheel, traffic had consisted largely of horn-honking speeders who did not hesitate to pass on the blindest of curves, secure in the faith that oncoming vehicles would simply move over, that even a narrow two-lane road could be stretched to three. Clermont did not share this certainty, and his head throbbed each time his knuckles tightened around the wheel in another tense situation.

The sports car swelled like a furious red hornet. The peace and coolness of the mountains beckoned. Clermont raised his eyes heavenward, then hooked the wheel left and accelerated gently, hoping Lisa would not awaken.

In the next half hour, it almost seemed that they had crossed a line into a magical kingdom. The rolling vineyards and carefully groomed fields of the coastal foothills began to give way to the shade and scent of pines. Traffic dwindled and dwellings grew sparser until both seemed on the verge of disappearing altogether. The road rose steeply, twisting through large rock formations, passing an occasional spring seeping down a stony face. The air through the car windows, unbelievably, grew cool.

Eventually, the tightening turns brought Lisa out of her slumber. She sat up, pushing back her hair from her forehead, looking confused. In faded cut-off jeans and a T-shirt touting a band called the Grateful Dead, she was very much a teenager; yet he was pierced by her resemblance to her mother. Just beginning to move from adolescent awkwardness to fulfilling her promise of dark blond beauty, she possessed the same tawny skin and litheness; and her face showed the same expressions, sometimes haughty with awareness of her developing power, sometimes frightened of it, that had tormented. and thrilled Clermont during his courtship, twenty years before.

3

Only now was he beginning to realize how much he still loved his wife.

"How you feeling, baby?" he asked.

She shook her head groggily. "Thirsty." Then, after a pause: "Where are we?"

"On the way to Nîmes," he said. "A little northwest of Montpellier. There's Cokes in the cooler."

She opened one of the small French bottles of Coca-Cola and surveyed the countryside, her eyes beginning to clear.

After a moment, she said, "We're not on the main road any more, are we."

"I thought this would be a nicer drive," he said carefully. "Looks like I was right. Don't you think?"

"Oh, Daddy, where are we going *now?*"

He winced, but said firmly, "Nîmes, honey, like we decided. This really isn't out of our way. We just swing a little north and over, instead of straight east and up." When she did not reply, he added, "The heat and traffic were terrible down there. My head was killing me."

The bid for sympathy did not succeed. She hugged her knees to her chest and sipped the Coke, face gone sulky. He exhaled, guilty in the knowledge that in truth, he had no idea where the road might go, and he considered turning back. But the idea alone wearied him, and he consoled himself with the time-honored parental thought that it was not necessarily good for her to get her way: that some day she would thank him for seeing to it that she had not gone through France with blinders on. He began to phrase a commentary on the Pont du Gard, awaiting them at Nîmes: the massive aqueduct still intact

4

after almost two thousand years, a monument to the genius and might of Rome.

Instead, he kept silent—some variation of the same speech had grown all too familiar to both of them over the past days—and soon, he sensed with relief that her annoyance was yielding to interest in their surroundings.

"Sort of like the Sierras, huh," he said, playing on her love of camping trips they had taken in Yosemite and Kings Canyon.

"The mountains aren't as high," she said, but both of them understood it was a quibble. He started to relax, and tried not to think about the memories his words had conjured up, of tramping through the High Sierra with Charlotte and Lisa as a little girl, in the happy, early days of marriage.

The road wound on for a time, passing occasional clusters of forsaken-looking houses that could hardly be called hamlets, then emerged onto a high plateau that showed nothing but scrub vegetation and rock for miles. At its end, the mountains rose again, beyond a frail one-lane bridge over a heart-stoppingly deep gorge. Clermont drove slowly, and paused in the middle to gaze at the slender silver torrent that rushed through the gorge's bottom. Its banks were lined with trees that looked like poplars, leaves flickering gold-green in the breeze. The water's spray cast small ephemeral rainbows in the sunlight.

Just as they were coming to the bridge's far end, while Lisa was still leaning out the window, entranced by the beauty below, he saw the ruin.

At first his gaze passed over it, mistaking it for a crag in the rocky cliffs ahead. But a second look left no doubt. The massive gray stones were hand-hewn, in the shape of crumbling arches.

During previous visits to Europe, his interest in ruins had been slight. But this time, a fascination had awakened; and though he tried to justify it as a facet of Lisa's education, he had admitted at last that the ancient buildings interested him morbidly because their isolation and decay seemed to reflect the wreckage of his marriage.

He glanced at his watch. It was just five. He still had no clear idea of where they were, but he was starting to suspect that they were not going to make Nîmes by nightfall. Fifteen minutes of wandering through history would hardly make a difference.

"Let's stop and take a break," he said. "I could stand to pee."

Lisa nodded uncertainly. "Are we coming to a town?"

"Not that I can tell. But I see some friendly bushes."

There was a turnout at the base of the cliffs. He parked, and as they stood beside the car and stretched, his eyes found a narrow, disused-looking trail twisting uphill toward where he had spotted the ruin.

"Bet we'd get a great view from up there," he said.

Lisa's gaze followed his pointing finger, and the corners of her mouth turned down. When she faced him again, her head was cocked to one side and her fists were on her hips.

"Are we ever going to get to the Riviera? Really?"

He raised his eyebrows and framed his hands around an imaginary crystal ball.

"I see beaches in your very near future," he intoned. She giggled, shaking her head in exasperation, but then allowed him to take her hand and lead her up the path.

It was overgrown with weeds—clearly, the ruin was not much of an attraction—and steep. By the time they reached the top, both were panting. Not much was left of the original structure, he saw with disappointment: a couple of arches and a few other crumbling sections of wall. He guessed that it had been a small church or abbey, probably not very important even in its heyday, and like countless other old buildings in Europe, long since devoid of interest to any living soul.

They walked across the empty courtyard to the western edge. From there, they looked down into the lovely river gorge, and over the miles of plateau and mountains they had just traversed. The hamlets and small farms showed as sprinklings of dollhouse-sized buildings. The sky was a pure pale blue shot through with translucent light, a color he had never seen anywhere but the south of France. With the bright yellows and violets of' wildflowers and deep blue-greens of the mountains, the overall effect was of a masterful impressionist painting.

"Worth it?" he asked.

She nodded, and lingered another minute. Then she said, with a recently acquired ladylike air that again reminded him maddeningly of her mother:

"If you'll *excuse* me"—and stalked off toward the scrubby forest. He moved in the other direction to drain his own bladder.

As he stood, he had the sudden sense of seeing his reflection mirrored in the rock he faced: a pleasant but unremarkable looking man—medium size and build, balding slightly—with a pleasant but unremarkable life.

Pleasant and unremarkable, at least, until the day four months earlier when Charlotte had announced her intention to leave.

He zipped up, glancing down at his apparel: neatly pressed slacks, button-down Oxford cloth shirt, Bass moccasins. The long-haired, tie-dyed, ragged fashions of San Francisco and Berkeley, and the accompanying life-styles, had not yet penetrated to the sedate Sonoma wine country.

But Charlotte had gone to them.

Perhaps, he had thought many times, she was right: at the age of thirty-nine, he was stodgy, with the mentality of an old man. Perhaps an outward change would have brought about an inward one. But at heart he was convinced that the truth lay nearer the reverse: that those who were most flamboyant outwardly were compensating for a lack of inner resources. Endless hours of excruciating self-examination over the past months had assured him that if nothing else, he was a conscientious businessman and a loving husband and father, that he had done well the things he considered truly important.

In short, he liked himself; and dull though he might seem, agonized though he was by losing Charlotte, he had refused to go through the pathetic motions of trying to adopt styles of appearance and behavior that simply were not his, in the desperate hope of pleasing her. It was difficult enough bearing the scandal, among his equally stodgy colleagues in the wine industry, of a younger, beautiful wife who had "dropped out" to be a hippie.

Whose newfound contempt for the middle classes had not prevented her from demanding a full half of his estate in the settlement.

Whose bearded, wild-haired, dope-smoking, bell-bottom sporting boyfriend was known as "Wayout."

Clermont thought of him as Furbrain.

The sun was falling toward the cliffs to the west; the afternoon was making the imperceptible passage into evening. He paused for a final look across the landscape before turning, a bit reluctantly, to continue the journey to the Côte d'Azur.

And saw, perhaps thirty yards below him, a small, energetic-looking Frenchman making his way up the slope.

"*Bon après-midi,* monsieur," the little man called "*Ça va?*"

Clermont's surprise amounted almost to shock; the site had seemed so remote that the idea of encountering another human had never entered his mind. But in the Old World, he reminded himself, there were precious few unpopulated places. He mustered a cheerful face and answered:

"*Oui, ça va bien. Et vous?*"

"*Pas mal, pas mal,*" the little man wheezed. His progress up the hill was vaguely insectlike, a scurrying zigzag that changed direction abruptly and was aston-ishingly rapid. Clermont wondered suddenly if he and Lisa had trespassed, and that the Frenchman's seeming cordiality was a prelude to a lecture the likes of which he had suffered more than once, featuring the ignorance and vile manners of Americans.

But when the newcomer arrived, it seemed clear that his good humor was genuine. He was of indeterminate middle age, with a sharp face and sparkling eyes of a strange sea green. Despite the heat, he wore a beret and wool jacket; along with heavy brogans, they suggested that he was a farmer or perhaps a shepherd, although his continually gesturing hands were small, soft—even vaguely feminine.

"A beautiful view, is it not?" he said, sweeping his arm theatrically to include the countryside below. The gesture was somehow proprietary, as if he owned the world.

"Truly," Clermont said. Though the Frenchman's speech carried the heavy accent of Languedoc, Clermont had spent his childhood among the Provencal and Italian vineyard workers imported to California by his grandfather, in the days before the labor force had become predominantly Mexican; the dialect came to him without difficulty.

"You live nearby?" he asked.

"Not far," the little man agreed. "And yourself?"

"We're American," Clermont said, and turned to look for Lisa. She was standing across the courtyard, watching him with clear exasperation. When she caught his gaze, she nodded pointedly toward the car, then started walking in that direction. He sighed inwardly, guilty again. She understood little French, and he could hardly blame her for her disinterest in listening to her father jabber with a stranger in an unknown tongue.

When he turned back, he saw that the Frenchman was watching her too.

"My daughter," Clermont said. The words came out sounding defensive; why, he was not sure.

The Frenchman's' eyebrows lifted in appreciation. "A young beauty," he murmured. Then: "If I may inquire, monsieur, do you come on business? Visitors to Saint-Fabrisse, you see, are quite rare."

Saint-Fabrisse, Clermont thought. So that is where we are. "No, by chance."

The Frenchman smiled slightly. "No one comes here by chance."

Clermont glanced at him, uncertain that he had understood correctly. But the Frenchman offered no explanation: only continued to gaze inquiringly.

"We're on our way to Nîmes," Clermont said. "This road will take us there?"

"Ah, yes," the Frenchman said, nodding vigorously. His eyes were slightly reproachful, as if Clermont had insulted him by suggesting that he lived near a road that went nowhere. "In not too long a time. Perhaps fifty kilomètres past the village, it joins with a main road."

"And the village is nearby?"

"Just beyond these cliffs. In old times, it was a fief of this abbey in which we stand."

He had been correct, then, in his surmise. He gestured at the desolation around them.

"I take it that the good monks of Saint-Fabrisse fell on hard times."

"As well they should have," came the answer, with sudden, surprising fierceness. "They pandered to the Inquisition, monsieur. A terrible, bloody time for the poor people of this region."

Clermont's grasp of European history was general rather than detailed. He knew that endless wars had ravaged the countrysides from early civilization into the present century.

But the Inquisition had occupied itself chiefly with combating heresy. Through Toulouse and the whole of Languedoc, there was evidence everywhere of the Albigensians, perhaps the greatest threat the Roman Church had faced between its inception and the Reformation. The Church's merciless thirteenth century crusade had all but wiped them out, ravaging southern France in the process. Perhaps survivors had found their way to the then-remote, wild Cévennes—only to be followed by the ever-patient Inquisition and weeded out, slowly but surely, with fire and iron.

"*Les Albigeois?*" he asked.

The Frenchman shrugged in partial assent. "*Il y en avait, oui.* There were some. But mainly, *les sorcières.*"

It took Clermont a moment to comprehend the term: witches.

He had been about to politely end the conversation. He did not want to jeopardize the truce that had sprung up with Lisa; it was time to get back on the road, to hurry her off to the promised land of sunlight and happiness.

But the Frenchman was still speaking, with the same angry vehemence.

"Dozens burned, monsieur, at this very spot," he declared. His pointing finger indicated the barren rocky field below the abbey's entrance. "That monster De Lancre, the judge who was himself a devil, set up his tribunal here. With monks, he commenced his reign of terror." He turned and spat.

"Are you telling me," Clermont said, half-amused in spite of the horror of what he had just heard, "people actually took witchcraft seriously around here?"

The Frenchman's expression went appraising, and he studied Clermont's face. Then he seemed to make up his mind.

"If monsieur will come with me."

Clermont hesitated, thinking again of Lisa, but his guide was already striding briskly toward the southern edge of the ruin.

From there, the view of the cliffs above was unobstructed. The Frenchman pointed at a peculiar rock formation, perhaps a quarter mile from where they stood—about as much farther as the abbey was from the road. Only the tops of a few great upright stones could be seen; whatever else there might have been was hidden in a forested glade where the cliffs leveled off. Clermont had glanced up there earlier and noticed nothing, but looking now, he realized that the visible stones did not appear to be part of any natural formation. They seemed instead to have been deliberately planted there.

"*Les Gaulois anciens,*" the Frenchman said. "That was a site sacred to them. There is a spring among those stones. They built a temple and worshipped a goddess, whom they believed descended there to bathe.

"Then the Christians came. In forcing the people to worship their god instead, they destroyed the temple and built this church. They even stole the water from the sacred spring, diverting it down here for the use of the monks.

"But like all such coercion, monsieur, it was doomed. That Christian god was seen as the god of the oppressors, as a usurper. The people rebelled against him, continuing to worship instead their goddess on her ancient sacred site: among those very stones, fittingly, that the Christians had pulled down. The monks were overlords of the peasants by day, but by night, when the cries of the revelers reached their ears, they cowered in their abbey, too terrified to interfere.

"Until at last they called in the Inquisition, and the goddess's followers were branded as witches. The petty minds of such men lumped together under that label all who dared to believe differently than themselves, and they punished such people indiscriminately, whether or not they were guilty of any true crime."

The breeze around them had paused; they seemed to be standing in a hushed spot of warm, dead air.

"Does she have a name?" Clermont said, realizing that like his guide, he had referred to her in the present tense. "That goddess?"

"She has many names," the Frenchman said quietly. "And three aspects. By day, she hunts in the forests. By night, she guides the moon. In these roles, she is beautiful, chaste, and most often, benevolent to men.

"But when the moon is dark, she reigns as queen of hell." He turned his gaze on Clermont, steady and level.

"It is thus, monsieur, that she is to be feared. Like any great being, she rewards those who serve her—and punishes without mercy those who have brought her harm. You may be assured that when those Inquisitors who tormented her followers arrived at her abode, she was awaiting them."

Absurd though the words sounded, there was no doubt of the Frenchman's seriousness. Clermont realized with shamed amusement that goose bumps had risen on his arms.

He had been raised Catholic, and although his church attendance had dwindled to the few obligatory appearances per year, he had never questioned the basic tenets of his faith; his own understanding of the nature of pagan deities was quite different from what the Frenchman seemed to suggest. But while he did not want to enter into a theological argument, he could not resist a question.

"And those who worshipped her—did she truly reward them?"

If there was a hint of irony in his voice, his guide did not seem to detect it. He shrugged.

"It is said that those who served her well prospered in their worldly affairs, and that if they became victims of persecution, their payment would come in the next life. Whether or not this last is true, only they themselves know. Records tell us that when they went to the stake, all of them shrieked alike."

Then he glanced at Clermont sidelong, almost coquettishly, and again there seemed a touch of the feminine about him.

"But records tell us too of the goddess's special gift to those who joined her worship: a spirit"—he added a word that sounded like *dewze*—"which would take the shape of whatever lover one most desired. Do you not agree, monsieur, that a man, or a woman too, would go to extraordinary lengths to obtain such pleasure?

"Imagine the lives of those people, four or five centuries ago: hemmed into a tiny village of some few dozen families, where marriage took place only for reasons of property. One was more than likely to be tied for life to an ugly or ill-natured mate, or to no mate at all. There were no journeys to pleasant places, no motion pictures or even books for diversion: only endless labor, and oppression and disease from which there was no protection. Life was too often a hellish prison. In such a situation, monsieur, what do you think you would give for a lover who embodied all that you desired, who appeared at your bidding, and who brought pleasure beyond your power to imagine?"

After several months of celibacy, and several years before that of a sex life that had depended increasingly on Charlotte's moods, Clermont admitted sardonically that the idea, at least on its surface, was quite attractive.

A shame the *dewze* isn't still around, he started to say.

But the Frenchman had stooped, and with his forefinger, was scratching an odd-looking design into the dirt: a crescent, like a quarter moon, pierced by what might have been a dagger.

"This mark," he said, "was the means by which the novices signified their submission to their new mistress.

16

They drew it in their own blood, for even spirits grow hungry.

"If you climb to those stones, monsieur, you may still see such marks, left from the days when she was in her glory. Few come here nowadays, but once, there were many. How are we to explain that if there was no reward? You seem a man of the world, monsieur. Surely you will agree that no one does anything for nothing."

Clermont's gaze rose again to the ancient temple. So: not only a rumor of witchcraft, but tangible proof. He gauged the difficulty of the climb. It would take perhaps ten minutes, with a bit of scrambling through brush. The Frenchman was watching him, the fey expression back on his face.

Abruptly, the thought came to Clermont that this was all an elaborate joke at his expense, that the object was to send the gullible American to look for the blood marks of witches, a story to be told amid much laughter at the village tavern–that even his guide's seeming vehemence was only a well-practiced part of the jape.

Then an even more outrageous thought occurred: was the little man making a pass at him? Trying to get him alone in the bushes, as it were? Clermont considered the flirtatious looks, the oddly feminine hands, and the way the conversation had turned almost immediately to sex.

He smiled coldly. "Very interesting," he said, "but I'm afraid I haven't got time. I'm keeping my daughter waiting as it is." He nodded toward where Lisa was no doubt stewing in a rising pique. "Thanks for the information." As he started across the courtyard, he half-expected his guide to follow and importune him.

But the Frenchman did not move. "People forget, and come to disbelieve," he said quietly. "What the Inquisition began with terror, the modern world has finished through neglect.

"But spirits remain in spite of what people think. *Au 'voir,* monsieur."

"*Au 'voir,*" Clermont said, waving without looking back.

He hurried down the trail, slipping on the loose dirt. Lisa was standing beside the car, arms folded, back to him.

"Sorry, honey," he said, touching her arm. "The man had some interesting things to say." She neither replied nor looked at him.

He stepped away, angry at first—at the Frenchman, at Lisa, at Charlotte, at all the pressures that seemed to have descended unjustly on his shoulders—and then, simply exhausted.

The car seats were hot. A fly buzzed with idiot persistence against the rear window. He drove slowly, unable to countenance the thought of traveling fifty more kilometers to a highway, and then an unspecified distance farther, in the main road's hellish traffic, to Nîmes. He wanted a stiff drink and dinner, soon. A glance at Lisa told. him that a peace offering was in order.

"I'll make you a deal," he said. "Let's stop, the first decent place we find. Have a bath and dinner and a good night's sleep, and we'll drive straight to Cannes to-morrow."

For half a minute, she acted as if she had not heard. Then she swiveled in the seat and said:

"No more lectures? No more ruins?"

"Promise," he said. He held out his hand. She took it and gave it several exaggerated pumps. He smiled, and with the tension broken, relaxed back into the seat.

It soon became clear that the Frenchman had been correct about at least one thing: the village of Saint-Fabrisse was hardly more than a mile from the abbey. Near its center, across from the courthouse square, a sign announced the Hôtel du Coq d'Or. The building was handsome, a solid, two-story structure of weathered masonry, with dark wood beams exposed in a vaguely Tudor style.

He pulled the Citröen over. Together, he and Lisa gazed into the street-level windows. Three or four people were gathered at a bar, while tables were set for dining in the next room.

"Looks clean," he said; and, thinking again of the drive that lay before him if Lisa did not approve, added, "There might not be another place for an hour or more."

"Just as long as there's no bedbugs," she said, referring to an unfortunate experience in Poitiers the previous week, when she had learned that the insects were more than a figure of speech.

"I'll make them guarantee it in writing," he said, relieved, and they walked into the Coq d'Or to negotiate the passage of the night.

TWO

The hotel was not only clean and reasonably priced, but miraculously even had reliable plumbing. Clermont took adjoining rooms with a bath between them, on the second floor, overlooking the village square. By dinner time, both of their moods had improved considerably, Lisa's from a soak in the tub, his from the goodly measure of Johnnie Walker he had sipped, sitting with his feet up, gazing vacantly out at the wooded slopes of the Cévennes.

The dinner, too, was better than he had allowed himself to expect: pâté, escargots drenched in garlicky butter, chicken with a savory mushroom sauce, salad vinaigrette, and a cheese tray which included an unusually tart *fromage bleu,* among his favorite delicacies. He chose a bottle of robust Fitou, allowing Lisa a judicious portion.

She had put up her hair and changed to a powder blue summer dress, making her look like a young woman rather than a girl; their conversation was quiet and relaxed; the fading light through the windows gave the wine glasses a deep rich glow, adding an intimate and even romantic air. Clermont wondered if he was only imagining raised eyebrows on the part of the hotel staff at the sight of the American traveling with his "daughter." If so, he decided, the governing emotion was envy; and he nodded expansively at the several other diners as they entered and left.

Afterwards, Lisa retired to her room. She was deeply engrossed in *The Lord of the Rings,* a work Clermont had not read but was nonetheless a fan of because it had occupied many of her evenings throughout the trip, easing the strain of their constant togetherness. He had brought books of his own, intending to inform his journey through France by rereading Fitzgerald and Hemingway.

But the nineteen-twenties seemed further removed in time even than the ruins he had taken to exploring; nor was this the right point in his life for stories of hopeless love. He had not slept a night through since Charlotte had left; he had never imagined he could miss so much her presence, her warmth—even just the sound of her breathing.

He considered working on the notes he had taken during their stops in Bordeaux; but trying to inventory the sapling vines he intended to import, or reviewing a process for controlling the acid content of cabernet as it aged, could not capture his attention. After standing for some moments with the unopened notebook in his hand, he quietly replaced it in his suitcase and walked downstairs, with the vague notion of finding a bistro and drinking a cognac.

The evening was fine, the air clear, with an almost autumnal crispness. Perhaps an hour of daylight remained. He strolled slowly at first, looking in the windows of the few shops, then examining the architecture of the *mairie,* the village hall. But it quickly became clear that there was nothing of much interest. The stores were closed, the streets deserted, the buildings all too similar to those in hundreds of other towns in France. A glance in the window of the single *brasserie* he passed showed three men and the bartender gathered in the idle conversation of those who had known each other for long; intruding would only make him feel more the outsider. Whether Saint-Fabrisse's dullness stemmed from a lack of tourist traffic or vice versa, he did not know or care, but he found himself agreeing with Lisa about this much: he had had enough of lonely restless nights in torpid villages.

He stopped, about to retreat to the hotel to try to read himself to sleep, when his gaze rose to the western cliffs, where lay the ruined abbey. A switchback trail leading that direction from Saint-Fabrisse was clearly visible–probably the remnant of an old road connecting abbey and fief. The afternoon's strange conversation with his unsolicited guide came back into his mind.

Although his skepticism remained firm, Clermont was suddenly less certain that mockery had been intended. He remembered the Frenchman's earnestness, his undoubtedly genuine anger at the Inquisition–and his calm but striking words at the end: *People forget, and come to disbelieve. But spirits remain in spite of what people think.*

Were there really marks such as the ones he had described? Drawn, by worshippers of a pagan goddess, in their own blood?

It was precisely the outlandishness of such a notion that made it intriguing: that people had believed enough in this madness to practice it—even at risk of the persecutions many of them had endured.

What do you think you would give for a lover who embodied all that you desired, who appeared at your bidding, and who brought pleasure beyond your power to imagine?

Absurd, of course. He had a vague memory of reading in some book or article, perhaps in college, that the so-called witches' sabbats were mainly the invention of superstition, enhanced by drugs, alcohol, and fevered imaginations.

But still, to actually stand on a site where such delirium had taken place—to see with his own eyes the blood marks painted by credulous peasants in the hopes of winning the favor of their dark goddess, and the demon lover she promised to send them—

Would it not be worth a little effort to investigate?

He gauged the distance to the cliff tops. The walk should take no more than twenty or twenty-five minutes; there was ample time for him to get there, explore, and return by nightfall. At this hour, the site of the old temple would be deserted: there would be no witnesses to his gullibility, if that was all it turned out to be. And he certainly had nothing better to do.

At worst, it would make a good story for his return to California, a piquant addition to the recounting of an otherwise dull journey. He glanced at his watch. It was just after eight. He hesitated a moment longer, then strode toward the cliffs.

He estimated correctly both the trail's destination and the time it would take to get there; it was just eight-thirty when he reached the clifftops and looked down to see the abbey, perhaps a half-mile below. It took him a moment to spot the temple in the fading light, but then he saw the little glade with its upright sentinel stones. Though the main path continued on to the ruin, a faint line that might have been a game trail wound down the few hundred yards to the glade. The going was easy, and in another couple of minutes he was standing in a small natural amphitheater.

There were several of the upright stones, about his own height, arranged in a rough circle some twenty yards in diameter. Other long slabs that lay nearby might have once stood among them, then been toppled during the temple's destruction by the zealous Christians.

And, as the Frenchman had said, a weeping rock face nearby gave evidence of a spring. *They built a temple and worshipped a goddess, whom they believed descended there to bathe.* The hollow beneath would have collected water for her chaste and solitary baths—until the monks of Saint-Fabrisse had appropriated it for themselves.

It was then that Clermont realized that his question as to her name had never been answered: Diana, presumably, or her Celtic equivalent. Although decades had passed since he had read mythology, he remembered that she was the goddess of the hunt, and that forest glades,

24

preferably with pools, had been her preferred haunts. Was there not a legend of an unfortunate young hunter who had chanced upon her bathing and, too mesmerized by her nude beauty to conceal himself, incurred her wrath in some terrible form? He could not quite remember the rest of the story.

But he remembered suddenly another of the Frenchman's statements: *When the moon is dark, she reigns as queen of hell. It is thus, monsieur, that she is to be feared.* Automatically, his gaze scanned the horizon. The silvery orb would have been visible even though the sky was still light, even as a sliver, but there was no trace. Perhaps it was rising behind the cliffs to the east—but he seemed to remember that it had been waning when they were in Bordeaux a week or ten days ago. Unease touched him, and though he scoffed immediately at his own suscep-tibility, he could not keep from glancing around. *Like any great being, she rewards those who serve her—and punishes without mercy those who have brought her harm.* The Inquisitors who had persecuted her followers, if the Frenchman were to be believed; perhaps even the monks who purloined her sacred water. Who else might have fallen into that unhappy category, to have some dreadful retribution waiting in the life to come?

The lovely trill of a nightingale stood out from the muted twittering of the evening birds, bringing his attention back to his surroundings, making him realize how thoroughly his few minutes' walk had removed him from all traces of modern civilization. He had been entertaining thoughts worthy of a primitive.

25

But even as he tried to recover his skepticism, a sense of mystery, even of awe, overpowered him to the extent of prickling his nape. At such a time and place, it was not difficult to understand how the ancient races had peopled their landscapes with spiritual beings. In truth, he could almost imagine the glade full of unseen presences, watching him with keen interest; and for seconds or minutes he stood unmoving, both frightened and exhilarated at the fancy.

He had to shake his head to break out of it, and it took him a moment longer to remember the ostensible reason for his visit: to examine the stones for the rumored marks. What daylight remained was disappearing fast. He walked to the nearest column.

At first his gaze found nothing. His sardonicism was gaining, when he realized that if any of the marks had survived the ravages of weather and time, they would be in sheltered spots. He moved to a tilted stone, roughly diamond-shaped, whose downward face was protected by the cliff.

And yes, this one did seem to have several dark patterns near its base, not unlike the markings of a snake. Though crude and irregular, they were similar to each other in shape. He knelt and leaned close.

After a moment, he rocked back on his heels, raising his face to the darkening sky. There was no doubt about it. The designs were not lichens or natural discolorations. They had been deliberately, even painstakingly, etched onto the rock face with paint, or ink—or blood. And while some were clearer than others, there was no doubt either that they were intended to approximate the crescent insignia the Frenchman had scratched in the dirt.

That much, then, was true. And the rest? Were they really a facet of something as bizarre as a worship that amounted to witchcraft, whatever the fine theological distinctions might be: that involved a goddess, magic, demon lovers? He supposed they could have been made for a different purpose, or even as pranks. But he did not think so. Their obvious age and seclusion spoke to their authenticity.

Whatever had actually happened in such goings-on, it seemed clear that the worshippers had believed.

And suddenly, a picture formed in his mind with startling clarity. It was as if could see the ancient revelers around him, performing their secret moonlit ceremonies, falling to the ground to copulate with bestial fury, imagining that their dark goddess watched over them.

The vision of the panting, writhing bodies faded. He was alone again, a lonely man in a lonely forest in a land far from his home. The sky had gone the final deep luminescent blue before full night. The first sprinklings of stars were showing. As he listened, it seemed that the crickets' song had taken on a sorrowing tone, and the nightingale's trill had become a lament. Without warning, his loneliness hardened into chilling despair. His world had become a desert, a bleak and empty city–a ruin–whose only light was his daughter. But much as he loved her, that fatherly love could not fill the void of his own adult needs. For the first time, he understood that everything he had undertaken as a man–his child, his work, his life itself–had been dependent on the support

27

of a mate. Without her, it seemed as purposeless as the laboring of a rat on a treadmill.

Was this the emotion that had driven the peasants of centuries before to seek even such patently mad means to lighten their burdens?

His feeling changed abruptly to defiance, the cold fury to rebel against all the forces responsible for his impotent anger and unhappiness. It was a passion he had never known before, intoxicating and giddy. Yes, he could see how those worshippers of old had come to live for such moments, founded though they were on fancy. A quick slice of the knife, the pain adding another sinister thrill; solemnly painting your vital essence on a rock; and the reward of freedom, at least in your mind, from all the strictures that had hemmed you in throughout your life.

Heightened by the very real pleasure of unrestrained revels with a partner who, though in truth only another lusty peasant, was made by your imagination more than human.

And as if that tumult of emotion triggered a retreat into the mind of an ancestor who might have walked these very cliffs and taken part in the delirium he had envisioned, as if a thousand such entities were clustered around him, whispering, tugging, urging him to throw off his civilized veneer and yield to the primal man within, Clermont found his penknife in his hand.

He put the point against the soft flesh of his forearm, pressing lightly, then harder. The pricking turned to pain, hot but bearable: strangely, almost pleasant. Hardly aware of what he was doing, he pressed deeper yet, drawing the blade in a two-inch slice. Blood trickled warm and dark down his wrist. He crouched at the column's base, and with his forefinger, painted a small, neat reproduction of the mark.

When he stood, he was panting, and he took a dizzy step back to keep his balance. The world began to come clear, as if he had gotten instantly drunk and as quickly sober again. He looked ruefully at his arm, hardly able to believe what he had just done.

"I suppose now I've joined the ranks," he said aloud, realizing it was a feeble attempt to cover his feeling of foolishness.

But ranks of what, came the question. Rebels? Pagans?

Believers?

With his handkerchief, he cleaned away the blood as well as he could, and shoved the damp wad in his pocket.

It was night now. The moon had not materialized, and when he stepped from the clearing into the woods, darkness closed over him. After stumbling several times, Clermont paused to let his eyes adjust. He had spent his share of time in the forests of the American West without ever finding them sinister—without its ever occurring to him. But here in this dark Old World thicket, surrounded by the gnarled and twisted shapes of unknown trees, his earlier sense of awe began to come upon him again.

Or was it unease—a sense of being watched by those same unseen presences, who had guarded this spot for an untold length of time, who had jealously defended their territory against the first invasions of humankind, until men had learned to propitiate them—often, with blood? *Even spirits grow hungry.*

Were those spirits dormant—or lying in wait?

When he could make out the path as a lessening of the blackness through the woods, he began to walk again—only to become suddenly aware that silence had fallen around him; both crickets and birds were stilled.

It was because of the sounds of his passing, he told himself. But the sense of presence was growing, and becoming increasingly malign. He realized that his jaw was tight, his hands stiff: that he was restraining himself from breaking into a run.

The trees seemed to converge across the path; again and again he found himself almost blundering into them, until he raised his forearms in front of his face to hold off the whipping branches. Was he still on the path? Had he mistaken for it a false trail that would peter out and leave him thrashing helplessly till dawn?

He paused again, panting. The dim shapes of the branches looked like clutching fingers, gleefully poised to strike. The menace around him was rising like a wave, with a force that lifted the hairs on his arms, that pulled his lips back taut in a grin of terror. He whirled, fists clenched, desperate to pinpoint some tangible source of threat—

A dark cluster of branches exploded into a thundering mass, coming straight at his face, screeching. His own answering yell was instant, involuntary, torn from his throat, and he flailed his arms blindly.

Then it was gone. For seconds, he remained motionless, half-crouched, arms protecting his head, while his brain registered what his fingers had touched.

Feathers. He had spooked an owl.

Slowly, he exhaled, then straightened. Although he was still shaking, the fear was gone; he even managed a wry smile at the thought that the poor bird, probably wakened by his blundering about, had undoubtedly been far more frightened of him than he of it.

Perhaps because of adrenaline, his vision seemed to improve. He followed the trail without difficulty through the remainder of the woods. Bird song and the rustling of small animals resumed. As if his encounter with the owl had been a catharsis, a release from the growing terror of the superstitious primal man within him, that man had become free to enjoy the sense of night: another atavistic emotion lurking in his subconscious, one that emerged only when the far more powerful fear and warning systems were assured that all was safe.

He reached the far side of the cliffs and came into open country, striding briskly toward the lights of Saint-Fabrisse; and absurd though it was, he felt as if he had ingested a subtle but heady drug that set him apart from the dull world of ordinary men.

He went straight to his room. A glance next door showed Lisa's light still on, but her book was collapsed on her chest and her face turned to the side amid the mass of tousled blond hair. He tiptoed across the floor, kissed the top of her head, and put out the light; then he quietly washed and bandaged his cut.

And while he should have gone to bed too, he was restless, and he knew he would only toss. Tonight, it went beyond the usual ache of loneliness for Charlotte: it was as if his newfound clarity and energy refused to depart. More and more, he had the sense that he had experienced something inexplicable but profound, something he could not yet grasp, but whose meaning would in time become clear.

His rational mind assured him cynically that this was only the need to convince himself that he had not really behaved like such a fool as it would probably seem in the morning. But for now, the feeling was not at all unpleasant, but even vaguely exciting. He paced, stared out the window, sorted through his collection of books, then took the bottle of Scotch from his suitcase and started to pour a drink.

But he was simply not ready for the night to end.

He looked in once more on Lisa, briefly envying her youthful untroubled sleep, then changed his shirt and walked downstairs to the bar.

Business had picked up in the Coq d'Or. Half a dozen men, probably locals, were talking animatedly at the bar, while several other people, singles or couples, sat at tables; these, he guessed, were fellow occupants of the hotel. He ordered a Rémy Martin and took it to a seat in the corner.

There he lit a cigarette and surveyed the room, idly guessing at the other guests' occupations. They seemed uniformly middle class and uninteresting, just as, he suspected, he must appear to them; and yet, there was something comforting about that. It had to do with a sense of aloofness: that while he might look ordinary, his experience of this night had in truth set him apart. The cognac was delicious, full-bodied and mellow, but with a fine sharp bouquet and flavor that burned in his throat, then blossomed into a rich glow when he swallowed. While he had intended to have only one, he rose and went to the bar for a second.

When he turned back, glass in hand, he saw the woman.

He blinked. She was sitting, alone, at the table next to his. It seemed impossible that he had not already noticed her, or that she had entered in the brief time it had taken him to get his drink. She must have been at the bar's other end, he decided, and walked to her seat while he was ordering; he had been too involved in his reveries to pay attention.

He paid attention now. Her age was impossible to pinpoint; she looked thirty but could easily have been older. She wore a close-fitting sleeveless black dress of some soft material; it came well above her knees, revealing elegant crossed legs. Glossy black hair was fastened behind her head in a loose chignon, a striking contrast to her ivory, almost pallid, skin.

But mainly it was her bearing that captured him. She seemed to embody the dignity and charm he associated with women entirely aware of their desirability. As if she sensed his thought, she glanced at where he stood rooted–staring, he realized with sudden shame, like a boor–and smiled faintly.

His embarrassment deepened, and he considered finishing his brandy quickly, right there at the bar, and leaving. He had always been shy, and he knew perfectly well that he could only make a fool of himself in such a situation. The fact that he imagined he had seen invitation in her eyes only made it worse.

But his cigarettes and lighter still lay on his table; besides, she was undoubtedly married, and would soon be joined by her husband. In Europe, women like her did not travel alone. He crossed the room and sat. Again she glanced at him–appraisingly, he could not help but think–and inclined her head in acknowledgment when he said, "*Bonsoir.*" As she reached for her drink, he saw that a single silver bracelet adorned her wrist, and that her nails, like her lips, were painted a subtle dusky red. He saw, too, that his expectations were confirmed: she wore what was undoubtedly a wedding band, although, oddly, it too was silver. Disappointment warred in him with a sort of cowardly relief.

He sipped the cognac slowly, mind and senses filled with this woman a few feet away, whom he had never even heard speak, but with whom he had already made love, even embarked upon a life, in his imagination. In his marriage he had never strayed, and had rarely been tempted; but his marriage was over, and he realized distantly that this momentary intoxication had forced Charlotte to the edges of his mind like a ghost.

It was as if he was again a teenaged boy in the unending heat of adolescence: too long deprived, not just of sex, but of companionship, of needs as simple as being touched, with the torment suddenly accelerated to the breaking point by the presence of the unapproachable answer to all those dreams. He lit another cigarette, more to mask his emotions than because he wanted it, and decided that when it was finished, he would leave.

Then he saw that she had taken out a cigarette of her own–long and black, with a gold filter–and was rummaging through her purse. Automatically, his hand went to his lighter; he hesitated for a second, but then held it out inquiringly.

She smiled, murmuring, "*Merci.*" As she leaned forward, he saw that her eyes were a strange sea-green. A memory flickered, but was extinguished by the faint shock of her fingers touching his while she drew the cigarette into life.

He replaced the lighter on the table, trying to appear nonchalant, but cursing himself for his ineptness; certainly this was license to start a conversation, but he had not the faintest idea what to say.

But her gaze remained on him, friendly, curious; and it was she who said, in a Parisian accent:

"You are American, are you not? I noticed you with the young lady at dinner."

What Clermont could not understand was how he had failed to notice *her* at dinner. And was he imagining, yet again, a thinly veiled interest in the identity of "the young lady?"

"My daughter," he said. "Yes, we're from the States."

"But your French is excellent. You must have spent a great deal of time in our country."

"A fair amount. My grandparents were French." He hesitated, then added, "They had a vineyard near Périguex, then moved to California and started a winery. Our family's still in the business."

"Ah, yes. I have heard that your California wines are quite as good as our own." It was clear from her amusement that, like every other French native he had ever met, she thought the idea absurd. Under other circumstances, he might have bristled. But he smiled back.

"I'm afraid not," he said. "We've only been doing it a century or so. But we're working on it."

There was a pause. He searched for something more to say, but his treacherous mind had gone blank again.

"And your wife?" the woman said suddenly. "Does she travel with you too?" Her gaze was steady on his.

"We're separated," he said.

"A pity," she murmured. "But perhaps it is preferable to being married without love." She twisted the ring on her finger, an absent, perhaps unconscious gesture, and turned back to her drink.

Clermont's heart was beating like a faintly heard drum. He stubbed out his cigarette, gathered his courage, and leaned toward her.

"And your husband," he said. "Is he with you?"

A moment passed before she shook her head. When she spoke, it was in a low voice, looking down into her glass as if she were addressing it.

"He is in Paris. Every summer, he sends me off to our house in Juan-les-Pins, while he stays with his mistress." When her eyes met his again, they had gone defiant and yet frightened, wounded. "She is younger than I, you see."

"She couldn't possibly be more beautiful," he declared, amazed at his own boldness.

She did not, as he bad expected, shrug off the remark, or even thank him. Her lips curved slightly, and the appraising look returned to her eyes, this time open and frank.

"*Vraiment?*"

"'Truly," he repeated. For long seconds, they stared at each other. Then she leaned back, the fingers of her right hand again toying with her ring. This time she took it off and dropped it deliberately into her purse.

"I would like one more drink," she said. "But in a more private place. My own room is not possible; I am traveling with my husband's sister, you see. She went to bed early."

"Then my room," he said immediately. "Number twenty-four. I have a bottle of Scotch."

"And your daughter?"

"She's in an adjoining room." He paused, then added, "She sleeps heavily."

The woman nodded, an almost imperceptible gesture. "Then I will join you in a few minutes."

She turned away. Clermont picked up his glass and drank the last swallow of cognac, trying to appear casual, but giving the room a covert glance. It seemed that such an exchange, like the woman herself, must have been noticed by everyone there, but no one seemed to be paying them any attention.

He stood, and said to her, a little more loudly than necessary, "It's been very pleasant talking with you. Good night."

"Good night," she said, extending her hand. As he took it, he again felt that tiny shock. Their gazes met once more, and just as he was realizing that he did not even know her name, she murmured, "I came down here, you know, hoping to meet you."

He walked swiftly up the stairs to his room, restraining himself from taking them two at a time, with the agony of uncertainty already beginning: would she really be at his door in a few minutes, or would some trick of fate—her losing her nerve, or unexpectedly being joined by her sister-in-law, or this whole thing having been nothing but a tease on her part to begin with—arise to cheat him?

And if the dream came true, what about Lisa? For a moment, he stood in her doorway. She was deep in slumber, the bathroom lay between them, and the walls of the old hotel were thick. But suppose for some reason she did awake, and found him in the embrace of a woman who was not her mother?

I came down here, you know, hoping to meet you.

He closed the door silently, then hurried to the sink to wash and brush his teeth.

When a light tap came at the door, Clermont moved swiftly to open it. The woman stepped inside, then leaned back against the wall with her arms folded, surveying the room.

"She sleeps?" she said quietly, inclining her head toward Lisa's door.

He nodded dumbly, hardly believing she had come. He had set two glasses on the table, and he picked up the Scotch bottle.

But as he was about to pour her a drink, take it to her, and dare to embrace her, she spoke again.

"*Eh bien:* it is too bright." Moving without hesitation, she switched off the light, then walked to the wide window and threw open the curtains. The few streetlights of Saint-Fabrisse filled the roam with a faint, ghostly illumination, like a false moonlight.

Then she turned to face him, and with a motion that was neither fast nor slow, unzipped and let fall her dress. A second sure movement of her hands, a shake of her head, and the cloud of ebony hair fell free to her waist. Then she stood, one knee slightly bent, hands at her sides: posing for him as Eve might have posed for God.

Clermont stood there, stunned, clutching the bottle in his hand.

"Am I still beautiful?" she murmured.

Through the burning in his throat, the hammering of his pulse, he understood that it was not an empty question: that he was meant to look. He set the bottle down carefully, then stood with his hands at his sides, not yet approaching. Slowly, measuredly, he let his gaze travel up her body, absorbing every detail: the shadowed veins that crossed the bones inside her slender ankles, the narrow vee beneath the round of her belly, the ivory swell of her breasts, with their dark centers puckered hard in the cool night air.

"You're the most beautiful woman I've ever seen," he said, hearing the thickness in his voice.

She laughed, a thin, silvery sound, and extended one hand. "Then come."

In a trance, he moved toward her. He shivered as his hands touched her waist. Her skin was cool, with a texture so fine it seemed to caress his fingertips, to separate the molecules and penetrate with an indefinable essence to his naked nerves. The faintest scent of perfume, musky rather than sweet, stirred his nostrils.

"I'm older than you think," she whispered teasingly. He shook his head, tongue-tied. She laughed again, and her fingers moved to the buttons of his shirt.

He caught her hands. "I don't even know your name."

She looked up swiftly, her eyes narrowed. But then she smiled secretively, her fingers at work again.

"You must not ask," she said. "It is not necessary. You will know me in a much more important way."

Released from his clothing, electrified by her touch, Clermont felt his concern—all the other concerns in his life—slipping away. She pushed him gently back onto the bed.

In later days, the word that would come to his mind when he remembered her caresses was *adoring*. Not Charlotte in their greatest moments of intimacy, not any of the half-dozen other girls he had known before marriage, had made love to him like this. She teased with her tongue, nipped with her teeth, pricked with her nails, until the teasing was unbearable, and then took him inside her. Again and again, her slow, careful motions brought him to the edge and then stopped, as if she was precisely attuned to the pitch of his nerves; and each

40

time he thought it was impossible to go further, she would hold him for seconds, then make some tiny movement that, sent a fierce new surge of pleasure rippling up his spine. Her lips brushed his face, and she murmured to him in what might have been French or might have been a language never spoken, until he could hardly tell if his eyes were open or closed, if he was dreaming or awake.

In the vision that overcame him, he seemed to float down a placid unseen river, twisting and flowing through a dream castle too real to be a dream, its spires rising impossibly high into a vast indigo sky. In chamber after chamber, through colors richer and materials finer than anything known in the world of men, lovely shapes, sensed more than seen, surrounded him, caressing, soothing, promising; and he opened himself to them, surrendered as he never had done before, knowing for the first time the agonized longing to be gone from a life of trouble into promised unending bliss. From far away, he heard the sound of weeping, and understood that it was his own.

At last, while his fingers twisted helplessly in her luxuriant hair and some distant, unimportant part of his mind suggested that his heart might literally burst, her movements quickened and became almost brutal. His sobbing turned to cries, and his body was wracked by spasms of pleasure so nearly unendurable as to cross the line into agony.

His trembling quieted, and he opened his eyes to the lovely face that looked into his.

"Did I please you?" she murmured.

To speak was impossible; a languor almost as sweet as the pleasure of her body had come over him. He could only nod. Sleep was coming on with alarming speed. He fought it, suddenly aware that she could not stay much longer, that he was about to lose her forever; but it was like a black tide sweeping through the night, tearing him loose from consciousness with irresistible force.

As his eyelids flickered, he was distantly aware of her raising his wrist and pulling loose the bandage he had taped across his wound. Her eyes gleamed with a coquettish look that was disturbingly familiar—but this time it seemed confident, powerful, triumphant.

Now you must pay.

But her lips did not move. Instead it was as if another entity was speaking: not with her voice or any voice at all, but with words that seemed to sound in his brain rather than his ears, reverberating harshly down into his being. Alarmed, he tried to sit up, but he could not overcome her feathery weight.

His last memory was of her touching the uncovered wound to her lips, with her dark, mocking gaze fixed on his.

In dreams that seemed more real than waking, Clermont drifted again through the exotic landscape. But it had become distorted rather than wondrous. This time there were no welcoming caresses or sylphlike shapes: only a cold, alien emptiness that gave way increasingly to a sense almost of pursuit—or rather, the feeling that he had awakened something which, once aware of him, would never again let him out of its sight. He struggled,

42

trying to escape the unseen but growing menace, but the bonds of sleep held him fast. Like a drowning swimmer, he knew he must break the surface of the water to save himself, but the harder he thrashed, the deeper he sank.

Finally, it was cries that awoke him. He lay motionless, hands clenched in his twisted sheets, uncertain of where he was. The faint scent of perfume confused him further: Charlotte? But it was the wrong perfume, the wrong bed—

The scream came again, a shriek of real terror, from the next room. In that instant, he remembered it all: the hotel, the woman.

Lisa.

He threw off the bedclothes and lunged toward the sound, shouting her name. But as his feet touched the floor, weakness came over him with the force of a blow to the stomach. His legs gave out and he fell hard, sliding, crashing into the wall. Blackness crawled around the edges of his vision. The screams rose in pitch. Panting, cursing, he scrabbled on his knees and tore at the knob of the bathroom door. It refused to budge. As his strength slowly returned, he clawed and pounded, his own shouts answering the sounds of struggle beyond.

It could have been seconds or minutes before the cries at last died off, and the door gave into his frantic assault. He slid across the tiled bathroom floor and burst into Lisa's room.

She was pressed back against the headboard of the bed, her legs splayed before her, her eyes dark and filled with shock. She looked like a broken doll. The bedclothes lay in a twisted bundle on the floor. Clermont strode forward and took her limp hand.

"Baby, are you all right?" he whispered.

"It–*attacked* me," she said, in a choked, disbelieving voice.

"*What* did?" he said, gripping her shoulders.

"There was this man in my dream, he was talking to me, really sweet, and then I woke up and he was here." Her brimming eyes rose to his. "Only it wasn't a man, Daddy. He turned into a–a *goat*."

Hugging her close, feeling her sobs as if they were his own, he glared murderously around the room for signs of an intruder. The hall door was chained from the inside; there was no balcony outside the second-story window. He strode to the wardrobe and threw it open: empty.

He returned to Lisa, looking anxiously up and down her body, noticing that her nightgown was bunched up around her hips. He automatically reached to pull it down as if she were a little girl, and his fingers seemed to brush a slick dampness on her thigh. Embarrassed, he told himself he was imagining: that it stemmed from his sudden shamefaced awareness that he was naked himself, with the woman's scent still on him.

Excited voices were sounding in the hall outside. A sharp, authoritative knocking came at the door.

"*Qu'est-ce qui ce passe ici?*" someone demanded.

Clermont hesitated, then stooped to pick the covers off the floor, surreptitiously glancing under the bed as he did. A gray band of light showed unbroken along the other side. There was no other possible place for an intruder to hide.

He arranged the sheets over Lisa and leaned close to her.

"Honey, it had to be a dream," he said gently. She did not answer; she might have been shaking her head. Helplessly, he rose. "*Un moment,*" he called through the door. He hurried into his own room to put on his robe, then went to answer the persistent pounding.

Four or five people stood outside in nightclothes, their faces expressing varying degrees of concern and curiosity. Clermont recognized the knocker as the hotel manager, a small round man named Pelissier; the others would be staff or guests who had heard the screams.

"Is all well, here, monsieur?" Pelissier said anxiously.

"Everything's fine," Clermont said, blocking the doorway with his body. "My daughter had a nightmare." The guests looked disappointed, the manager suspicious, and anger flared within him. Did the man think *he* was somehow responsible?

Keeping his voice cool, he said, "I'm sorry to have disturbed you. It won't happen again. I'll sit up with her."

With obvious reluctance, the manager accepted his assurances and shooed the guests back to their rooms. Clermont returned to sit beside Lisa. Her weeping had died off into sniffles. He took her hand and asked, as gently as he could:

"Lise, do you want to see a doctor?"

"No," she said. Her voice was soft.

"What did this—goat—do?"

Perhaps half a minute passed before she answered. "It wasn't just him. There were other things watching."

"What do you mean, *things?*"

45

She was silent again. Then she said, "I have to go to the bathroom."

Her absence lasted perhaps ten minutes. It seemed to him like half the night. At last, when he was about to go after her, the sound of running water stopped.

In bed again, she turned on her side with her back to him, but held his hand clasped against her shoulder.

"You're right," she whispered. "It had to be a dream."

This time, she did not fall quickly asleep. Clermont sat without moving or speaking, no longer able to hold at bay the memory of the instant when the blocked door had finally given way and he had stumbled into her room.

Absurd though it was, he could not rid himself of the distinct impression that some invisible presence—no, *presences,* a crowd of them—had rushed past him, taunting him with laughter that rang in his mind.

There were other things watching.

Had Lisa, in some inexplicable way, become attuned to the woman's presence—perhaps even overheard, in her sleep, what her father was doing next door—and reacted with the nightmare? Or was just it a matter of too much brandy and too much excitement for so staid a man?

He waited until her breathing at last evened, then freed himself gently from her grasp. It was time for a bath and bed—although he knew there would be no sleep for him.

While the tub filled, he opened the window in his room and leaned out, as if the empty village streets might give some clue to what had happened this night. They were as still and silent as a cemetery. The window faced east, and his view of the sky was unobstructed. There remained no sign of the moon.

Had he imagined, too, his final vision of the woman raising his bloody wrist to her lips? The words which, like the taunting laughter as he burst into Lisa's room, had sounded in his mind?

Now you must pay.

He shut the window and stepped into the bathtub, as if water could cleanse him of all the guilt and unease simmering in his heart.

THREE

"I suppose I can say my trip to Berkeley was a success," Clermont wrote. "I came home with an armload of books on witchcraft, demonology, and the like. Felt like a fool inside the store—one of those places with incense burning, lady proprietor dressed like a gypsy, even a black cat I heard her call 'Asmodeus.' The rest of the clientele looked like the cast from a B production of *The Hunchback Of Notre Dame*. But nobody paid any attention to me. Apparently, occultism transcends the bounds of appearance.

"I've spent a good deal of time in the past days going through the books. Most of it, of course, is hogwash. But it's opened up a part of history—a very unpretty part—I never knew existed."

He set his pen down and sat back in his chair. The room was dim and cool; the big frame house, built almost a century before, had been surrounded by sapling oaks now grown into shade-giving giants. But outside, where he had spent dawn till noon, and where he would soon return until twilight, the September sun was blistering, the temperature over a hundred. It was the busiest time of year: the grape harvest followed by the dreaded crush, weeks of frantic nonstop work punctuated by inevitable mishaps that only tremendous effort and plain raw luck could keep from turning into outright disasters. Clermont performed the multiple functions of supervising, managing, troubleshooting, and when other duties relented, stepping in with his own curved knife to fill crates with bunches of the lush ripe grapes. His khaki shirt and jeans had been soaked through with sweat since early morning, and were stained with sticky purple juice.

At crush time during previous years, he had usually managed to catch an after-lunch nap of a half-hour or so, enough to fortify him for the long afternoon to come. But this fall, sleeping in the day was impossible for him; it was difficult enough at night. So, for the first time in his life, he had taken to keeping a journal during his restless rest time, hoping to bring to the surface and clarify the murky inner troubles that disturbed his peace.

Except that not quite all the troubles were inner.

Lisa was refusing to return to high school.

Since they had come back from France, she had gotten increasingly isolated to the point of no longer seeing her friends, and she ignored both his attempts to encourage her to socialize and to get her to talk. Possessed of a strange, distant calm, she spent most of her time in her room or walking alone through the winery lands; and she had reacted with outright hostility, obviously underlaid with fear, to his suggestion that they meet with her teachers or a counselor.

As to *why* she had made this decision, her answers were superficial and varied. She didn't think more education would help her just now, or she wasn't feeling well, or—in her more barbed moments—she wanted to go live with her mother. She was sixteen; she could not be forced to attend school. Clermont had exhibited saintlike patience, partly out of compassion for her unhappiness, partly out of guilt, and partly out of sheer stubborn unwillingness to admit that he had failed with his daughter as he had with his wife.

But he had exhausted the possibilities of reason, and of coercion short of threat. Today was Thursday; school would begin Monday. At last, reluctantly, he had telephoned Charlotte. She was due to arrive this afternoon.

He picked up his pen and hunched over the journal, rereading what he had written. The lighthearted tone struck him abruptly and forcefully as false: seeking to cover something that in fact had come to concern him more and more, to the point of pervading his dreams.

What *had* happened that night in Saint-Fabrisse?

In the journal, he had recounted the events themselves as precisely as he could remember them. At first it had seemed innocent enough: a chance encounter with a woman who happened to be both beautiful and lonely, and who had found him acceptable for easing that loneliness. At worst, her motives might have involved revenging herself on a philandering husband.

But as he had written, questions sprouted like noxious weeds, a sensation like an unpleasant twisting, as of a serpent, in his subconscious; and he had come to realize that this was what had given birth to the idea of

50

the journal in the first place—that his unrest was driving him to try to sort the whole mess out.

At the bottom of it lay the suspicion that had dawned after the incident that in some incomprehensible way, his absurd action at the ruin, together with the nonsense the little Frenchman had put in his ear, had conjured up a demonic image in the depths of his unconscious imagination, an image corresponding to his vague conception of a medieval devil—a being part man, part goat—and that that image had translated itself to his daughter's dream: propelled, perhaps, by his guilt at making love to a woman not her mother while she slept in the next room.

He had spent the remainder of that night in Saint-Fabrisse in anxious, sleepless thought. How, first of all, was it possible that he had not noticed such a striking woman at dinner? Perhaps it had to do with the sister-in-law with whom she traveled—he had not paid the same attention to two women as he would have to her alone—or perhaps they were entering as he and Lisa left, or vice versa. But somehow, he found it difficult to believe that he could have been in the same room with her even briefly without seeing her.

That was only one of many things he began to wonder.

It had happened so quickly. Although he was not familiar with the complexities of love affairs, he was not naive enough either to believe that such sudden encounters were common outside of books and movies. And why had she refused so strangely—even fearfully—to tell him her name?

But, while unlikely, those things were within the realm of possibility: the marks of a once-in-a-lifetime adventure with a woman who wanted to play a game of mystery. Harder to explain was the sudden black sleep into which he had fallen; his fatigue and slight drunkenness would not seem to account for it.

But by far the most disturbing recollection was his certainty that he had neither dreamed nor imagined his last vision of her, raising his sliced wrist to her lips. He had found the bloody bandage in the bed.

Now you must pay.

He had risen at dawn, shaved, and, packed—weary, but anxious to be gone from Saint-Fabrisse. Around seven, while Lisa still slept, he had gone downstairs in the hotel. A few people were breakfasting; the woman was not among them. But as he scanned them, he had realized yet another odd fact: the lovely face that had seemed so clear last night had become a featureless blur in his memory—all except for the sea-green eyes.

He asked to speak to the manager. Not surprisingly, Monsieur Pelissier was cool; he accepted noncommittally Clermont's repeated apology, and made no secret of his relief at hearing that he and Lisa would not be spending another night.

Clermont was intent enough on his mission not to be angered. He offered his hand, which Pelissier took reluctantly, until he felt the crisp fifty-franc note folded in it.

"For your trouble," Clermont said.

Pelissier's manner warmed instantly. "*Merci bien,* monsieur. I am sorry you had difficulties in my house. May I offer you a *café au lait* for your journey?"

Clermont accepted; Pelissier spoke sharply to the desk clerk, who hurried off to the kitchen. The two men were momentarily alone.

"I have a question of some delicacy," Clermont said quietly. One of Pelissier's eyebrows rose, giving his round face an almost comical look of sly curiosity. "Last night, I encountered a very lovely lady, staying here at the hotel. But I did not learn her name. Is it possible–?" With a nod, Clermont indicated the guest register.

Pelissier frowned. "Unfortunately, monsieur, this is a thing not permissible"–but his words stopped at the sight of another fifty-franc note. The bill vanished and the book opened. "Who was this lady with?"

"She was alone when we met. She said she was traveling with another woman, a sister-in-law."

Pelissier's frown deepened. "I do not recall two women together." He turned the book so Clermont could see it, and his finger moved down the list. As he neared the bottom, he began to shake his head.

"I might have misunderstood," Clermont said. "She could have been alone."

Pelissier shook his head again, this time firmly. "I am certain there were no single women staying at the Coq d'Or last night, monsieur. I would remember; it is a rare thing in France." He looked up, his face conspiratorial. "Perhaps she was married?"

Clermont hesitated, then said, "Yes."

Pelissier smiled slightly. "But she tells you she is not traveling with her husband. *Eh bien,* perhaps she finds you so irresistible she is not quite truthful. Can you describe her?"

"Beautiful," Clermont said simply. "Black hair and lovely figure. She came into the bar last evening, wearing a black dress."

Pelissier, obviously interested by now, put his finger to his cheek and thought. "No,' he said at last. "'There are three or four women here with their husbands, but none who answers that description. I would remember such a remarkable guest." He paused, then said delicately, "Had monsieur had a great deal to drink?"

"I'm not exaggerating," Clermont said curtly.

"Then let us ask Julien; he tended the bar last night." The desk clerk was just returning with two cups of coffee. Pelissier launched into a blistering thirty-second tirade concerning his laziness, then sent him scurrying off to find Julien, who presumably lived in or near the hotel.

"Tell me," Clermont said to Pelissier. "Do you know anything about that ruin?" He gestured vaguely in the direction of the old abbey.

Pelissier shrugged. "There is not much to know, monsieur. Long ago it housed monks; it was abandoned around the time of the Revolution. There are many such places in France, and this one is of no particular interest. You have been there?"

"We happened by and stopped for a minute," Clermont said, unwilling to tell of his second visit. He hesitated, then added, "We met a man there, a local, who told us some wild stories about witchcraft in the old days."

"Ah, yes," Pelissier murmured. "There were such stories, of sacrificing babies and the like. Even when my grandfather was a boy, a great stone remained that was said to have been used as an altar. It was thought that such goings on continued at the time, and one day the priest and a group of men went up there to overthrow that stone. My grandfather swore that all of those men who touched it came to bad ends soon after, and it is a fact that the priest died. But I think we may be sure that those other stories were the work of old peasant women on lonely nights, perhaps with too much wine in them." He smiled. "Monsieur has nothing to fear from witches, I think. This lady's husband, however–" He rolled his eyes roguishly, and Clermont managed to laugh, a forced, unnatural sound.

Pelissier went back to managerial chores. Clermont sipped the sweet milky coffee and waited, nodding at guests arriving for breakfast, on the alert for the woman's appearance. In perhaps five minutes, the desk clerk reappeared with an unshaven, rumpled-looking young man whom Clermont recognized as last night's bartender– probably dragged from his bed or breakfast. Pelissier dismissed the desk clerk once more and confronted the wary-eyed Julien.

"This gentleman was with a lady last night. Do you recall her?"

"I recall monsieur," Julien said. His manner was anxious and earnest. "He drank a Rémy, and then a second one."

"But the lady?"

Julien looked doubtful. Clermont described her again, and then said in exasperation, "For God's sake, there were only half a dozen people in the bar. You served her a drink."

Julien looked helplessly at his master. "It does seem to me that monsieur was with someone," he said at last. "But I can remember nothing about her."

"*Salaud!*" Pelissier growled, pointing an accusing finger. "You had your nose in the cognac again, *n'est-ce pas?*"

Disturbed and confused, Clermont lingered a moment in the midst of the accusations and protests that began to fly, then murmured his thanks and left.

Upstairs, Lisa had risen and was starting to pack. He put his arm around her shoulders and said:

"How you feeling this morning?"

She smiled bravely. "Fine, Daddy. Thanks for sitting up with me."

"No more bad dreams?"

She shook her head. Then, primly, she said, "I guess I got my period last night. It's early, I wasn't expecting it. Maybe it freaked me out. In my sleep, you know?"

He remembered, with a touch of embarrassment, his fingers brushing dampness on her thigh; but he was relieved at having a concrete explanation for the nightmare, especially as it seemed to satisfy her.

"I'm glad you're okay. So let's make tracks for the beach, huh?"

But over the next few days, her well-being gave way to withdrawn brooding. In Cannes, she hardly set foot on the fabled beaches they had crossed an ocean to see, showed no interest in the young French men who showed a great deal of interest in her, and accompanied him on excursions with increasingly obvious apathy.

Finally, after several days of staying in her room rereading Tolkien, she asked quietly but firmly to be taken home.

Thus they had returned two weeks early, and as Lisa's isolation and uncommunicativeness deepened, his own inner life, and his sleep, had become increasingly troubled. He would awaken sweating, able to remember only vague, fragmented images, aware only that they involved a host of presences that were stealthy, cold, and grotesque—and that what they promised was menace.

In short, he was beginning to feel that Lisa and he were two carriers of a psychic disease, constantly re-infecting each other so that neither had a chance to recover. And irrational though it was, try as he might to dismiss it, he could not evade the growing conviction that somehow, his action at the ruin—the awakening of a mysterious, malignant force—was at heart responsible; and that that force had pursued him back across the Atlantic Ocean and the whole continent of America, to claim as victim not only himself but his daughter.

But irrational was the key word, he reminded himself. It was guilt over his brief, only, and justifiable infidelity that was poisoning his thoughts and communicating itself to Lisa. Exploring the roots of the sickness was the first step toward curing it: thus the journal. If he failed on his own, he was prepared to seek whatever form of help seemed appropriate.

As for the books on witchcraft, they had been a whim, purchased half in a spirit of self-mockery. He had decided it was only fair that he try to bring to the surface whatever archetypal memories and superstitions might lie buried in his subconscious and been awakened by what his guide at the ruin had hinted of.

About this much, the little Frenchman had certainly been correct: between the approximate dates of 1450 and 1750, upwards of one hundred thousand and possibly several times that many people had been executed in Europe—many by burning alive or in other inhuman ways, and many cruelly tortured first—on the suspicion that they had been in league with diabolical powers.

The name the guide had mentioned as the architect of the persecutions at Saint-Fabrisse, De Lancre, had cropped up several times in Clermont's reading. Convinced that entire provinces of France—men, women, children, and even priests—were "infected" with the witchcraft heresy, he had burned at least six hundred.

A number of his near-contemporaries had left similar marks on history: Sprenger and Kramer, celibate churchmen who wrote the infamous *Malleus Maleficarum,* the work that was seminal in providing the Inquisition both justification and formula for its persecutions—which were aimed primarily at women; Bodin, who believed an accused witch should never be acquitted, and who tortured children and adults alike; Rémy, who had boasted without hint of irony, "So good is my justice, that last year there were no less than sixteen killed themselves rather than pass through my hands"; and a host of others who had made their names, and sometimes their fortunes, out of blood, hysteria, and delusion.

But *was* it all delusion? Had he not seen the marks on the stones with his own eyes?

His reading had acquainted him, too, with Ovid's description of *strigae:* demonic birds that flew by night—often owls—in search of human blood.

He closed the journal and stalked to the window, forcing his mind to the issue at hand: that of getting his daughter out of her shell and back into school. Not many minutes later, he heard the sound of tires crunching on gravel in the driveway outside.

Charlotte's Volkswagen bus—blue, with large red peace symbols painted on both sides—came to rest in the same shady spot where she had always parked the succession of Mercuries she had driven when they were married. Trying to harden his heart, he watched her gather her purse and other belongings, a process that always seemed to take several minutes.

But when she stepped out of the van, his cold facade fled, and he exhaled in misery. She was wearing a thigh-high fringed leather skirt, sandals that laced above her calves, and a loose white peasant blouse. Her hair was parted in the middle and held by a beaded headband, falling past her shoulders with sunlight catching auburn and gold highlights. Few women of any age could have looked anything but silly in such an outfit. Charlotte looked, simply, superb. At thirty-seven, she could have passed for Lisa's sister. But the deeper attraction lay in her very unpredictability, her capacity to be now loving, now harsh, now vulnerable, and suddenly, without warning, irresistibly seductive.

He supposed that in some sense, he had been punished for his greed in once imagining that he possessed her. But he knew with certainty that he would welcome her back in a heartbeat, take the chance of experiencing again the agony of her leaving and the ongoing ache of her absence, for the delight of having her with him. It was even true that he missed the bad moments as much as the good.

She entered without knocking, as if the house were still her home.

"The flowers need watering," she said, tossing her oversized purse on the couch.

"I'll tell Angel," he said. Without slowing or looking at him, she strode on to the kitchen. He heard the refrigerator open and close, and a moment later, the sound of a cork being pulled. She returned with a bottle of chilled chardonnay and two glasses. After filling them, she sat back, fanning herself with her hand.

"It's hotter than hell out there," she said.

"I know," he said. "I work in it all day. Or have you forgotten about all those little grapes that pay your rent?"

"It was foggy in San Francisco." She crossed her ankles, knees slightly apart, and the skirt had ridden high. It was clear that she was not wearing a bra. Lips compressed, he looked away.

"Are you going to drink this?" she said, pushing the glass toward him.

"I'm going back out to work. It would give me a headache." She shrugged, drained her own glass, and picked up the full one.

"Is learning to drink like a fishwife part of the liberating experience?" he said coolly.

"Maybe. Maybe if you were more liberated, you'd be able to communicate with your daughter."

Maybe if you were home where you goddamned well belong, it wouldn't all be up to me, he started to say, but caught himself.

"She's upstairs." As he walked to the door, he added, "It might be nice if you weren't completely in the bag when you talked to her."

He made a point of not slamming the door, but its closing cut off any answer she might have made. The force of the sun was stunning; he stood, half-blinded, disoriented, helpless with anger and frustration. Was it so much to ask that Lisa's mother—her *mother*—be an ally instead of an enemy in a time of crisis?

Absently, he noted that she was right, the flowers in the beds around the house did need watering. But Angel, the grounds keeper, was out in the fields picking grapes, like every other able-bodied human on the estate.

All but one: Lisa.

Trying to remember which vineyard he had to visit next, he trudged across the driveway to his Jeep.

Less than another hour had passed before Clermont, standing atop a flatbed truck loading crates of grapes, noticed a cloud of dust coming along the road. In front of it was Charlotte's van.

"I'll be back in a few minutes," he said in Spanish. Angel nodded and immediately assumed an air of importance, jumping upon the truck and shouting at the harvesters to move faster. Clermont strode along the road to meet the van.

"Get in," she said without preliminary. "You're not going to want to hear this here."

61

He glanced back at the crew. Angel was standing on the truck cab and gesticulating like a general. Clermont climbed into the van.

Charlotte wheeled it around in a quick, expert three point turn. She drove approximately twice as fast as he would have–she had obviously ignored his request to stop drinking–and he bounced in his seat on the rough road, but held his tongue. Surreptitiously, he studied her profile: fine, slightly arched nose, accented cheekbones, hair blowing in the breeze of the open window. But her face was uncharacteristically tense, and that undercut the resentment that had smoldered in him during the last hour.

At the fork of the road that would take them back to the house, she turned left instead, heading into the part of the estate too rocky and steep ever to have been cultivated.

"Mind if I ask where we're going?" he said.

"For God's sake, will you relax for once? Angel's been picking those fucking grapes for five years. They can survive an hour without you."

The road was growing weedier and rockier. When she turned onto a trail that was hardly more than two faint ruts, he realized she was taking them to the waterfall: a place where the small stream that flowed through the property tumbled some twenty feet down a steep rock face into a pool just big enough to jump into.

"So she told you what's bothering her," he said.

"Yes."

They did not speak again until they had parked and walked the last hundred yards. This late in the summer, the waterfall itself was down to a thin stream, but the pool was full and clear. She took another bottle of wine and a corkscrew from her handbag and gave them to him. Then she shrugged off her clothes, letting them fall.

At the edge of the pool, she looked over her shoulder, deliberately meeting his eyes for the first time.

"She's pregnant," Charlotte said, and stepped in.

He stared at the froth on the water where she had disappeared. The wine bottle was cool in his fingers, its surface slick with moisture. Birds and crickets sang dutifully nearby. The heat of the sun was dizzying.

After several seconds, Charlotte's head broke the surface. As if the sight of her brought him out of a trance, he took a lunging step forward.

"What the hell do you mean, *pregnant!*" he shouted.

Facing him, treading water, she said, "How much clearer can I make it? In a family way. *Enceinte.* Knocked up."

Slowly, he crouched, then sat.

"If you're not going to open that bottle," she said, "give it to me."

He looked down at it as if he had never seen such an object before. Slowly, his fingers started to peel the foil around the cork.

She nodded. "I thought you could probably use a drink. There's glasses in my bag. If you're smart, you'll take a swim, too. It's like a breath of new life."

"I can't believe," he said, voice shaking, "that you can tell me our daughter is pregnant as if—as if you were talking about buying a new dress."

"If you'd been able to *communicate* with her, maybe you wouldn't be so surprised." She paused, then added archly, "Maybe she wouldn't have gotten herself screwed in the first place."

"She wouldn't have gotten herself *screwed,* as you so delicately put it, if you'd been here at home with her like a mother goddamned well should be, instead of running around like a deranged teenager yourself!" As he yelled, he rose again, pointing at her, the bottle clenched in his fist. "Don't you dare blame it on me! It was probably one of Furbrain's friends, while you were somewhere getting liberated."

"Even if it happened," Charlotte said coolly, "while she was with you in France?"

Blinded by sweat, feeling nauseous, he turned away and stared unseeingly across the sunbaked hills.

Then Charlotte was standing in front of him, dripping wet, her hair smooth and slick like a seal's pelt. She gripped his lapel and tugged.

"Your face is red as a fire engine," she said firmly. "Get in that water right this second." His mouth opened to protest, but she put her hand over it. "Just settle down. It's not the end of the world. Cool off and then we'll talk, okay?"

Suddenly drained of energy, he obediently gave her the wine bottle and struggled out of his sweaty shirt and jeans. The sun-warmed water was a perfect temperature, bracing but comfortable. He came to the surface, inhaled deeply, then returned underwater and released his breath slowly, making the stream of bubbles last as long as he could. After three exhalations, he admitted that physically, at least, he felt a little better.

When he paddled to the pool's edge, she was kneeling, filling the two glasses in front of her. As he watched, a memory tugged at him, and he realized that her body was a mirror image of the unknown woman that night in Saint-Fabrisse, the type he had always found most attractive: small high breasts, waist he could still almost circle with his hands, slim legs–

And a face he could not remember. For the first time, it occurred to him to wonder if the truth were precisely the opposite: if the French woman's body was the mirror of Charlotte's.

But records tell us too of the goddess's special gift to those who joined her worship: a spirit which would take the shape of whatever lover one most desired.

He shook his head and accepted the glass Charlotte set in front of him. The wine, a chardonnay he had bottled three years before, was cool, dry, and sharp. She lay back on an elbow. The graceful swell of her hip led his gaze irresistibly to the dark triangle of fur still glistening with droplets. Helplessly, in spite of the absurdity of the situation, he felt an erection growing. Since the night in France, three months before, there had been no one. As if she could see through the pool's rock lip, she smiled lazily. He turned away, determinedly ignoring both her body and his own.

"I don't see how it could have happened," he said. "I was with her practically every minute."

"You're not the only one who can't figure it out. She swears she hasn't let anybody near her."

"What the hell is that supposed to mean? The second immaculate conception?"

Charlotte shrugged. "What I suspect it means is, she was necking with some boy and things got away from her and she doesn't want to admit it, even to herself. Maybe she was drunk, or honestly didn't know what was happening. Or maybe she's trying to protect somebody."

"If she says it didn't happen at all, then how do you know it happened in France?"

"I'm guessing," Charlotte admitted. "Because of the timing. Doctor Soames can tell us."

"You're guessing, meaning you jumped at the chance to hang the blame on me."

"I'll apologize for now. Until we find out I'm right." She stretched out gracefully, reaching for her purse. His erection, momentarily forgotten and wilting, sprang back into life. Exasperated, he went underwater to blow bubbles again.

When he emerged, she was lighting a thick, wrinkled cigarette, its end twisted to a point. The smell of the smoke was pungent but not unpleasant. She inhaled and offered it to him. He shook his head curtly.

"Do you good," she said.

"I'd rather continue this conversation while one of us is still on earth."

She laughed, and said without rancor, "God, what an asshole you can be."

Gloomily, Clermont hung suspended in the water, prevented by the treachery of his own flesh from exiting with dignified anger.

"I've got to get back," he said. "What do we do about finding the father?"

"That's the least of our worries right now," Charlotte said. "It'll come out in time. She's very frightened. She needs to know we still love her."

"Christ," he muttered. "I wish she'd told me."

There was a pause. Then Charlotte said, "She mentioned a dream of being attacked, maybe raped, one night in some little town in France. She doesn't seem quite clear on what actually happened. I wondered if somehow, there really could have been a man."

He shook his head. "There was no way anyone could have gotten in or out of her room. I even looked under the bed." He thought about confessing to his own activities that night, perhaps to defend against any ugly suspicion that he himself might have been the dream attacker—disguised by Lisa, even in her own mind, by some trick of her subconscious. But he knew that if the idea ever even occurred to Charlotte, she would dismiss it without a thought. It was not a proof of love, perhaps, but certainly of respect, which he had often tried to believe was more important.

"Do you know what she asked me?" Charlotte said dreamily. Her gaze had gone absent; the joint, forgotten between her fingers, was out. "If a man's cock was supposed to be freezing cold."

"For God's sake," he said, getting angry again. "First she's still a virgin, then she comes up with something crazy like that. Maybe we should take her to a shrink."

"Not yet," Charlotte said. "Maybe down the line. But right now, we keep everything low key and make it clear we're not angry."

Then she rolled onto her belly and reached to cup the back of his neck, her lips tantalizingly close to his. "It gave me a way to prove to her she was dreaming," she murmured. "I assured her they're nice and warm,"

Their coupling was short, and he could not help sensing the insincerity of her response. He climaxed silently and without joy.

"Come home," he said. The words were unplanned, and his own intensity surprised him. "She needs you. So do I."

Charlotte lay unmoving beneath him, her head turned to the side. "I can't think about that right now," she finally said, and pushed him gently off. She stepped again into the pool, and he followed, an ablution that had the air of ritual. They did not touch again.

He dried himself quickly with his jeans, then put them on and sat to lace his boots. Charlotte, in white cotton bikini panties, hair still slick and damp, looked hardly older than Lisa. He watched miserably as she stepped into her skirt, gone from him once more, an he ached to grip her shoulders, shake her, make her understand that she would never again find a love like his.

But he no longer had any such right, and perhaps that was the single hardest part of seeing her, that loss of the ability to simply touch her, to summon the comfort of physical contact that demonstrated to them both and to the world that she was still his.

"One more little problem," he said, forcing his stern facade to return. "What do we do about the baby?"

"She wants to have it," Charlotte said. "I brought up the idea of an abortion, but she didn't even want to think about it. All that good Catholic upbringing."

Clermont had never been faced with a personal situation involving abortion, and was not sure how he felt. But it struck him for the first time how remarkable it was that a superstition as unverifiable as those of the medieval peasants of Saint-Fabrisse could have such a profound impact on modem, supposedly enlightened lives.

In any case, if that was what Lisa wanted, that was how it would be; and he admitted that the thought of a grandchild, legitimate or not, was already beginning to excite him. Raising a baby without a father would present difficulties, but money was not a problem, and the winery's isolation would ease whatever social strain might come to bear on Lisa. They would keep her out of school for the year, and if she wished, send her to a private school the next. No one would even have to know. And with the way the times were changing, it hardly stood to ruin her life, the way it might have a century, or even a decade, before. There remained every possibility of a marriage and happiness.

It even occurred to him that this might snap Charlotte out of her dream world, and make her accept again her responsibilities, bring her back where she belonged.

She had not said no.

She drove more sedately on her way back to the vineyard, as if the business that demanded haste had been concluded. In a way, he supposed, it had. She stopped little short of the harvesting crew, which, he noted with approval, had made substantial progress in his absence.

"I bought a roast yesterday," he said, opening the door. "Feel like getting it started?"

"I can't stay, Don."

He turned and stared at her. "Not even a night?"

She hesitated. "I have a date."

"A date? You can't spend an evening with your pregnant daughter because you have a date?"

"It's a concert, Country Joe and the Fish at the Fillmore. Tonight's the only night."

Disgusted with her, and with himself for allowing an air castle to begin constructing itself in his mind, he got out.

"Well, how was I supposed to know what was going on?" Charlotte said. There was an edge of pleading to her voice; and abruptly, he understood that she had offered herself as a receptacle for his anger, as a way of expiating her own guilt. "She can come see me any time, and stay as long as she wants."

She needs to know we love her, huh? he thought. He said only, "Be careful driving. You're not exactly grounded in reality just now," and stalked off to join the crew.

Angel relinquished his command poet with obvious reluctance and went back into the field with his knife. Clermont bent his back and worked ferociously, slinging crates, glad for the sweaty grunting work to absorb his energy.

If the woman in Saint-Fabrisse resembled Charlotte physically, they had at least one other characteristic in common: both had used him for purposes of their own,

70

then abandoned him to take care of whatever difficulties arose.

FOUR

February twenty-fourth was the third day of a rain-storm that had settled across northern California as if it were determined never to leave. Dawn seemed to take hours, giving way to a twilight that lasted all day long, only to fade imperceptibly again into darkness. In the mountains, the steady downpour would be punctuated by great gusts of wind, the clouds sweeping down the canyons like invading armies in the first rage of battle. The ground had turned to a sea of muck; even the trees seemed cowed by the unending wet that battered and soaked them and hung like a heavy translucent blanket from their foliage. There was apprehensive talk of flooding in the valleys.

It was the slowest time of year at the winery. Most of the pruning in the vineyards was done; bottling would not begin for a few more weeks. Angel and the rest of the year-round crew busied themselves with maintenance chores. Clermont went out to supervise halfheartedly for a few hours each morning, but the long gray afternoons would find him writing in his journal, or paging through his now-considerable collection of books on the occult, or simply sitting in the living room, staring into the fire. He slept poorly, lying awake until the small hours, then only with great effort dragging himself out for work. For the first time in his life, he drank frequently during the afternoons, and often continued on into the evenings. His face had taken on a haggard, uneasy look, and pouches under his eyes greeted him in his morning mirror.

He took a sip of the Scotch at his elbow, then picked up his pen, all the while listening for a sound from upstairs, where Lisa now spent most of her time, drawn ever further into herself. The baby was due in just two weeks. By all indications, both mother and child were in top health.

The problem was not physical.

While his reading had started off whimsical and become an education in a grim, little-known phase of history, it had taken yet another turn, fueled by the solemn proclamations of churchmen like Augustine and Aquinas, whom he had been raised to believe were nearly as wise as God. He had encountered several passages which held most seriously that there were, or at least once had been, such beings as familiar spirits capable of having sexual intercourse with humans.

"The same evil spirit," a Dominican had written, "may serve as a succubus to a man, and as an incubus to a woman." It was even thought that such spirits could father children.

He had also come across general agreement that familiars had the habit of sucking at a teat or wound on the witch's body to draw nourishment—sometimes milk, but usually blood.

And he had finally remembered where he had seen the other pair of sea-green eyes.

However the Frenchman had couched what he had spoken of in terms of pagan worship, was he not really talking about a bargain of the same kind the Inquisitors accused the witches of? Had not the peasants of Saint-Fabrisse, in making their blood offerings, attempted to court the favor of an entity whom they believed would give them actual rewards here and now, instead of an aloof and inscrutable God in heaven, who allowed, even if He did not cause, all the misery and helpless suffering in the world?

Had not he, Donald Clermont, enlightened, skeptical, twentieth-century man, done precisely the same thing: offered his blood, with the idea burning inside him, however deep and unrecognized, of easing his desperate loneliness?

And had he not gotten what he had bargained for?

Now you must pay.

Charlotte was due to arrive the coming weekend, to spend the final days of Lisa's pregnancy. She had visited dutifully two or three times a month; although she usually spent the night, there had been no repeat of their intimacy at the waterfall. And while they had agreed not to formalize the divorce until after the baby's arrival, she continued to evade his suggestions that she return permanently.

He thought of calling her and asking her to come tonight, immediately; but what reason could he give other than the same one as always: she needs you, and so do I? How could he tell her about the movements he sensed increasingly as the old house filled with shadows in the gloomy twilights, the half-seen flitting shapes, the whispers that seemed tense with lewd excitement, the presences that had gradually intruded from his dreams into his waking hours, that he could not bring himself to ask Lisa if she sensed too?

He had cautiously consulted physicians, psychiatrists, and a clergyman, and had received a unanimous response: a look that came into their eyes, an intent focusing accompanied by a slight lifting of the head, followed by questions whose conversational tone did not disguise wariness–the conviction, already established, that he was moving toward the outskirts of sanity. He had considered flight: taking Lisa somewhere warm and sunny and carefree.

But then he would remember the night of her dream in Saint-Fabrisse: his sense of the shapes rushing past him as he had broken into her room. If they–whatever they were–had followed from France, where was there to hide?

And if they were developing apace with the growth of the baby in Lisa's womb, what was yet to come?

The gray afternoon was sliding perceptibly into evening. He swiveled in his chair at a sound that might have been a creaking of the floor joists, a shifting of the old house in the wind–or a stealthy footstep.

He stood, glaring into the darkening corners of the ceiling and the shadowy border of the living room beyond the stairwell. The footsteps had been Lisa's, he decided, stirring from the napping, dreaming, and fantasy reading that had become her life. He hesitated, reluctant to intrude, but then climbed the stairs. A light tap at her door brought no response. He pushed it quietly open.

She was sitting up in bed, wearing a print flannel nightgown, an open book face down in her lap. Though the room was unlit and gray, she was not asleep, but gazing out the window opposite. He had found her like this many times before, and suspected she might have been staring, motionless and seeing only whatever was taking place inside her mind, for hours. The bedclothes swelled over her belly, but her face was drawn. Though she ate ravenously—the only times she seemed to come to life—she had gained hardly any weight but that of the baby. Clermont gazed at her, his heart aching, torn by a question that had occupied him increasingly over the past weeks: was this only the unhappiness of a pregnant, unmarried teenaged girl? Or did she have suspicions, even knowledge, similar to his?

He sat on the edge of the bed. "How, you feeling, Lise?" His voice sounded hollow and sepulchral. He had rewallpapered the room in a bright lemon yellow, painted the trim, bought books and teddy bears and posters; but still, in the half-light, with the unending rain pattering against the window, it had the feel of a crypt.

Without turning her head, she answered, "Fine." Her voice was hardly more than a whisper.

"I'm going to make dinner soon. You hungry?"

She nodded.

Groping for conversation, for any contact, he said, "What are you reading?" and reached for the book on her lap. It was a collection of baby names that Charlotte had given her, complete with purported origins and meanings. "What do you think?" he said, trying to put a teasing note into his voice. "Boy or girl?"

"Girl," she said firmly.

His eyebrows rose, more at her tone than the answer. This assurance was new.

"How do you know?"

Her silence stretched. A gust of wind hurled a barrage of raindrops against the glass, smearing the outside world into a gray-green mass.

"I just do," she finally said.

"That's wonderful," he said heartily. "What are we going to call her?"

With the same assurance, she said, "Selena."

"Beautiful," he said. "Let's see what it means." He began to page through the book.

"It's not in there," Lisa said. "She's a moon goddess."

His fingers stopped. "Well, where did you hear it?" he said, managing a laugh. "I don't think I ever have."

She paused again. This time, he had the distinct sense that her hesitation did not stem from uncertainty, or from the groping attempt to continue a fantasy, but from having information she was not sure she should pass on.

"*They* told me," she finally said.

Something moved at the edge of his vision, a flitting shadow in the far corner of the room. His head swiveled sharply, causing a burning pain in his neck. There was nothing.

Careful to keep his voice light, he said, "They?"

77

"You know," she whispered.

He cleared his throat. "Do they—talk to you?"

"Sometimes. More, now that she's almost here."

"What do they tell you?"

Another silence. Then, shaking her head, "They don't want me to say any more."

Tell me, he started to say, *I have to know.* Instead, he patted her hand and rose. It would not do to push her. This was a significant breakthrough, he assured himself, and must be handled delicately. Over the next days, he would gently probe for the rest of this fantasy, this shared nightmare that had turned them both into prisoners. Exposed, it would shrivel up and blow away.

"Okay," he said. "I'm going to make dinner for you and Selena. About half an hour, huh?"

She nodded.

"You want a light on?" he said as he reached the door.

"No," she said quickly.

He was stepping out into the hall when she said, "Daddy."

He turned, suddenly frightened of what he sensed he was about to hear.

"It wasn't a dream," she said. "I ached for days. It wasn't my period, either. That stopped."

Clermont stood there, gripping the door jamb.

"It was cold," she whispered. "So cold it burned." She turned her face to the side.

He walked back into the room and stroked her hair.

"I'll call your mother," was all he could think of to say. "I'll tell her to come right away."

"Yes," Lisa said, her voice eerily clear again. "I'd like to see her. There's no moon tonight, you know."

He stopped the question on his lips and strode downstairs, his heart beating hard, his mind filled with confusion, anger, and fear.

No moon tonight. She must have been watching its progress, he told himself.

It is thus, monsieur, that the goddess is to be feared.

On his way through the kitchen to the telephone, a movement in the sink caught his eye. Loathing rose in him as he realized what he was looking at: a scorpion that had come up through the drain and gotten trapped. It was perhaps two inches long, shiny black, with a disgustingly bloated abdomen.

In the wild, he let them go, like the black widows that nested in the milk cartons used to protect baby grapevines from deer, and like the rattlesnakes that lingered around the property's springs; and ordinarily, he would have trapped it and taken it outside to release it.

But as it crouched, watching him, tail poised above its back to inflict its vicious sting, he imagined a malignant intelligence emanating from it, as if it had become infected by the sensed presences: as if it were their agent, sent to lie waiting in darkness for a chance to do him or Lisa harm.

He grasped a heavy cleaver, and with sudden violent anger, brought it down on the creature's back. The tail flicked with eyeblink speed at the blade, in a death agony he could almost feel.

When the thrashing stopped, he scooped up the parts onto a dish, carried them to the parlor, and scraped

79

them deliberately into the fire, realizing that he required seeing the loathsome object completely destroyed, that he did not trust it, if tossed out into the night or put in the garbage or even flushed down the toilet, not to somehow regenerate itself and come creeping back to finish what, in his fancy, it had begun.

The ringing of the telephone brought Walter Soames from a sleep which, after twenty-five years of general practice as an MD, was habitually light. Although he growled a curse, anxiety, as always when he was called late, held the forefront of his mind; and as he reached across his stirring wife, he was already trying to guess which of his patients and what order of business it might be: a neurotic who had suffered some minor ailment for weeks, only to decide in the middle of the night that it was no longer endurable, or a genuine emergency that would have him dressing hurriedly, adrenaline pumping. He noted automatically that the time was a little after two AM.

"Soames," he said into the phone.

The first words of Donald Clermont's tense, tightly controlled voice erased any doubt as to which sort of situation it was. Pulse quickening, Soames listened for thirty seconds, then said:

"You can't bring her to the hospital?"

The reply was an anguished stream of words that even Anne, sitting up now, could hear.

"All right, all right," he said soothingly. "I'll be there as soon as humanly possible. Go sit with her, hold her hand, and try to keep her calm."

He put the phone down hard, already moving across the room to clothes set out on a chair–another years-long habit. His medical paraphernalia waited in his car.

"What?" Anne said.

"Don Clermont's daughter," he said, pulling on his slacks. "Her water broke half an hour ago and she's already in labor. She isn't due for two weeks, and there was absolutely no indication she was going to deliver early. Christ, Mike Travis just saw her three days ago."

"Where is he tonight?"

"Clermont couldn't raise him. I seem to remember he was going to a conference in San Francisco. Do me a favor, honey. Call the hospital, have them send an ambulance to Clermont Vineyards, and see if they can round up an O.B. man." He quickly kissed her offered cheek.

"Walter," she said anxiously. "How long's it been since you delivered a baby?"

"Too long," he said, and strode for the door.

In fact, it had been almost five years; with the last decade's increase in medical specialization, childbirth had become almost exclusively the province of obstetricians. But in his younger days, he had handled his fair share of deliveries, and it was not the sort of thing one forgot how to do. He only hoped that Clermont's urgency, and what it implied–at best, mistaken diagnosis on the part of Dr. Travis; at worst, genuine trouble–was the result of nervousness.

But he did not think so. He had been their family physician for twenty years. Clermont was not the sort of man to fly off the handle.

He jumped into the car and raced down Highway 29 through the rain, ignoring speed limits and St. Helena's single red stoplight.

During the next years, the images of what greeted Walter Soames when he entered the Clermont house would come to him almost nightly, usually in the moments of half-dream before his consciousness gave way to sleep—jerking him abruptly back to wakefulness, and leaving him there with open eyes and thumping heart, sometimes to toss restlessly until dawn.

It was not any fancy about saving Lisa that tormented him. When he found her in an upstairs bedroom—after hurrying with increasing apprehension through the silent house, his calls echoing unanswered in the stillness—there was no doubt that she was already beyond hope: unconscious, breath almost stopped, pulse fragile as the beat of a butterfly's wings, skin gone the color of sour milk. He lifted the single sheet that covered her and recoiled, exhaling with a hiss. She was torn as if the baby had clawed its way into the world. The bed was literally soaked with blood.

But Soames was no stranger to physical horrors, and he steeled himself to the necessity of triage: leaving the dying, and saving those who might yet live.

Except there was no sign of the child.

Or of Donald Clermont.

And as he stood in that room, with the dripping from the eaves outside like the whispering voice of something vast and bleak that noted all human anguish with cold dispassion and could or would do nothing to help, he imagined, with a prickling chill that rose from the base of his spine up the backs of his arms and neck, that there was movement, shadowy, sensed more than seen, in the room: that beneath the voice of the rain there were other faint whispers and murmurs—even laughter.

Abruptly and sternly, he tore himself from his rapture of fear. It was only the presence of death, hovering over Lisa like a dark angel. He had felt it on many occasions. And this was no time to indulge such morbid foolishness: finding the baby, immediately, was imperative. He wheeled and strode out of the room, fighting the fear that, given Lisa's condition; the child might be grotesquely deformed: that that might have driven Clermont into destroying it, out of madness born of grief, or even revenge for the loss of his daughter's life.

The suspicion leaped when, after a quick tour of the empty upstairs, he looked at the bed Clermont had once shared with his wife, and saw a mound of bedclothes and pillows piled in the center.

At the bottom, the covers were squirming tinily.

Bracing himself, Soames tore the pillows away—and stared down at a bloody but perfectly formed infant girl.

In the next few minutes, he again allowed his reflexes to take over, caring for the child, then gratefully giving her to the obstetrician when the ambulance arrived. Only later did he realize that the baby—in spite of hunger and nearly smothering—had never made a sound.

It was a little after that, combing the house for some clue as to what had happened to Clermont, that he found a journal on a table in the parlor; open to a page blank except for one sentence:

They dance as my daughter dies.

And then, as if led by some terrible guiding instinct, he had walked out into the gloomy night, down the little slope that led to a picnic spot overlooking the vineyards. The rain had paused, and the light from the windows reflected faintly off the low clouds, just enough to show the slumped shape of Donald Clermont. A .45 caliber service revolver was still in his hand, and the side of his skull was a mask of blood and shattered bone.

But what Walter Soames remembered most during those sleepless nights in the years to come, ever more frequent after the death of his wife and his subsequent retirement, was what occurred when he returned inside the house and informed the ambulance attendants that they had not one, but two, corpses to take back to town. Numb with shock, he had leaned over the open diary, searching for some clue as to what might have happened.

Beneath the final line in Clermont's hand, a single word was scrawled which he was certain had not been there before:

Selena.

PART TWO

June 1988

FIVE

On a glorious Saturday afternoon, Gene Farrell leaned against the veranda railing of the big white house overlooking Clermont Vineyards, sipped Beefeater gin, and surveyed with disinterest the stream of arriving guests. He did not know many of them, but he knew enough not to expect surprises.

Affluence showed in the cars and dress, sedateness in the deportment. Most were older by at least a decade than his own thirty years. He shook his head wryly and took a long drink of the tart gin. It was true that he had moved to the wine country to get away from a frenetic life in San Francisco. He just had not expected quite this degree of success.

Although he was vague about the precise circumstances of the party, he gathered that it was a sort of housewarming. The Clermont family mansion had been unoccupied for some time, but an heiress had appeared and commissioned an extensive revamping. The event today marked her official occupancy and her entry into wine country society. Farrell envisioned a brittle, aging, high-strung woman, probably several times divorced, who had come to this part of the world because she had worn out others, and would only last until she wore out this one, too. Doubtless, she would be about as interesting to him as the other guests. He finished his drink too fast, already beginning to regret that he had come.

As he was starting a second trip to the bar, he saw a cloud of dust speeding along the rough stretch of dirt road that climbed to the winery from the county highway. He squinted, surprised, at the vehicle in the midst of it. He was no expert on sports cars and could not identify the make right off, but it was exotic, possibly even a Ferrari or Maserati. Most striking of all was the color: a strange glowing silver he had never seen anything quite like before. The driver was speeding along the deeply rutted road, plunging and bouncing, endangering the car's tires and undercarriage. Some vineyard owner's spoiled kid, he thought with a touch of distaste; but as the vehicle slid to a stop beside the house and the dust settled, he found himself still gazing at its eerie color–almost as if moonlight had been captured in paint–and he admitted that it added a refreshing contrast to the neutral-tinted, sensible sedans.

"I see you've spotted our hostess," said a voice at his elbow. "Late for her own party." Farrell had just time to glimpse a tanned leg emerge from the open car door and a toss of long dark hair. He blinked in surprise: the mental picture he had formed was a million miles off.

"Hello, Elaine," he said, turning to the handsome, fiftyish woman who had come to stand beside him.

"You don't need to pretend I'm very interesting by comparison to Selena Clermont," she said archly.

He grinned and leaned forward to kiss her cheek. "You'll always be my first love," he said gallantly.

Elaine Ross had been a college friend of his mother's, and during his childhood had been to him the equivalent of a favorite aunt. She had lived in Sonoma most of her life, and was a well-established member of local society; it was she who had arranged his invitation here today. She had lost her husband, a gentle, soft-spoken man Farrell had grown up calling "Uncle Bill," to cancer two years before, and while she never spoke of her loneliness, it had been a factor in his choosing the Sonoma Valley when he was deciding to resettle: as if he were drawn to her as a fellow refugee from life, in some ways closer even than family.

A glance back over his shoulder gave him another glimpse of the tanned legs flashing beneath the hem of a white dress, before Selena disappeared into the crowd.

"So that's the lady we're here to honor," he said casually, knowing it would open the floodgate of gossip. For the first time, he was interested.

"Yes. She's been living in New York the last couple of years, and Europe before that. Her family used to own the winery, but her grandmother sold it off a few years ago—all except this house. Selena's inherited it, and a good deal more besides." Elaine tapped his forearm for emphasis. "The rumor is that she spent close to a hundred thousand dollars getting the place redone."

"Jesus," he said. But a glance through the windows into the living room, with its rich carpet and drapes, new leather furniture, and white-coated waiters carrying trays of champagne among the milling guests, made it clear that there was no shortage of money.

"Yes, it does seem rather a lot. But the house was quite run down; no one had lived here for more than twenty years. Since she was born, as a matter of fact. But that's another story."

"Oh, yeah? Do I smell scandal?"

"We really shouldn't talk about it," Elaine said. "It was a terrible tragedy."

"No fair," he protested. "You can't set me up like that, then pull back."

"Well," she said, glancing around. She leaned forward confidentially.

But another woman had stepped out onto the deck and was approaching; Elaine turned to her graciously.

"Robin, dear, how lovely you look. Have you met Gene Farrell?"

Annoyed, he forced a polite smile. Robin looked to be a few years younger than himself. She was softly pretty, but her chiffon dress, complete with a beribboned straw hat, made her look like an outsized child, and she wore too much makeup. Her smile was coquettish to the point of being vaguely offensive. When she offered a plump hand, he noted automatically the absence of a ring, and began phrasing the words, *Excuse me, I was just on my way to the bar*.

But Elaine, as if sensing his impending escape, laid a hand on his arm and said, "Darling, I've just remembered, I must have a word with Mary Layton. Do excuse me. I'm sure you young people, will have plenty to talk about." She smiled innocently and went on her way, leaving Farrell to cover his exasperation.

"And what do you do, Gene?" Robin said. He could sense her appraisal of him, so far neutral at best: he was a not very prepossessing man in this elegantly groomed crowd. His shirt and blue jeans were clean but rumpled, his Nikes nearly worn out from actually having been run in. His sandy hair was longish, curly, and also rumpled, his slightly beaked nose crooked from high school football. He was not tall, and his thick chest and shoulders, with a small waist, gave him an almost gnomelike look.

"I'm a physician," he said.

A gleam appeared in her eye. "Really." One hand rose to toy with the hat's ribbon. "What sort of practice?"

"Emergency room."

He watched the gleam diminish a notch, dampened by doubt as to whether this particular specialty shared in the important facets of practicing medicine: six-figure income, country-club memberships, status. Did ER doctors even play golf?

"It must be very–interesting."

Farrell shrugged. "Most of the time it's coughs and cuts and mining impacted shit out of old folks who haven't been taking their Metamucil. But once in a while you get a pretty good one, like when the Saturday Night Knife and Gun Club meets, and you get to wallow around in body cavities till hell won't have it. Up to the fucking elbows. I've decided that mesentery is my *medium,* you know what I mean?"

Her hand, still holding the ribbon of her hat, had stopped moving. Keeping his gaze locked on hers, he took a half-step closer.

"Or a motorcycle wreck where nobody's been wearing helmets, they"re my real favorites," he said, his voice husky with passion. "Where you got a couple teenaged kids who've been out showing off, and now they're looking at fulfilling, productive futures on life-support systems. You know what it's like going into one of those skulls to see what's left of the brain? It's like picking the shell off a hard-boiled egg you smashed for breakfast. Except, you know, a *huge, hairy, blood-soaked* hard-boiled egg."

Her mouth had become a small round O, her eyes glassy.

"But hey, this is no time for shop talk," he said, dropping back into a conversational tone. "It's a beautiful afternoon, it reminds me of this really beautiful poster I saw one time: today is, like; the first day of the rest of your life. Could I get you a drink?"

"No," she said faintly. "Thank you. I have to–find my sister."

"Next time, let's talk about what *you* do," he called after her.

He shoved his hands into his pockets and started off at nothing, feeling sour. That had been unfair. But it was not just her. It was the whole business of pretense and forced politeness and social convention, of form without substance, of status without underlying value: a vast amorphous anonymous blob of bullshit that crushed people under its weight.

Or perhaps what really angered him was himself, for the feeling that he succumbed to that bullshit a little more, fought a little less hard, each day. The syndrome was impossible to escape–its unseen tentacles were everywhere–and battling it was like trying to punch out the Pillsbury Doughboy.

And maybe erupting against the occasional target, even a not-so-innocent sacrificial lamb like Robin, was a needed form of catharsis: the psychological equivalent of going to bed with a woman even though he knew it was a mistake. Within seconds after orgasm, he would be wishing it had never happened–and, yet, he knew he would do it again. He had stopped pretending it was ever going to be different, and had begun to envision a future as an ineffectual curmudgeon, cynical because of his own failure to maintain a peculiar form of integrity he could not even put a name to.

He walked glumly into the house and made his way through the crowd toward the bar, declining a glass of champagne from one waiter and a tray of hors d'oeuvres from another, nodding at people who seemed as though they might be interested in striking up an acquaintance, but moving steadily on. There was no sign of either Elaine or Selena; his curiosity was doomed to remain unsatisfied, at least for the present. With a fresh drink, he headed outside again, not sure what he was looking for except breathing room. The parking area was bordered on one side by thick, leafy oaks. He walked down from the deck, and with relief, leaned back against one, letting his gaze wander.

The mansion was like a feudal castle, overlooking the fiefs below; there was even a scattering of bungalows, no doubt for the estate's modern serfs. The surrounding vineyards sloped down to the Sonoma Valley, perhaps two miles distant; up its center, a constant stream of traffic marked the winding route of Highway 12 to Santa Rosa. To the south he could see the town of Sonoma itself, and to the west, the small coastal mountains that separated the valley from the Pacific, their foothills already browning in the midsummer sun. If he had been another few hundred feet in elevation, he would have been able to look over the mountains to San Francisco, perhaps even see all the way across the city to the towers of the University of California hospital on Parnassus Heights—where Valerie was probably in her office right now.

Calling it "stopping out" doesn't fool anybody, Gene. You're jeopardizing the career you've worked for all your life.

"'In a world of fugitives, he who takes the opposite direction will be said to be running away,'" he muttered aloud. Val had snorted in disdain when he had quoted the line to her. He admitted there were times when it had a hollow ring, even—especially—to his own ears.

He let his black slide down the tree trunk until he was crouching. His gaze moved restlessly, stopping at the gleaming silver of Selena Clermont's car. Whatever it was, he would have bet it had cost well over fifty grand.

But money did not much interest him; and he had all the woman trouble he needed with Valerie. He stood, drained the gin, and decided to allow himself one more before admitting that the day was a bust.

The party was in full swing, the inside of the house and the veranda resonant with talk, laughter, and the clink of glasses. He was just stepping away from the bar when a cluster of bodies shifted, and he got his first good look at Selena.

She was standing with a group of older people, perhaps ten yards away, wearing a simple, close-fitting white dress and sandals, with several bracelets and rings. Her hair was like a dark mane halfway down her back, with auburn highlights glinting in the sun. Shadowy lines of definition played up and down one arm as she gestured to make a point; the tendons behind her ankles were like tight-strung cables. Her face was too sharp and intense to really be called pretty.

But what his first glimpses of her had not revealed, and what struck him now with almost stunning force, was an altogether different quality than mere physical beauty: a freshness, a vitality, that showed in the gloss of her hair, in the intelligence in her eyes, in the vibrant way she moved. She made him think of a splendid wild animal deigning somewhat impatiently to consort with lesser creature—a living human in a room full of wax figures. Above all, there seemed to be a total lack of self-consciousness—replaced by some mysterious inner quality, unheeded and unrestrained, as if it were a facet of herself she could not control, and which unawareness only caused to shine the brighter.

In his entrancement, he hardly realized he was staring until, as if sensing his gaze, she flashed him a quick, piercing look. It was knowing, cool, even contemptuous. He averted his eyes, feeling his face grow hot. Very good, Farrell, he thought grimly. The lady is doubtless sick to death of just that kind of stare, and here you are ogling like a drunken Shriner at a convention.

Well, it was a sign, an omen of what he had been feeling anyway: for him, the party was over–if it had ever really begun. He decided to down the final drink and make a quiet, unannounced exit. With combined relief and moroseness, he started toward the door.

Only to see Elaine Ross making her way toward him determinedly.

"What happened to Robin?" she said.

He winced. "She had to go find her sister."

"Well, that's an acquaintance you should cultivate. She's a very nice young woman, from a good family. She has a little boutique in St. Helena, and she's doing quite well with it."

No doubt, he thought. "I'm sure she's a sweetheart."

"Do I detect a note of sarcasm there, young man?" she said, folding her arms.

He saw a tiny flicker in her eyes, anxiety or calculation or both, and he realized that there was another dimension to this.

"What's going on, Elaine?" he said. "Why are you all of a sudden concerned about my love life?" The remark attracted glances from a couple of people nearby. He smiled tightly at them and drew her aside.

For several seconds, they studied each other's faces, and for the first time, he realized that while he had watched her age, she had watched him form.

"Your mother's worried about you, Gene," she said finally. "And I agree. You're confused right now, and you're spending too much time alone. That can be very bad for a man, especially a man with your background." She nodded at the drink in his hand.

"My background?" he said, getting angry. "I had nothing to do with the old man's juicing."

"But you grew up watching it–watching him hide from his problems that way–and that's how children learn. Being half Irish doesn't help. You've inherited that moody temperament, along with the way of dealing with it. You've been depressed lately, haven't you?"

He said nothing.

"Haven't you?" she said again, more gently. "Neither your mother nor I blames you for leaving that residency. It sounded horrible. But you can't chuck your life along with it."

"And so Mom enlisted you to play matchmaker."

"I said nothing at all about matchmaking. I said you were spending too much time alone."

"I appreciate your concern, Elaine," he said, and looking for a way off the hook, went on with a half-truth: "But I'm still involved with Valerie."

"The Commissar?" she said, smiling thinly. "Gene, be realistic. She's a fine woman in her own way, but she has no imagination or sense of humor. Take it from an old married lady: if you can't play with your mate, you'll be absolutely desperate within a year of saying 'I do.' Be thankful that something in you recognizes that."

He raised his glass and sipped, trying to cover the confusion her words aroused.

"The proof's in the pudding, isn't it," Elaine said. "She's there and you're here. You left. If life with Valerie was what you wanted, you'd still be there with her—and still slaving away in that surgery ward."

I left because I needed a change, he started to say, It's only temporary, I *am* going back. But Elaine's words had made their mark. Instead, he defended himself with sarcasm.

"So I'm supposed to find contentment with a little Shirley Temple whose daddy bought her a boutique?"

"She's all human," Elaine said simply. "Not half machine."

A dozen biting remarks came to his mind; but he exhaled and forced a smile.

"I'm thinking it all over, Elaine," he said, "and I'll keep you posted on any major developments. Now, how about I get you a splash of champagne?"

"I shouldn't," she said doubtfully, but allowed him to take her glass.

As he went in search of a waiter, his gaze again caught Selena. She was talking to one man now, who might have been in his late forties. He was large and somewhat doughy, with oversized features and huge thick fingers, which Farrell could see even from that distance were beautifully manicured. He wore bright yellow sansabelt slacks, a white golf shirt, and a five thousand dollar Rolex on his wrist. When he smiled, he showed all his huge, perfectly capped teeth. Though his bearing indicated confidence, even arrogance, his eyes were small and watery. The look he fixed on Selena seemed ingratiating and hungry at the same time. Farrell felt a stab of cold dislike, and then realized, with jarring surprise, that it was mixed with jealousy.

He returned to Elaine and handed her the champagne, then glanced casually at Selena.

"You never finished telling me the story about our hostess."

Elaine followed his gaze and clucked her tongue in exasperation. "Gene, she's only twenty-one, and–"

"And what?"

"Well, wild."

He grunted. "Mom wouldn't approve, huh?"

Amusement came into her eyes. "The forbidden fruit is always irresistible, isn't it."

Forbidden fruit, my ass, he thought: I've never in my life seen a woman like that.

"Who's the sleazeball she's with?"

"Gene!" she said reprovingly.

Selena's hand was on the man's arm now; small eyes gleaming, he said something that made her throw back her head and laugh, a husky vibrant around that reached Farrell all the way across the room. He looked, Farrell thought, like the kind of man who would spray saliva in your face as he spoke.

"His name's Lyle Randolph," Elaine was saying. "And he is not a sleazeball, he's a dentist. He works with children, and by all accounts he's very good."

Thick fingers that spent a lot of time in little mouths, Farrell thought. Sourly, he turned away.

"You could follow those pants through a coal mine."

Elaine laughed. "Well, I confess, I hardly think he'd be right for Selena. But then, I don't think she's right for

99

you." She paused, and with her head cocked to the side, looked at him appraisingly. "Although I will say, I was married when I was only twenty-one, and not nearly as—worldly—as Selena. And I stayed married to the same man for over thirty years. How many of your smart modern women can say that?"

"Damn few," he conceded, putting his arm around her shoulders and steering her toward the door. "Now why don't we finish that little composition we started earlier: 'Scandal for a Boring Saturday Afternoon, key of C minor.'"

When consciousness returned to Gene Farrell, it was through the agency of several malevolent gremlins inside his skull, working steadily with picks and hammers to break out. For several moments, he lay unmoving, until what was left of his rational mind assured him that the pounding was really his pulse. Cautiously, he opened one eye. The inside of the lid felt like it was lined with steel wool.

He was in familiar darkness, and soon recognized it as his own bedroom. The luminous dials of the digital clock said 1:13; he had been asleep some four hours. He searched back through time, remembering the party—

And then, his conversation with Selena Clermont. He closed his eye again, trying to block the recollection out, but it lingered in the forefront of his brain, taunting him maliciously. Groaning, he swung his feet to the floor and stumbled to the kitchen in search of something to irrigate the parched desert of his throat.

He cringed from the light, and again at the sight of the half empty bottle of Tanqueray on the counter, amidst a chaos of slaughtered lemons. To one side, a gnawed cheese sandwich had turned gummy and pernicious in the warm night air. Carefully avoiding the carnage, he found a clean glass and filled it with ice and tonic. Then he went to his calendar to confirm that he did not go back on duty at the hospital until Monday morning. Relieved, he splashed a little gin into the tonic, put on jeans and a T-shirt, and went to sit in the quiet darkness of his living room.

Outside the window, a field sloped down to a creek, a dark slash across the silvery moonlit grass. Behind it rose a thick black wall of trees. Although there were other houses nearby, none could be seen. He had chosen this place largely because of its isolation, a feeling that came from a lifetime of densely populated areas; Los Angeles, Palo Alto, and San Francisco. Valerie had disapproved, arguing that he would miss the crowds, that he was foolish to think he could turn his back on civilization. But he had heard dearly beneath her words the truth of what she meant: that it was one more way of distancing himself from everything she considered important. And he supposed it was true; Valerie had never seemed further away.

"Scandal," he said softly, tasting the word. But it was not at all what he had expected, a spoiled rich girl's shenanigans; wild parties, recreational drugs, maybe an abortion or two.

No, the events that had surrounded Selena Clermont's entry into the world were of a profoundly more serious nature: her mother killed by the birth itself, a stigma no child could ever wholly overcome; her grand-father committing suicide on the scene–after trying to smother the infant girl, it was rumored; her grand-mother's subsequent abandonment of her to care centers and boarding schools.

"I probably shouldn't mention this," Elaine had said, "but some people suspected that her grandfather had–well, you know, that he was also her father. That would explain his suicide, and trying to smother her, and all. But I never believed it for a second. I knew Donald Clermont quite well. He was a fine man, and such a thing would have been simply impossible." She had raised her head and spoken the last words defiantly, as if challenging anyone who might have overheard to contradict her.

Whatever the truth was, it must have been a hell of a way to go through childhood, money or no; and his annoyance at Selena washed away in a wave of compassion. You'd be bitter too, he thought, and remembering his own loutish stare at her, added: especially if every man who looked at you was jumping you in his mind.

How much of his own cutting edge stemmed from a genial drunk of a father, who had regarded his children with bemusement and spent virtually no time with them, who had literally passed Gene on the street more than once without recognizing him?

He returned to the kitchen to fill his glass. The pleasant glow of the liquor was creeping around him like fire on a cold night, taking the edges off the hangover, sliding him back into the caress of drunkenness. He shrugged. Thirty hours remained before he had to face the world. He would sleep late, work out and eat well tomorrow, and by Monday, be fit as ever. Until leaving San Francisco four months before, he had hardly ever been drunk in his life. But Elaine was right: it was a routine that was becoming disturbingly familiar.

In fact, he thought, wincing again, it was gin that had made him bold enough to approach Selena, at a moment when the dentist Lyle Randolph had gone off to the bar. Hoping to efface his former rudeness in staring at her, he had given her his best boyish grin.

"I've been admiring your car," he said. "What make is it?"

When she glanced at him, her gaze held neither surprise nor interest, only that same level coolness.

"If you've been admiring it, how come you don't know?"

Flustered, he. said, "From a distance."

"A distance," she said, "can be a good place to stay from things you admire." She had then turned deliberately and stalked away, leaving Farrell to stare at her back. When he recovered, he managed an inane smile at the several nearby people he was sure were barely holding in their laughter, and hurried out to his own battered little Datsun pickup—to find that one of the front tires had gone flat.

He had owned the vehicle only since moving to Sonoma, and had not yet had to change a tire. He had bought it used; there was no owner's manual. Although the operation of jack and spare ultimately turned out to be quite sensible, the system was unlike any other he had ever encountered.

And toward the end of the forty-odd minutes he spent wallowing in the dust, cursing the bad road, the Japanese auto industry, the heat, and his luck, he had heard the smooth growl of finely tuned engines starting up, and turned just in time to see two cars vanishing down the road: ahead, a bottle-green Porsche driven by the canary-trousered dentist, and following it, the moonlight-colored sports car of Selena Clermont, with her unmistakable dark hair and profile behind the wheel.

He slumped onto the couch, shaking his head ruefully. It was, after all, absurd for him to be interested in a twenty-one-year-old–he said the word deliberately aloud–"girl."

Although there was nothing girlish about the way she had handled him. It stung, and it stung worse that she had taken off with a man who was, despite Elaine's disclaimer, an obvious creep. At least, he thought sardonically, you couldn't say she did not like older men.

He finished the drink and decided to allow himself one more before dutifully putting something into his stomach. Perhaps there would be an old movie on TV that he could watch until he dozed off on the couch. As he entered the kitchen, the phone rang, startling him. His immediate flash was, the hospital. It was a sensation like an unpleasant electric shock, with the attendant memories of years of sleep caught in few-hour snatches, of endless weary rushing, of his time and his life itself belonging, not to him, but to medicine.

But those days were gone, he remembered with a flood of relief. Nowadays, when he left the emergency room, his job was done. He deliberately had no phone in his bedroom, and closed the door on the one in the kitchen when he wanted uninterrupted sleep, a luxury undreamed of in his former life. Wondering who could be calling at two o'clock in the morning, he answered.

"Where have you been?" came Valerie's agitated voice. He closed his eyes, wishing he had foreseen the obvious and let it ring.

"Asleep," he said, hearing the faint slur in his own voice.

"All evening? So soundly you didn't hear your telephone?"

"I went to a party and got a little drunk."

"Oh, wonderful. That makes me feel much better. The term for that is 'passing out,' Gene, not 'falling asleep.'" He said nothing.

"Did you drive home?" Then, with sudden suspicion, "Or did someone take you?"

"Val, I'm not feeling so hot. Why don't we talk tomorrow."

"Is someone there?"

"No," he said patiently. "I am absolutely, entirely alone. I have had no sexual contact with any species of being, male or female, human, animal, or extraterrestrial, since I last saw you. Okay?"

"I want you to promise me not to drink any more."

"Jesus Christ," he said with sudden heat, "everybody in the fucking world knows what's good for me."

There was an icy silence. Then she said, "Well. I was going to offer to drive up and visit tomorrow. But since you're feeling so touchy, maybe it's not a good idea."

The words, You're right, it's not, hovered on his lips. Then he exhaled and stepped into the dutiful role he knew so well how to play.

"I'd love to see you, honey," he said. "I apologize for my churlish behavior, and I promise I'll be Little Lord Fauntleroy when you get here."

"I'll think it over," she said, aloof now, "and call you in the morning." With undisguised sarcasm, she added, "That is, if you're answering the phone."

He hung up, stared vacantly at the wall for a moment, then freshened his drink. Glass in hand, he walked into the bedroom and switched on the desk light. Valerie's photograph smiled sternly at him. Her face was attractive, square and strong, framed by a short, no-nonsense haircut. She kept her body trim and firm with an unyielding regimen of diet and exercise. She always slept nude, was warm as a furnace in the foggy chill of San Francisco dawns, and was as matter-of-fact and professional about fulfilling sexual needs, both his and her own, as about everything else.

The Commissar, he thought: Elaine's term for her. *She has no imagination and no sense of humor.* There was some truth to it. At twenty-eight, Val was one of the rising assistant administrators at one of the West Coast's premier hospitals. She was driven in the same way as some of his former surgery colleagues: a drive he had often associated with precisely that lack of imagination.

106

And she wanted, or at least *had* wanted, to marry a promising young resident named Gene Farrell.

If you can't play with your mate, you'll be absolutely desperate within a year of saying "I do."

He shrugged; it seemed increasingly like something that had happened a long time ago to somebody else. Beside her photo was one of himself, in cap and gown, taken a few short years before, upon his graduation from UCLA med school: smiling confidently at the life he had envisioned. But now he was no longer a surgeon, no longer promising–perhaps no longer even young.

He found a frozen Swiss steak dinner in the refrigerator, put it in the oven, and turned on the TV. With pleasure, he realized he had come upon Casablanca: Claude Rains was villainously demanding a lady's virtue in return for arranging her and her hand-wringing husband's passage out of Africa.

Farrell settled back, and as he grew drowsy with the gin and the warm smell of the pseudo-food baking in the oven, he found himself half-thinking, half-dreaming of the vibrancy of Selena Clermont's presence.

The main cabin of Lyle Randolph's houseboat was decorated with photographs of smiling children, all with perfect teeth: presumably his patients. He was a bachelor, he had said, without a family of his own. Selena studied the pictures, with a combination of anger and excitement rising within her. The display was innocent enough on the surface–a man exhibiting his art, as it were–but she knew that beneath that lay something far more sinister. It was the reason she had come here.

Randolph was below, where he believed he was setting the stage for his seduction of her. In truth, it was just the reverse.

She stepped out onto the deck. The oval moon hung over the harbor in Tiburon, casting its chilly reflection to rise and fall in the dark waters of San Francisco Bay. To the south, she could see the brightly lit skyline of the city. Beneath her feet, the. boat rocked gently. It was large, comfortable, and richly if garishly appointed. The harbor's gentle swells and the warm light exuding from surrounding craft suggested peace, affluence, and safety.

You give us poor sustenance, Selena.

She tossed her head angrily as the familiar voice sounded in her mind, at first refusing to acknowledge the presences that were gathering to hover around her.

But it was no use. Her own mind framed a cold reply: *Then go find your own, Hasmoday.*

With pleasure, came the immediate, mocking reply, even as she was regretting her words. *Would that you would free us to do so.*

Resignedly, she opened her inner vision to the cluster of predators who had been her companions since birth. They bristled with coarse hair, sprouted trunks and horns and sex organs, suddenly opened eyes or gaping mouths in the midst of bellies, then subsided into hideously naked, featureless lumps of flesh, only to begin again. It was like watching a living painting by Bosch. She focused on the imp called Hasmoday, largest and strongest of the swirling, cavorting group. Stabler than the others, he usually maintained the same appearance, as a faunlike creature with pointed ears, shaggy legs, and a malicious smile.

She had seen him in aspects not nearly so pleasant.

I give the same as always.

Yes, diseased cattle, came the imp's contemptuous reply. *It is no longer enough.*

Hard talk for an eater of table scraps, she thought scathingly.

Not so, he answered with wounded dignity. *I am of a higher nature than these.* He swept a hand to indicate the other shapes. *You force me into the shame of sharing their wretched food. But far worse, you betray our mistress.*

Since when do you speak for her?

He ignored the question. *She is furious, Selena. Your evasions have gone on too long. The time has came for change.*

Below the deck, a door closed. Footsteps sounded on the stairway.

I am not her slave. The thought came out less certainly than she had intended.

The imp smiled with icy charm. *We will talk again soon.*

The shapes began to retreat. Although she always knew intuitively the precise phase of the moon, she gave it a quick glance. It was on the wax, not quite full.

"In two weeks, Hasmoday, you will feed," she called hoarsely.

You waste your breath protesting to me, Selena, came the mocking, silent words. *You have a much greater worry now.*

The footsteps were reaching the top of the stairs. The moment was near, and she felt the familiar tightening in her stomach: the combination of anticipation and disgust she had come to know all too well over the years. As always, she consoled herself with the knowledge that it would soon be over—at least until the next time. Hurriedly, she composed herself. When she turned to Lyle Randolph, she was smiling.

"Did I hear you talking to somebody?" he said. He scanned the surrounding boats suspiciously.

"To the moon," she said.

He glanced at her sidelong. "Oh?" He began to open the bottle of champagne he held in his thick, perfectly manicured hands. His motions were careful, patient, precise. "What were you telling it?"

"*It* is a *she*," Selena said. She stepped closer to him, turning her smile seductive, but at the same time carefully keeping her tone girlish. "I was telling her how lucky I was to run into you."

"I'm the one who's lucky," he, said, looking pleased. Then, as if he were joking, "You're young enough to be my daughter." As he spoke, he filled glasses.

He handed her one, leaning forward to nuzzle her throat. The scent of sweet cologne was so strong it almost stopped her breath.

"To my little girl," he said. She touched her glass to his with a soft ringing clink. She drank, staring boldly into his eyes, seeing his sickness close to the surface now.

"Would you like to meet her?" Selena said. "The moon?"

He shrugged. "Sure."

"You will," Selena said. "As soon as she's dark. When you don't see her in the sky, that's when she's down here on earth, walking through the night. Hunting with her hounds."

Randolph laughed. "I didn't know she was such a tough lady."

"You better believe it," Selena said. "She hunts people down and eats them. Only not their flesh and blood, she gives that to the dogs. She want their souls."

His laughter rose again, but it was an uneasy sound, and a wary look came into his watery eyes.

She laughed too and stepped closer, coyly putting her hand on his arm.

"You think I'm strange, don't you."

He did not answer.

"I can get even stranger."

Randolph paused with his glass halfway to his lips, his eyes measuring the intent of her words. He drank, slowly, deliberately, and she watched his mind trying to determine whether this was a tease, or outright craziness—or if she was truly the wild rich girl his imagination craved.

"Yes?" he said. "Like how?"

"I'd have to show you."

His eyebrows rose. Too casually, he said, "I think I'd like that."

"But I need inspiration."

He finished his champagne and refilled the glasses. He was smiling, his big teeth very white in the moonlight.

"You tell me what kind of inspiration you need, honey. I've got just about everything you can think of

111

right here on this boat: booze, prescription pharma-ceuticals—even laughing gas."

She held his gaze, letting her fingers toy with her dress between her breasts.

"What turns you on?" Randolph said thickly, watching her fingers.

She half-turned away, letting the silence stretch, until she sensed his concern, rising to near panic, that he was losing her. Then she wheeled to face him.

"Secrets," she breathed. "That's what turns me on. What have you got that you've never shown anybody else?"

Randolph swallowed thickly.

She stepped toward him and let her fingernails lingeringly brush his groin.

"What's your very *very* most secret thing?" she whispered.

For long seconds, he neither moved nor spoke, while excitement, fear, and guilt warred in his sweating face.

"I have some movies," he finally said, his voice low and hoarse.

"Movies!" she said, stepping back in scorn. "You think I haven't seen every kind of movie there is?"

He shook his head. "You can't buy these."

And then, the word she had been waiting for, that brought into focus what she had sensed the instant she saw him: the evil black bulk of the predator, clinging like a leech to the base of his brain, urging him on and feeding off his sickness:

"Kids."

Her smiled deepened as she took his hand.

"Show me," she said softly, and turned to lead him down the stairs.

SIX

The next afternoon found Gene Farrell once again on the dirt road to Clermont Winery, gritting his teeth at the truck's bouncing and his own annoyance. He had not planned on returning so soon. Or for that matter, ever.

But after he had gotten the flat tire fixed in town, and then gone to replace the spare where it rested beneath the truck's bed, he had discovered that the jack handle, and the key to the chain hoist that raised and lowered the spare, was missing.

There was only one place he could have left it, he decided unhappily: in the dust outside Selena Clermont's house. He remembered putting the jack itself back in the truck, but could not recall having touched the handle again; he had, after all, been frazzled, angry, and a little drunk. He supposed he could buy a new one, but on Sunday, the Datsun dealer was closed; and he suspected he might have to buy an entire new jack assembly, which would certainly be expensive and possibly take days or even weeks to get.

In short, it was worth the twenty-minute drive to take a look; with luck, there would be no one around Selena's house, and he would find it immediately and be gone. The idea of facing her again, especially branded by yet another act of stupidity—or even worse, to have her suspect that he had left the tool there deliberately as an excuse to return—was a grim one, and he spoke sternly to himself as he drove, with a wary eye for the welfare of his tires, the final rocky quarter-mile. His hangover and the afternoon's sultry heat did not help.

The truth was, he thought as the rooftop of the house came in sight, that even if she were home, she would not remember who he was. She was probably still off playing with Lyle Randolph.

But her silver car was back in the driveway, alone. Although there were no signs of life, the veranda and grounds were as spotless as if a team of elves had come in during the night and obliterated all traces of the previous day's festivities. He pulled the pickup over to the place where he had changed the tire. As he was stepping out, a flash like sunlight on glass caught his gaze, up a hillside a few hundred yards away. He swiveled toward it, staring, but it was gone. A broken bottle, maybe, revealed for an instant by a breeze parting the thick green foliage.

Deliberately ignoring both her car and house, keeping his eyes on the ground, he paced slowly. The jack handle was about three feet long and painted red, but after four or five minutes of careful circling, there was no sign of it. Either it was buried completely in the dust, or more likely, someone had noticed it and taken it inside.

He shoved his hands in his pockets and stood, trying to decide what to do: knock on the door, and take the chance of ridicule? Or just fork out the money for a new one?

He had admitted defeat and chosen the latter, and was reaching for the truck's door handle, when a rough male voice with a distinct Okie twang called out:

"You got business here, mister?"

Startled, Farrell turned. The man striding toward him was tall, lanky, thick-wristed, with a slicked-back ducktail haircut and a narrow, long-jawed face. He was wearing grease-stained jeans and a faded work shirt with the tail hanging partly out. At a guess, he was a caretaker or vineyard hand. No guessing was necessary to see that he was not friendly. Farrell's own bad mood bristled in response, but he immediately quelled it. There was no percentage in trouble.

"I was at the party yesterday," he said. "I changed a tire, and I think I left my jack handle here. You wouldn't happen to have seen it?"

The tall man squinted suspiciously, then turned and spat a brown stream of tobacco juice.

"What's a jack handle look like for one of them Jap toy trucks, a toothpick?"

Farrell smiled slowly. "That's clever," he said. "You think it up all by yourself? Or maybe you heard it on TV. I mean, I can tell you didn't *read* it."

The tall man went very still.

"Except maybe in a comic book," Farrell said.

Whatever might have happened next was stopped by the sound of the house door opening. Both men turned.

Selena, wearing a short terry-cloth wrapper, stepped out onto the veranda, folded her arms, and surveyed them coolly. Farrell felt like a small boy caught in mischief by a teacher. It was all he could do to keep from hanging his head.

"Roy, are you finding a way to help Doctor Farrell?" she said, surprising him: she not only remembered him, but knew his name.

"He says he lost a jack handle," Roy answered sullenly, not meeting her eyes.

"Have you seen it?"

"Nome," Roy mumbled.

"Then thank you. Doctor Farrell, won't you come in?"

She stepped back into the house, leaving the door open. Farrell glanced at Roy and met a stare of such antagonism that his breath stopped.

"If I do find the son of a bitch," Roy said softly, "I'll bend it into a pretzel. Round your neck, if I catch you here again." He wheeled and stalked down the hill.

Rubbing his jaw, Farrell started for the big house. Whatever else he might or might not know about Selena, this much seemed clear: her effect on men was not neutral.

The house's inside, like the outside, was spotless and in perfect order; cleaning must have started as soon as the party was over. Selena was leaning into a closet, the robe riding nearly to one hip, exposing a long, tanned thigh. Farrell looked pointedly away. When she turned back to him, she was holding the jack handle.

"Is this what you're looking for?"

117

"Yes," he said, relieved that at least there was evidence that his mission was not altogether contrived. "I'm sorry for disturbing you. I thought maybe it would be in the parking lot, and I could just grab it and go."

"One of the cleaning crew found it," she said.

They met halfway across the room. Her skin glistened with a fine film of oil, and its warm fragrance filled his nostrils. She must have been sunbathing, he realized. The thought made him a little dizzy. If Lyle Randolph was still around, there was no sign of him, or of anyone else.

The cool metal of the jack touched his hand with a tiny shock of static, and he almost blurted, *Look, we've gotten started all wrong, I think you're very attractive, could I take you to dinner?*

But if her eyes were not hostile, they were not friendly either; there was only that same level coolness he had already grown used to. Her seeming politeness, he realized, was simply that of good manners.

"Thanks," he said, and started for the door, congratulating himself on not compounding his buffoonishness yet again.

He was almost to his truck when she called after him, "It's a Lotus Esprit."

He turned, and thought he saw her smile slightly before she stepped back inside and closed the door.

Selena walked back upstairs to the balcony off her bedroom. Her gaze went automatically to the hillside opposite, although she knew that Roy Lutey—with his binoculars—hadn't had the nerve to return to what he

118

supposed was his secret stake-out spot for spying on her. He had the instincts of an animal, she thought, almost amused: on the arrival of another man, he had rushed down to do battle. The intrusion into her privacy was annoying, and she had considered putting an end to him. But while he was hardly admirable, neither was he in a class with the victims she preferred; and she felt sorry for his wife.

A chaise lounge and novel awaited her, the trappings of another long afternoon ahead. She started to take off the robe, to stretch out again in the sunlight; but her fingers stopped untying the belt as she caught a glimpse of Gene Farrell's truck leaving the last stretch of the vineyard's dirt road. She had been deliberately hard on him, as she always was with decent men who were attracted to her, and she was already regretting her friendly parting words. If he took them as a sign of encouragement, she would have to hurt him again—this time with real cruelty. Trying to explain that it was for his own safety would be useless.

The angels had looked upon the daughters of men, she thought, *and found them fair.* How many people who had ever lived had any idea how close that could come to the literal truth? Not Farrell, certainly; although he was merely naive, not venal or stupid.

Nor was the term "angels" quite correct.

Her gaze swept across the property her grandmother had left her, an object of envy to all who saw it. They would not envy other facets of her heritage. She 'd been four years old before she understood that while

119

other children also had imaginary playmates, theirs did not actually appear.

Or haunt—even destroy—anyone she got close to.

What would it be like, she found herself thinking while Farrell's truck disappeared from view, to unite with a man out of attraction instead of hatred? A normal woman might be so bold as to call him, invite him to dinner, take the first tentative steps in the game that all mankind played, that made life worth living.

But the question that arose was larger. Did not her momentary softening toward him speak to her growing weariness? In the past, she had been cold and strong. But recently, after each man, it had gotten worse, as if the human side of her, long subdued by the stronger half of her nature, was struggling to rise, to demand recognition—to refuse any longer to be what she had perforce become. The emotions she had tried long ago to kill in herself were not dying, but growing, especially in those rare instances when she encountered a man like Farrell, who had in his makeup an extra element that touched on the mystical—a longing for something beyond the narrow confines of this world. It complemented her own desire for precisely the opposite: for humanity, for a touch of normalcy. She had not realized how powerful that desire had become; it was beginning to treacherously affect her behavior.

She turned and walked into the bedroom. There she paused, her gaze moving restlessly around. When the house had come into her possession on her twenty-first birthday, a few months before, she had entered and found this room with its once-bright wallpaper faded, its ceiling streaked with cobwebs, and the pathetic mementos of dust-caked posters from two decades before. Although no one told her—or at least no person—she understood that it was the room in which she had been born. The rest of the house, she had decreed, must be completely overhauled: walls patched and painted inside and out, floors refinished, drapes and rugs and furniture replaced. But this room, she had only cleaned and made her private place: a sanctum sanctorum, with its bed no man would ever share.

In one corner stood a lovely oak china closet, with intricately carved doors and panes of beveled glass. She had found it in London a decade ago and understood immediately that it was what she needed to house her collection—in those days, just beginning. She smiled faintly at the memory of the antique dealer's patronizing reaction to an eleven-year-old girl, unaccompanied by parents or guardian, demanding to make a purchase of several hundred pounds—until she had produced the cash.

The shelves were lined with vessels, all different shapes and designs, but all of silver. Each contained a small quantity of dark liquid; in most, it was congealed or dried. There were forty-one of them, three or four per year since she had begun the collection.

In number forty-two, a delicately chased perfume vial from Spain, the liquid was still fresh rich red.

Her thoughts returned to the dim light below the decks of Lyle Randolph's houseboat. Again, she saw herself rising from the bed and padding barefoot to her purse. Silver razor in hand, she turned back to him. He lay in a deathlike sleep, as they always did when she had finished with them. In repose, his face had turned heavy and dissipated; his tanned skin looked sallow, his hair thin, his muscles flaccid.

At the foot of the bed, a stack of video cassettes, labeled only in a numbered code, rested beside the over-sized television. She remembered the images that had played: young faces frightened, or blank from drugs, or eager to please the masked adults.

And in Randolph's avid eyes, she had seen the fierce hunger of the predator to which he had given himself. It watched her too, hating her with an inarticulate rage, knowing it would soon be dispossessed; and though it was powerless to harm her, she felt the same thrill of repulsion and fear as if she were watching an angry cobra in a glass cage. It belonged to the most evil and virulent species: those which joined with humans to prey on the young.

She knelt beside the man and performed the familiar ritual, drawing the blade slowly beneath his jaw, from below his ear to just past his carotid: a slice of perhaps two inches, almost, but not quite deep enough to sever the artery. When he awoke and found the wound, he would like as not think it was from her nails. Then she filled a silver vial with his blood, pausing to wet one fin-ger and raise it to her lips.

The first time she had stood above a sleeping man with a knife in her hand, she was nine years old, and she had intended to kill him. But Hasmoday's voice had whispered of the far more special fate that awaited him, and she had contented herself with a souvenir.

As if the imp had been listening, his voice came suddenly into her mind.

Congratulations, Selena. Your performance last night was exceptional.

She exhaled in exasperation as he appeared to her inner vision. Today, he was alone. The others would be following Lyle Randolph, preparing for their coming feast, grooming him psychologically to extract from him maximum terror. Like all humans whose perceptions opened to see or even sense them, he would learn quickly what their company entailed.

"I wasn't calling you," she said, but her cross tone belied her unease.

He ignored her, as she had known he would. *The more you despise a man, the hotter your passion seems to grow. You should have seen yourself.*

She closed her eyes, trying not to remember. Randolph had been not only frightened by what he had revealed to her, but drunk by then, enough to require coaxing. For what the experience cost her, she had wanted to make sure of the outcome, and had gone to extremes.

"There's no need for you to watch, Hasmoday," she said, then added tauntingly, "But then, there's not much else a eunuch can do, is there?"

Not a eunuch, he answered smoothly. *A far higher order of being than humans, not hemmed in by the troublesome limitations of sex. That is, after all, a peculiarity of animals. Spirits make use of such crudity only for particular reasons. Such as the creation of those meant to serve them.*

He paused. She refused to rise to the bait.

You should be proud, Selena. You carry our mistress's immortal essence.

"Yes, and look what it's brought me."

That is your choice. You were born to far greater dignity.

"Hah! What that means is, to be a high-class whore instead of a streetwalker. And a link in a food chain all the same."

The imp was silent. Then, *But a very important link.*

She tossed her head and stalked back out to the balcony. Hasmoday hovered close, with his puckish face creased in a cunning smile.

It was decreed that you would be left to your own devices until you came of age in human terms. She hoped that you would serve her willingly. Instead, you make a mockery of the purpose for which she brought you into the world.

"My creation was none of my doing," she said bitterly.

Ah, but your all too human grandfather accepted her gift. Like all who do so, he paid a price in turn. You are the descendant of that transaction, Selena, and you must share in it; that is the nature of things. Have you not heard how the sins of the fathers will be visited on the next generations?

How we waited for a man like him! What a rare thing in these times, to find one who would allow himself that precious moment of belief! Centuries had passed since such propitious circumstances. The phase of the moon, your mother's fertility—all had to be precise.

But you continue to deny her who gave you life. Instead of bringing her the offerings she requires, you cheat her—and us, her servants, too.

The afternoon had gone from merely hot to sweltering. The air was thick and still, with even the drone of the insects sounding stupefied.

"She only made part of me," Selena said defiantly. "I'm half human, too."

How am you be proud of that? The imp seemed genuinely distressed. *Look at what they are, look at what they do.*

"Not all are like Randolph."

Most are good only because they have not the courage to be bad. You think you know them, Selena, but I have watched them since they first walked the earth. They combine the hearts of wolves with the stupidity of sheep—and arrogance unmatched even by spirits.

In truth, they are but the gods' cattle: it is why they were created. And yet, you risk our mistress's wrath to protect them.

"There is light," she said, "in all of them."

For an instant, the imp's face reflected impatient irritation; then the smooth smile replaced it. *True. And equally true that there are those who have tried to tell them so for millennia—to no avail. Selena, do you know the name Khasdiyeh? The great angel of destruction?*

When she did not reply, he went on: *Before earth or even time, an agreement was reached. The Sons of Light believed, in their naivity, that they could raise man from what he truly is. We knew differently. Thus the great war began.*

We have been proved right. Man will always give in to us, to serve his own lusts. Now the allotted time is up: the battle some have sensed but none see is all but over. Khasdiyeh has given them already the weapons that will bring about their devastation.

"They have agreed not to use them," she said quickly.

The imp laughed, a nonsound that fell silvery on her brain. *Do you think you can put such toys into the hands of children and not have them played with?*

Most remarkably, men of power seek to hasten the destruction. They foul the earth with waste, they seed strife, they profit privately from crimes they publicly decry—they even deliberately foster the overbreeding of the wretched, ensuring a misery that must soon erupt.

They do this believing they will survive and have a new earth to rule over. But the truth is, they are but the tools of the gods—even in their belief that the gods do not exist.

"What you call gods and angels, Hasmoday," she said, "men call demons."

As you wish. What matters is that only the predators will profit. Do you not see them all around you, swelling the streets of the cities, clinging to the backs of faceless, aimless humans in numbers never before known? There are too many mouths and not enough food, Selena—not just for humans, but on the unseen plane too. Hunger will force the crisis—and then the predators will prowl the earth in the aftermath of the deluge, reaping the rewards of chaos.

Soon, Selena, my brothers and I will grow fat indeed.

"Why do you tell me this?" she burst out. "Why the sudden concern?"

I do not speak on my behalf, but as our mistress's emissary—and for your benefit. She is willing to forgive you your youthful foolishness. But you are no longer a girl.

Cease your treachery. Dignify her, help to make her strong and beautiful. When the final days arrive, she will see that you survive. You have immortal blood, Selena. Death need not find you. Your prostitution will come to an end. Then, as her high priestess—as her daughter—you will be great in power in the world to come.

But should you die still rebellious—she has a very special fate awaiting you. There is nothing quite like the punishment reserved for traitors.

Selena watched a hawk circling slowly, waiting for its shadow to terrify some small bundle of fur into freezing motionless, to be snatched up in the sharp crushing talons and carried off to harsh death.

"And if I said yes?" she finally murmured.

Begin with a token of your submission, came the immediate reply. Offer her a man—but not one of the empty husks you make a practice of choosing. A strong, clean man; a man with a rich soul.

She laughed scornfully. "As if there were any such in my life. She has seen to that."

On the contrary, Selena. Your doorstep is still warm from one who passed through it.

For three beats of her heart she was motionless. Then comprehension dawned, and she whirled on the grinning imp.

"Isn't it enough what she's done to me already? Made me into a black widow and a whore?"

You made yourself into a whore, Selena. What you consider a curse was meant to protect you. She gave us to you as an entourage such as any great being must have, and charged us to keep you from falling into the swamp of humanity. She never dreamed you would deny that gift and turn traitor.

Would that you had never bitten that apple! Your life would be free of this torment.

She turned away, palms pressed to the sides of her face.

Why continue it, Selena? This path you have chosen harms everyone: our mistress, us, and you. These men you insist on offering are hardly a mouthful to us and useless to her. You suffer their embraces with loathing, only to needs be fly from one to the next. You fear for those who are good, but you cannot save them. Save yourself instead. Serve her as you were meant to. She will forgive you. You will be a queen in the new world, ruling over the cattle—and never again having to endure their bestial embraces.

His hovering presence began to fade. Then, as if in afterthought, he lingered, patting his belly, his face lined with mock pain.

My little brothers and I hunger. Perhaps it is time for us to get acquainted with your neighbor's charming children.

"You cannot!"

Things have changed, Selena. Now that you are of age, the strictures that have held us in check are dissolving. As you choose for yourself, so you must take the consequences.

"You lie," she said through her teeth.

We shall see, came the reply. *While you consider, do not forget to imagine how the Queen of Hell would punish betrayal by her own blood.*

Give her the man. Soon.

For a long time afterward, Selena stood without moving, staring at the distant hilltops. Some part of her had known that change must come, that she could not go on as she had been; now she realized that it was that which had driven her to return to this place of her birth, in the desire to find—what? Rest? Peace? Some justification for why she was as she was? Was it the absurd hope that this room—the doorway between two worlds, witnessing not only her own entry, but that of the companions— might absorb them all back someplace where they could do no more harm?

She knew the imp was lying, as he did much of the time. She just did not know precisely about what.

Slowly, she walked downstairs. In the kitchen, she poured a glass of chilled wine, then wandered into the living room. It seemed huge and empty. She found her gaze lingering on the place where Gene Farrell had stood when she had given him the jack handle: the closest they had come to touching.

Since childhood, she had been torn between warring voices. Because of her birthright, it was her fortune–or curse–to see and hear the imps; their messages and demands were abundantly clear. They could not kill, but could terrify, coax, pressure, lie; and because the fright of children was so powerful, those were their preferred victims. Every nightmare, every instant of childish fear, was a tasty morsel for an unseen hungry mouth–and like as not, caused by it.

There were innumerable such beings clustered around humans at all times: imps like the companions, leeches like those on Randolph, psychic vampires, and a horde of other species of greater or lesser virulence, all ravenous to feed on human pain and fear. Often, those who had seized on the weak were capable of pushing them over an edge, either into self-destruction or the destruction of others. It was the cause of countless seemingly unmotivated acts of violence.

Most humans had only ever sensed these entities dimly, as imagined glimpses into the darkest parts of their minds, or the residue of nightmares. The ancients had known them well–called them lemures, hungry ghosts, a host of other names–and sought to propitiate or defend against them. A few visionary artists had been haunted by them, and written about them or captured them on canvas.

While moderns largely scoffed, they had not gone away.

Selena had learned to disobey them, at the prompting of other, much subtler urges. These came from a source she had never perceived directly, but was certain

130

constituted a profound hidden intelligence. At times she believed she had sensed it as a spiral of light that enwrapped her inmost being.

And the goddess—that great entity who was in truth beyond sex, who existed beneath the faces of all the deities of destruction throughout time, whether styled as Hecate or Moloch, Kali or Quetzalcoatl, Magna Mater or Isis, the forgotten idols of primitive tribes or Satan himself: who, like a hydra-headed monster, had engendered the sacrifice of the living since humanity's beginning—required that light itself, to lie helplessly crushed forever within the prison of her serpentine coils, to nourish her as a stolen egg would nourish a snake.

In feeding her, Selena would become a Quisling.

And in allowing her will to be corrupted, she too would become a victim—

Ending with one of the evil predators clinging to her own back, and then live on through the centuries, existing only to feed humans to the great goddess of terror and destruction.

"Of all those such as I who have ever lived, Hasmoday," she murmured, "how many have died by their own hand?"

There was no answer. She took the empty wine glass back to the kitchen, and went upstairs to dress.

SEVEN

In the early afternoon, Dora Lutey emptied the old washing machine for the third time and carried the heavy basket of wet clothes outside to hang on the line. It was hot, in the high nineties, and growing hotter by the day. There was already talk of drought. She pushed her hair back from her perspiring forehead, thinking, the Lord won't allow harm to come to us. And even if He did, she would not dream of complaining, for His ways, if incomprehensible to man, were just.

As she worked, pinning up the endless stream of work clothes and towels and underwear that appeared every morning in the laundry room no matter how tirelessly she had emptied the hampers yesterday—almost like loaves and fishes, she thought, and then immediately murmured a prayer of repentance for her near blasphemy—her gaze strayed to the big white house on the hill, where Selena Clermont had taken up residence in a few weeks ago. The foreign car the girl drove was parked in the driveway, gleaming arrogant, pagan silver: a pure and simple object of sin. Selena herself was probably lying out in the sun right now, reading some shameless novel, or just lazing.

Of course it was wrong to envy, especially those who were paving their own roads to hell; but Dora could not repress a touch of resentment at the soft life of her new mistress. She had been pretty herself as a girl, but had been married almost half her thirty-three years, suffered two miscarriages (taken away by the Lord as punishment for her sins) before bearing her only child, and the hard years had left her looking rawboned rather than slender, her gingery hair lifeless and badly cared for, her eyes and movements perpetually weary. There had been no time for lying in the sun, no money for nice clothes or hairdos, let alone fancy cars.

There were times, she admitted, when she was troubled by the world's injustice. Why should she and her husband, who had worked hard all their lives, live in the shadow of a property, worth far more than they themselves would ever earn, that had simply been *given* to a girl hardly more than a teenager, who had never lifted a finger? In the five years they had been here, they had come to think of the big empty house almost as their own: wrong, she knew, but a hard habit to break. Their poorly constructed bungalow seemed like a hut by comparison.

But she lowered her head at the clear mental image that immediately formed, of the Reverend Emmett Tom Harner raising his forefinger in admonition, his heavy red face growing redder with reproach, his deep powerful voice growling.

Yea, sister, do you doubt the Lord's wisdom? Do you not remember His words, that the meek shall inherit the earth? That it is easier for a camel to pass through the eye of a needle than for a rich man to enter the kingdom of heaven? The Lord has blessed you with poverty, woman, that you might not fall into the worldly cesspool of temptation. When you have fought the good fight, and you pass from this veil of sorrows to your eternal reward, you will look down upon those lost souls thrashing in the snares of sinful wealth and pleasure, and you will rejoice as you watch them tumble down the primrose path to the eternal torments of hell!

And as that voice pierced her like a cold iron arrow, searching out her secret innermost self and impaling it until it writhed in shame, the others in the congregation of the Church of the Most Holy Redemption would murmur, *Amen,* and cast sidelong glances at her; and as the Reverend Harner's voice rose again, huge and almost threatening now—*Let us join in prayer for our sister Dora, that her faith might not be weakened by the foul snares of the Tempter*—she would feel Roy's silent rage beside her, humiliated by her again—it was bad enough that she was an incomplete woman, doomed by a doctor's decree to never bear more children—and know, with a strange mixture of terror and excitement, that later that night, his breath heavy with beer, he would beat her; and that would inflame him; and they would end up struggling together for a few brief moments of forbidden passion.

Afterward, he would turn away from her, spent and exhausted, silent with reproach for her having led him into sin—it was always the woman's fault—and would leave her to spend half the night praying in tearful contrition. The procreation of children was the only reason the Lord had created humans with such vile parts, and of that, she was no longer capable.

But the truly perplexing thing was that during those moments when she held him inside her, his rage would turn to tenderness, his face become like the young man she had married, not yet hardened by years of frustration and anger: like someone she could love, who loved her in return.

And perhaps, she thought miserably, she was something far worse than just the naturally weak vessel, whose body was constructed around the very gates to hell: perhaps that shameful secret self of hers did purposely rouse him to rage, just to get those few precious moments of affection.

She pinned up the last of the laundry—that task, at least, was done for today, the Lord be praised—and thought with resignation that it was time to start dinner. There was no air conditioning, and the little kitchen was poorly ventilated; cooking a roast or a chicken was a hot job. She would have been satisfied with cool salads and fruit in such weather, but Roy liked meat, and feeding him properly was her duty. Sometimes it seemed there was no end to the chores, that one slipped right into another, with intervals of sleep, until a year, five years, a lifetime were past without a clue as to what it had all meant.

But that was the Lord's province, she reminded herself: not hers to question. In the shade of a giant oak, she paused and turned to survey this place that had become her home. With the wicker basket on her hip and her ankle-length dress and kerchiefed hair, she felt like one of the elder women of Israel, overlooking the Promised Land. Steep hillsides and thick woods of oak, madrone, and laurel stretched westward to the row of cliffs that met the sky. Behind her, the gentler south-facing slopes were planted with neatly ordered rows of grapevines.

It was beautiful, lush, and peaceful: a wonder after her first ten years of marriage, moving from Bakersfield north by stages through the hot dusty Valley, with never enough money and Roy quitting jobs in rage, and drinking and fist fights and jail, and more than once, decamping in the middle of the night from some hovel where they owed several months' rent. But all that had changed when they came into the Reverend Harner's flock. He had found Roy this place and this job, the first one he had ever seemed content with; and she was proud that they gave two-tenths of everything they made, a double tithe, to the church. It was a tiny price for salvation from their blackly sinful former lives.

In the driveway of the big house on the hill, a car door slammed, followed by the low commanding growl of an engine. Dora watched the sleek silver car nose down the winery road and out of sight. Roy said it cost more than fifty thousand dollars. To her, such a sum was stupefying, beyond her imagination, and she saw anger and envy in his eyes when he spoke of it. Their beaten, dust-colored Ford pickup was almost fifteen years old.

It was only after Selena had returned that the rumors began to be whispered among the winery staff. Something terrible had happened up in that house when she was born. Her mother had died. There were hints of a suicide. None of the family had ever lived there again—until Selena. Dora was glad she had not known any of that; the big empty house was spooky enough, especially on the dark rainy winter afternoons.

Selena's arrival had brought at least one bounty: she had hired Dora to clean, for fifty dollars per week (of which ten went to the church, and all but five of the rest to Roy). Dora had tried once to talk to her, while dusting the beautiful china cabinet filled with exotic and mismatched silver vessels: tried to tell her how the Lord had died to save sinners exactly like herself and Roy—exactly like everyone else in the world, exactly like Selena. The idea was Reverend Harner's, after Roy had described to him the car and house.

But Selena had responded by asking questions, of a type Dora had never thought about.

"How do you know your religion is the true one?"

"Because God said so."

"Every religion's god tells them that. Why should yours be special?"

"The Reverend Harner says the gods other religions worship are false idols."

"Hm. Where does the Reverend Harner get his information?"

"Well, from the Bible."

"And who dictated the Bible?"

"God."

Then, laughing, Selena had said, "Did it ever occur to you that the Reverend Harner might be lying? Or even God?"

That had stunned Dora—the idea of the Reverend Harner lying was impossible enough, but *God?*—but before she could begin to think of a reply, Selena had told her firmly that she would not allow any preaching, and that Dora did not need to dust in that particular cabinet any more. The Reverend Harner scowled when Dora told him the results, but urged her to persevere.

Other than that, Selena had been both polite and generous. Nor had she engaged in any of the scandalous behavior they had expected, or at least none that they noticed. Although she occasionally spent the night elsewhere, doing Lord knew what, no men had stayed at the house or even called, and the only party had been a very proper one. Secretly, Dora was a little disappointed, and suspected Roy was too.

She shook her head gloomily. In spite of her resentment, in spite of Selena's blasphemy, that guilty secret self of hers liked the girl, even admired her strength and freedom. It made it all that much more important to bring Selena to her senses, to persuade her to die to death and live to life: one more burden on Dora's stooping shoulders.

She was about to start back to the house when she heard the sound of children's voices. A glance at the path a little way below showed her ten-year-old daughter Rosalie, a pretty girl with long black hair and sun-gold skin, walking with seven-year-old Emilio Vasquez, the eldest of the four children of Carlos, who worked the vineyards, and Estrelita, who was Dora's only friend up here, even if she was a Catholic. Head bent in earnest conversation, Rosalie did not look toward where her mother stood half-hidden by the tree. Dora started to call to her, to tell her to come help with dinner; but the girl's words stopped her.

". . . teaching me to dance," Rosalie was saying. "They want me to bring all my friends, and we can play with them."

"Meester Azdamay?" Emilio said uncertainly.

"Asthma-Day," she corrected. "And a bunch more like him. They've got hairy legs and beards and they play the bagpipes. Don't you want to learn to dance?"

Emilio shook his head.

"Well, you can just play with them, then. But you can't ever tell any grownups about this, okay? It has to be just us kids' secret."

They passed on out of hearing range. Dora was disturbed, but let them go. Mister Asthma-Day? From the description, it seemed that these friends were imaginary playmates; this far from town, in the midst of what was practically a wilderness, a group of strangers could hardly have wandered along, let alone hairy-legged, bearded, bagpipe playing strangers.

Undoubtedly, she should forbid the game; Roy would be angry if he knew. But she had had imaginary friends who eased the passage of her own ungentle childhood; and while the Reverend Harner considered dancing second in wickedness only to fornication, she was able to persuade herself that the kind of dancing Rosalie meant, children frolicking innocently, was not

139

included. She was lax with the girl, she knew, something Roy was forever grumbling about; she did not make Rosalie wear dresses and kerchiefs except when they went to town, and often allowed her to play when she should have been helping with chores. Let her be a child as long as she could, Dora thought wearily; it would be over soon enough.

Today was Friday, she remembered. Roy would be home all day tomorrow, watching sports on television and drinking beer–while the Bible made no mention of the Lord ever having danced or, forgive the thought, having sex, the Reverend Harner pointed out that He *had* turned water into wine–and Sunday, of course, they would spend most of the day at church and the rest in the Sabbath's mandatory inactivity. Sundays were a relief; besides their being the Lord's own day, Roy, subdued by a hangover and fiery words from Reverend Harner's pulpit, was usually quiet. Saturday nights were when his drinking–and, she feared increasingly, her weakness–were apt to lead them into sin.

Although it had happened twice on weeknights over the past month. Perhaps that was why Roy seemed even more sullen and restless than usual. Unease touched her heart. Strait was the gate, wide the primrose path. She would have to exert every quiet influence to see that he was not beginning that downslide.

As she turned to the house, her gaze fell on Rosalie's bicycle, and abruptly she thought, Mister Asthma-Day? Where could such a name have come from? When she had been in grade school, children with asthma were excluded from cleaning the blackboard erasers. Could the modern school system have dedicated a day to that now?

But hairy legs? Bagpipes? Rosalie had never been an imaginative child. Dora supposed she must have seen pictures in some forbidden comic book or TV show, perhaps at the Vasquez house. She would have to talk to Estrelita, try to make her understand, in the pidgin mixture of Spanish and English the two women used, that such things were evil, and that Rosalie–and Estrelita's own children, for that matter–should not be exposed to them.

She made her way slowly inside, to finish out the remaining tasks that awaited her in this day of the Lord's bounty.

The afternoon was hotter than hell, and as Gene Farrell trotted panting along the country road, his body reminded him with every step that this was not San Francisco, where the weather rarely got out of the seventies. Here, it had to be nearly a hundred. He kept a close monitor on his own physical symptoms, to make sure he was not about to succumb to heat stroke.

But when he got his second wind, he started to enjoy the fierce baking heat and the sensation of sweat pouring out of his body. It was like running in a sauna, with the same cleansing effect. Staying in good physical condition had always been of primary importance to him. He had been a three-letter athlete in high school, and had gone out for freshman football at Stanford. But he was small, he hadn't cared for the win-at-all-costs attitude of the coaches, and the rigorous academic demands of his premed curriculum had mounted each quarter. Sophomore year, he had declined the opportunity to sit on the varsity bench in favor of his studies.

There was almost no traffic on this small backwoods road, one of the great advantages to his house. Instead of having to drive to a park or deal with city streets, he simply walked out his door, spent a few minutes stretching in the yard, and began to trot. Although he hated the idea of "jogging," and, in symbolic rebellion against anything smacking of yuppiedom, always wore sweatpants instead of shorts even in the hottest weather, running had become over the years the only feasible exercise, something he could do in irregular moments of spare time, without needing to schedule a court or partner or travel to a gym. During the course of his surgery residency, even that had grown next to impossible: when he had time, he was too exhausted.

After leaving the residency, he had reviewed his body along with the rest of his life; decided that while the second had rigidified, the first had grown alarmingly soft; and when he moved to Sonoma, bought a wall-mounted weight stack, determined to alternate days of roadwork with lifting. So far, he was sticking with it, and he took pleasure in the noticeable tightening of his muscles, the added spring and balance in his movements, the overall heightened sense of being.

He reached the five-mile point on his loop and slowed to walk the last several hundred yards, a time to savor the satisfaction of the workout's completion and anticipate whatever would follow. It was Friday. He was scheduled to begin his next twelve-hour shift tomorrow night at eight. As the junior member of the emergency room team, he drew more than his share of weekends, with the attendant drama of vehicle wrecks, alcohol and drug related madness, and what was known as the Saturday Night Knife and Gun Club. Farrell did not mind–even liked the intensity and occasional real adrenaline charges, exhausting and frightening though they were. Time flew by, and it made other occupations–including much of surgery–seem pale by comparison. Most specialities worked under relatively controlled circumstances, but he never knew what might walk–or be carried–in the door. Even the fact that a goodly portion of his work, particularly on injuries stemming from violence, would remain unpaid, did not distress him. On the contrary, it gave him a sense of worth, of performing a vital service for those who could not afford it. He had. gone into medicine to improve lives, not to make money.

He stopped in the middle of the road and wiped sweat from his eyes. The dry heat surrounded him like an airy blanket. Birds hopped and chirped in the brush. Leaves fluttered in the faint hot breeze, green against the sharp azure of the sky, set off by the deep red of smooth-barked madrones. The scene was beautiful, peaceful, rustic.

Dull.

There remained more than twenty-four hours to kill before his shift, and. he was beginning to encounter the flip side of the monstrous efficiency he had acquired during his academic and medical career. He had spent the morning studying, in an ongoing conscientious effort to master the field of emergency medicine and stay abreast of new developments in others, and the early afternoon in dutiful house-cleaning and yard care. His bankbooks were balanced, his bills paid, his truck in top running condition. He was caught up on correspondence with his family and friends. He had exercised.

He started walking again, reviewing options. After a morning of intent reading, he could not face the thought of a book. Television and movies did not in general interest him, nor did concerts or other forms of public socializing. To spend another evening in solitary drinking would be both destructive and empty, a form of psychological masturbation.

There was, of course, Valerie. She would doubtless be working late and up early tomorrow, but she would be company, and—he felt a touch of guilt at the thought—a warm body for the night.

But immediately came the memory of her visit two weekends previous: more like a battle in an escalating cold war than a date, even between lovers who were drifting apart.

At her insistence, they had gone to dinner at one of the quaint, overpriced restaurants on the old town square, a prospect that had made Farrell gloomy, less because of the expenditure than because he knew it would be cramped and crowded with tourist shoppers, and because his healthy appetite would have to be satisfied with elegantly cooked but tiny portions of exotic food, instead of the thick steak and baked potato quivering with sour cream that he craved.

She gazed with disapproval at the two iced Beef-eaters he consumed while they waited—and waited—for a table.

"Are you thinking about becoming a career alcoholic?" she finally said.

"Runs in the family," he answered, shrugging. "That's about all the old man's done for the last thirty years. First it was martinis at lunch. Now that he's retired, he plays golf every day and knocks them down at the clubhouse. Only difference is, he doesn't have to quit juicing at two and go back to work."

"Calling it hereditary's just an excuse," she sniffed.

"You're right," he said. "Who needs one of those?" and pointedly ordered a third.

And after staring at the playing card-sized piece of breaded abalone on his plate for which he would shortly pay twenty-four dollars, and at the eighteen-dollar bottle of wine he could have bought in a store for seven, and at the expensive clothing and hair styles of the chic throng around him, he had leaned forward to Val and said:

"You know what I really feel like doing? Lighting a cigar."

She paused in her dissection of one of the four, finger-long scampi that another twenty-two dollars had purchased, and looked at him with exasperation.

"Honestly, Gene, where's this antisocial behavior coming from? I mean, maybe you should just move someplace where there's no people around."

"Montana!" he said, slapping the table. 'That's *it*. I'll go into agriculture—raise dental floss, say." He took her hand, face gone earnest. "Come with me, Val. Be my lady

145

tycoon. We'll be the Ferdinand and Imelda Marcos of the oral hygiene world. Think of the abject gratitude of all these beautiful mouths around us." He swiveled in his seat, making a grand, sweeping gesture to include the surrounding tables. A number of people paused in their meals.

Valerie's stony gaze remained on his face. For the first time, it occurred to him that she very likely had never heard of Frank Zappa.

You're not funny," she said. "In fact, you're a little pathetic. An adolescent trying to cover up for copping out on his responsibilities." She paused to let that sink in. "Do you know what Doctor VanKamps said to me a few days ago? That he could understand how you might want to take a little time to think things over before immersing yourself in a life's work as demanding as surgery. And that he'd be glad to see you back–as long as you didn't take too *much* time."

"Doctor VanKamps is a pompous asshole," he said, regretting the words even as he spoke them, unable to stop himself.

"Oh, Gene," she said, setting down her fork and staring.

"It's true, Val, and you know it." He could feel the words starting to roll out of control, his mind futilely trying to catch up with and curtail his voice. "He's big and tall and has this great deep voice and shaggy head of white hair and that fine piercing twinkle in his eyes, and everybody kisses his ass, but the truth is he's the most conceited son of a bitch I ever met. And after Stanford, that's saying something."

Voice full of controlled anger, she said, "He's been very good to you–"

"Yeah, because he thought I was a bright student who stood to reflect well on him some day down the line. If I ever did anything sharp, he could say, 'Ah, yes, that young Farrell was one of mine,' and if I fucked up, he'd drop me like a hot brick. 'I knew that young man was trouble from the first. Vacillated, you know, between the godlike status of surgeon and some lower form of life, emergency medicine or some such nonsense. Can you imagine?'

"Val, I don't care how good a cutter you are: if you're that scummy a human being, you're better off dead. I'd rather be going through dumpsters for beer cans."

"You're shouting," she said quietly.

He glanced at the oblique gazes and poised utensils at the surrounding tables.

"Okay," he said, exhaling. "Truce, okay? Let's finish and get out of here."

They were coolly polite to each other for the rest of the evening. They did not make love. And when she left in the morning, after accepting only a cup of coffee instead of breakfast, neither spoke of a next meeting.

He knew that she was hurt, disappointed, angry, and he supposed he did not blame her. About his own feelings, he was thoroughly confused. But he saw no way to continue, with her bristling dsapproval, spoken or un, about everything regarding his new life; and himself, increasingly resentful of another force trying to shape him, to make him become what someone else wanted. It seemed that such pressures had directed his entire

147

past—that he was only now beginning to realize it—and that this was almost in the nature of a last chance to break free, to become himself, whoever or whatever that might be.

He got a bottle of Anchor Steam from the refrigerator and returned to the porch. Sitting on the steps, arms crossed over his knees, he admitted that there was a woman on his mind. Only it was not Valerie.

But even if he had not just imagined that Selena Clermont's parting words to him were a first sign of friendliness, what could he have in common with a girl almost ten years younger than himself, whose life had been so utterly different?

And yet, often as he had pushed her out of his mind, she was back at every turn. It was that quality he had sensed, that vibrancy, aliveness, as if it were a hint that she partook of some mysterious power denied to ordinary mortals.

Forget it, Farrell, he told himself, taking a long drink from the sweating beer bottle. You're lonesome, she's attractive, and you're trying to turn this into something it's not. Valerie's right, you're acting like a kid, rebelling against all your education and training, and letting your subconscious pull this kind of hippie-dippie bullshit to justify it. Next, you'll be buying crystals.

And let's not forget the sleaze factor. Every man at the party was staring at the girl, and she takes off with the asshole with see-in-the-dark pants and a smile like a sheep-killing dog. Something, my boy, is amiss inside that pretty skull.

Ruefully, he finished the beer and went inside to shower.

He was toweling himself dry when the phone rang. It was his mother's friend Elaine.

"I'm calling to invite you to dinner one night soon. Whenever's good for you."

"Let me check," he said, running his finger down his calendar. "How about Tuesday?"

"Fine."

"White or red?"

"Pardon?"

"Shall I bring white wine at red?"

"Oh. I hadn't thought about it. White, I suppose."

Her voice sounded distracted, even troubled, and he had the sudden sense that the dinner invitation was not really what the call was about.

"Elaine," he said gently. "Is something wrong?"

There was a pause. Then she said:

"I just got some news, and I'm afraid it's shaken me. Remember Lyle Randolph?"

"Vaguely," Farrell lied.

"Well, he's dead."

"Jesus." His forehead wrinkled. "What happened?"

"He drowned. He lived on a houseboat in Tiburon. Early yesterday morning a neighbor found him floating under a pier. They haven't finished all their tests yet—you know more about that sort of thing than I do—but—"

"But?" he prompted.

"They're quite sure he killed himself. He could swim, and the neighbors say it would have been easy for him to get to shore."

"Maybe he slipped and hit his head or something."

Again the hesitation. "That's not quite all," she said. "Apparently he had–damaged his own eyes. Clawed at them."

"*What?*"

"I know, dear, I couldn't believe it either. But they found blood and, you know, tissue, under his nails. As if he'd tried to blind himself, then leaped overboard in despair."

"Good God," Farrell said, leaning back against the wall.

For a moment, neither spoke. Then she said, "I must confess, he wasn't one of my favorite people in the world, but that's too terrible for anybody."

"Yes," Farrell said. It was all he could think of.

"I've tried to call Selena, but haven't been able to reach her. She left the party with him, you know."

I'm afraid I do, he started to say, then remembered he would be insulting a dead man.

"Was she still seeing him?"

"I don't think so. In fact, I have it on good authority that she's–being a busy girl. Still, someone should make sure she knows, and offer condolences–to see if there's anything one can do."

Busy girl? Farrell thought.

"Have *you* seen Selena again?" Elaine was saying.

"Briefly, the morning after the party. I left my jack handle in the parking lot and went back to get it. Why?"

Another pause. He could almost hear her pondering. "Bad luck seems to follow her," the answer finally came. "Nobody wants to admit it, but I think that was why she was moved around so much from place to place when she was a child."

"You mean she was a troublemaker?"

"No," Elaine conceded. "There was just a feeling. It sounds silly, doesn't it."

"I guess some people just don't get any breaks," he said, trying to lighten the conversation's tone.

"Maybe. And maybe they manufacture their luck. First she starts running around with a man more than twice her age, and now–"

"And now," Farrell said, "what?"

Silence. Then: "Marlene Peterson talked to her the other day, and she mentioned blithely that she'd been in this awful roadhouse outside Santa Rosa, a place where no one goes but criminals."

Well, kiss my ass and call me Howdy, he thought. A busy girl indeed.

"Elaine," he said, "if I'd had a childhood where I got shuffled around on account of bringing down 'bad luck,' I'd probably have social adjustment problems too."

"I suppose you're right. Still, I hope you'll stay away from her. Just in case you were considering otherwise."

"I wasn't. But why don't you tell me about this den of iniquity, just so I won't wander in there by accident?"

"It's got some ridiculous name like Hoolie's or Toolie's, and I don't know exactly where it is. But from what I hear, it's hardly the sort of place anyone wanders into by accident."

"Okay, darlin'," he said. "Thanks for the invite and the advice. I'll see you Tuesday night. And, uh, sorry about Dr. Randolph."

151

He hung up the phone and stared out the kitchen window. So the man was dead. He could not honestly say he felt any sorrow, never having spoken to Randolph, and not much liking what little he had seen. But he had spent too many agonizing hours trying to save life to hear of its loss without regret. And he admitted to a twinge of guilt for having thought badly of him.

Especially when the death suggested despair. Even madness.

Especially when it was connected, however absurdly, to Selena and her reputation for "bad luck."

He went to the refrigerator and opened another beer. *A place where no one goes but criminals.* What was going on with the girl?

More to the point, why could he not accept the clear indications that she was trouble, and dismiss her from his mind? Elaine had been correct in almost every particular about Valerie, and doubtless she was right about Selena too.

And yet, as he walked to his closet to dress, his hand paused at the usual selection of a clean button-down shirt, and he found himself flirting with the notion that it might be time to do a little exploring of this area he held come to live in. The half-dozen times he had been out to bars had been with his hospital colleagues or Valerie, usually en route to dinner; all had been establishments of the same upper-class stamp.

Perhaps it would be entertaining to foray into the downbeat side of town, places with more of a gritty edge.

A roadhouse, say, where no one would go but criminals—and one wild, rich, obviously disturbed young woman.

EIGHT

The "roadhouse" turned out to be a place called Foolie's, and Farrell drove around for some time before he found it: a quonset hut in an industrial district on the outskirts of Santa Rosa. He spent more time sitting in his truck, working up his nerve, before he went in. The parking lot was full of older-model American cars, most in an ongoing state of repair; the ambient color seemed to be primer gray. In front of the door, a dozen custom-painted Harleys with low-slung seats and extended forks waited in formation like a row of menacing giant wasps.

There was no sign of a silver Lotus.

The inside was a single cavernous, dimly lit room containing several pool tables and a juke box. Shadowy shapes moved like specters through the thick smoke and heavy metal music. The dress code seemed uniform: tight dark-colored T-shirts and greasy jeans for the men, tank or tube tops and cut-offs for the women. Heads lifted and stares followed Farrell as he walked to the bar, his feet sticking in places to the scarred wooden floor.

He had worn faded jeans, boots, and a work shirt with cut off sleeves that displayed his thick biceps, and he tried to put a roll into his stride, but he sensed, with real fear, that he fooled no one: that if every person in the room were stripped naked and their heads shaved, all would still be instantly, instinctively aware of the unbridgeable gulf between him and them.

We are different orders of being, he thought, and we hate and fear each other. Except that right now, that fear ran only one way. In a hospital or courtroom it might be different, but here, he was on their turf. The bartender was built like a sumo wrestler: a Samoan, Farrell guessed, with an Afro-like shock of kinky blue-black hair and a garish Hawaiian shirt open at the bottom, exposing his tremendous belly. He folded his tattooed arms across his chest and stared impassively. Farrell had been about to ask what kinds of imported beer they had, but caught himself and ordered a Pabst.

He carried the bottle to the end of the L-shaped bar and relaxed a little; his back was against a wall, and the other occupants of the room had ceased to pay attention to him. Bursts of raucous laughter came from the pool games. The barmaid, a slatternly blond in high heels and cutoffs so short the cheeks of her buttocks jiggled as she walked, paid no attention to the fingers that caressed her thighs or hooked into her blouse for a better look each time she leaned over to serve a drink. Nearby, four men were hunched over a table talking, with the conspiratorial air of reliving old crimes or plotting new ones.

He drank the first beer quickly, out of nervousness and thirst from the sultry night, and worked his way more slowly through a second. A steady stream of arrivals, occasionally announced by the throbbing growl of motorcycles outside, was packing the room with shadowy figures that strutted grotesquely in the eerie dim light. There was a great deal of hearty hand-clasping, shoulder slapping, and other overt good fellowship, all undercut by a rising feel of wolfish tension, waiting only for a match to be struck to explode into violence. The sense was of an antechamber of Dante's hell.

It was not quite ten o'dock. The absurdity of this project was growing on him. He was admitting by now that he had come here with some notion of trying to correct Selena, even to save her: that she was too young to know what she was doing. But any woman, however unsophisticated, would understand instantly what a place like this was all about. And little as he knew about her, "unsophisticated" was hardly an adjective that would apply.

So chalk it up as another lesson in your neverending education, Farell, he thought: a transcultural experience. Interesting, but you grasp the general concept, and don't forget the very good possibility, mounting by the minute, of getting the shit stomped out of you. It was time to finish the beer, then make the move back to what he called normality. Elaine was probably just mistaken about Selena hanging around here. And if she had been, he could only conclude that she was just flat crazy. There was no percentage either way. Drink up. Beat it.

He turned to the bartender and said, "You got any real Mexican tequila?"

By the time he had downed the second shot, the complexion of his night was changing. The harsh edges of the music blurred, leaving it powerful and haunting. The loud voices and laughter, the aggressive posturing, even the simmering ferocity, seemed vibrant, strong, real, with the force of a deliberately barbaric society that had turned its back in contempt on its flabby civilized cousin.

Then the door opened, and the room quieted noticeably.

Farrell's head turned with the others to the group that had entered. The man in front stood like a bodyguard, feet apart, hands ready at his sides. He was not much over Farrell's height, but his body went straight down from shoulders that looked a yard wide. His head was big as a basketball; a turned-up nose with slitted nostrils, together with a bristly shock of dun-colored hair, gave him the look of an enormous boar. From one ear hung a glittering object as big as a cigarette lighter. At first, Farrell thought it was a climber's carabinier, but then realized it was the master link to a motorcycle chain. For several seconds he just stood, face devoid of expression, head turning slowly to survey the room.

Then a second man stepped into view. He was shorter and thin, but strung as tightly as a marionette; even from across the room, Farrell could see veins running like wires down his biceps. His hair was pulled tightly back and twisted into a knot held by leather thongs. His face was narrow and sharp, and his head moved with the quick feral malignancy of a snake about to strike.

But it was his eyes that fascinated, and Farrell sensed that everyone watching was taken by their spell. They were luminous, hypnotic, filled with sinister power: the

157

eyes of a Manson or Rasputin. They toured the room, seeming to demand, and receive, acceptance from all that the undisputed master had arrived.

Then he turned back to the door, holding out his hand, and a third figure stepped into the light. Farrell let out his breath in a hiss.

She was wearing a white tank top that did more to accent than conceal her breasts, and skin-tight jeans the color of blood. Her lips were painted the same bright crimson, exaggerated into a pout. Her hair was a tangled wild mass, as if from the night wind on the back of a Harley, and seemed to bristle with life. As she turned, he caught flickers of iridescent light from her cheek, and realized she had freckled herself with glitter.

He turned away, groaning softly, in time to see the bartender finish pouring at least three ounces of Wild Turkey into a glass and hand it to the barmaid.

"For Icepick," he told her. "On me."

Icepick, Farrell thought. The name had the ring of the kinds boys made up for themselves in clubs, with secret initiation ceremonies–although there was nothing boyish about the man who carried it.

Farrell ordered another tequila and covertly watched Icepick and Selena take a table, flanked by the standing bodyguard. Alone and in pairs, with studied nonchalance, the denizens of the bar began to approach, exchanging greetings and handclasps like knights paying homage to the king and his queen. So, Farrell, he thought unhappily. There she is, just crying out for you to ride up on your white horse and rescue her. Go to.

The tequila came. He raised the glass and downed it in a swallow. Then he stood and started for the door.

During the next months, Gene Farrell would think many times that what was to happen—the events of that night, and everything that followed—would never have come to pass but for the simple accident of eye contact. Concentrating on making his way through the crowd, sure she would not recognize him even if she saw him, he did not glance her way until he was past the table where she sat, and then, only for a last bittersweet glance at the source of his folly.

But she was staring directly at him; and in the instant before the mask of coolness returned to her eyes, he imagined he saw a hint of something very different: disturbed, unhappy, even imploring.

He stopped, and turned, and walked to the table.

The bodyguard and surrounding bikers fixed him with their stony evil stares, and then Icepick himself added his hypnotic gaze. Silence spread outward like rings from a pebble thrown in a pool. Farrell ignored them all, his eyes still locked with hers, and though he sensed the shifting of bodies and movement behind him, tequila and adrenaline combined to give him a sense of detachment, an absence of fear.

"Fancy running into a girl like you in a place like this," he said.

Her expression remained cool. "I seem to remember suggesting you keep a distance from things you admire."

"I don't always take advice. It's one of my problems."

"Not the biggest one, friend," Icepick said. His voice was soft, with a hint of sibilance, and amusement showed in his burning eyes. "Right now, that is far from your most important trouble."

That was when Farrell saw the tears tattooed down the corner of one eye over the pocked cheek.

"All you lack is scales, man," he said levelly.

The blow landed against his temple at the instant the last syllable left his mouth. It was like a white-hot painless explosion inside his head, sending him reeling sideways, arms windmilling, until he crashed into a wall. He slumped down it, trying to get a grip on its flat surface, understanding dimly that never in his life had he imagined it possible to be hit with such force.

He regained control of his buckling knees and pushed off the wall, staring blurrily at the refrigerator sized bodyguard who stood waiting. The laughing bikers were moving back to form an aisle. At its end, watching impassively like emperor and empress, sat Icepick and Selena.

Farrell shook his head, focusing. There was no pain: on the contrary, as strength began to return, the charge of adrenaline mounted into a tremendous surge of electric clarity. Perhaps two seconds had passed since the blow, and in the next eyeblink of time, his mind replayed, unbidden, a scene from high school.

His favorite football coach, a Chicano named Ruybal, had grown up street-tough in East Los Angeles during the days when the medium for settling disputes had been fists instead of automatic weapons. From time to time the players had prevailed upon him to give them some pointers in self-defense.

"If you're in a one-on-one situation with a more powerful man," he had told them one lazy afternoon during a practice break, "your best move is to get out. Just run like a dog if you got to. Fighting is no joke, my friends. It don't happen in real life like with John Wayne.

"But if you can't run, your only chance is to hurt him, bad and fast. Throat and balls are too hard to hit, I don't care what you see in the movies. What you do is try to kick his kneecap off. If you miss, you're a dead *hombre*. If you connect, it will at least stagger him. If he still don't go down, punch him very hard with your fist on the point of the nose. That will blind him with pain for a few seconds.

"And then, *muchachos,* is when you haul ass."

Farrell had practiced the maneuver countless times in his bedroom mirror, with his adolescent mind supplying fevered scenarios of heroism, but had never dreamed he might ever use it in real life. Some part of him was vaguely astonished to find that his body was already moving.

He lashed out with his left hand, a deliberately clumsy punch that the bodyguard reached up contemptuously to slap out of the way. But as he stepped in, Farrell was using the momentum of the returning arm to reverse his shoulders. His right hip swung forward, powering a vicious kick at the man's advancing kneecap.

He was surprised again when he felt the heel of his heavy boot connect solidly.

The bodyguard bellowed in pain and outrage, both hands flying down to grip his collapsing knee. In the instant of shocked silence that surrounded them, Farrell

161

stepped forward, crouched slightly, and drove his fist into the perfectly positioned nose. It connected with a sound like a sledge hammer hitting a watermelon.

As blood sprayed from the bodyguard's face, a forearm clamped around Farrell's neck, dragging him backwards. He had barely time to think, *Got the kick and the punch right, just didn't quite get around to hauling ass,* before he went down under a storm of fists and boots.

When he awoke, he was in darkness. He lay without moving, gradually aware of the smell of gas and oil fumes. His cheek was against cold metal. Seconds passed before he understood that he was lying in the back of a truck.

He tried to sit up, but at his first stirrings, his body was racked with pain. Groaning, he remained motionless while a detached, analytical part of his brain methodically took stock of his injuries: possible dislocated jaw, excruciating throbbing in right hand, several ribs almost certainly cracked, and various other contusions whose voices were muted by the general clamor, but would undoubtedly be heard soon.

He braced himself and tried again. This time, he managed to pull himself slowly upright. His rib cage felt as if something with claws and very sharp teeth was trying to tear its way out. Clenching his jaw awakened the new possibility of loose teeth. Carefully, he touched his face, feeling his lips swollen like sausages and caked with blood, his nose unbearably tender. He groaned again, gazing blurrily around. After a moment, he realized that the truck was his own. He pulled himself to his knees, then laboriously climbed over the side to the pavement.

With his liabilities enumerated, he began to take stock of his assets. Eyes and testicles seemed okay. Except for the shooting pain in the hand, probably a sprain, his limbs felt unbroken. His neck was stiff but undamaged; he remembered with a shiver the thick forearm clamped around it, dragging him to the ground.

A touch to his back pocket told him he still had his wallet. The keys were even in the ignition. He was parked in an alley among a row of warehouses; the realization awakened a dim memory of being half-carried, half-dragged across Foolie's parking lot, thrown into the truck, pockets roughly rifled; then a bumpy ride of indeterminate distance, until the whine of the Datsun's engine and the thunder of the several motorcycles that hovered around it disappeared into the night, and he faded out of consciousness.

The question remained: Why hadn't they killed him or even damaged him seriously?

Painfully, he lowered himself into the driver's seat. He had left his watch in the glove compartment, a prudent move, as things had turned out. He recovered it and saw that the time was not much after midnight. The bar would still be open.

But the little guy is not, in classic western style, going to go back and clean up on the baddies, he assured an unseen audience. The little guy is going to get the fuck out of here, and never get within five miles of that place again. The little guy is in fact extraordinarily lucky to be functioning, and we're not at all sure he deserves such luck. Anyone capable of doing something that stupid ought, properly, to be eliminated from the gene pool.

He drove slowly through the dark empty industrial streets, breathing shallowly against the tearing in his side, searching for a landmark to tell him where he was. In a few minutes, he came to a high overpass and green signs for Highway 101, and he hissed with frustration. He could not remember if there was an exit for Highway 12 to Sonoma.

But, he realized abruptly, 101 would take him to San Francisco.

If he had ever needed that warm body, it was tonight.

And if there was something despicable about turning to a second woman after being humiliated by a first, retreating to the sure thing after failing in the adventure, it was only following the downward course of his life in general.

Angrily, he jammed the vehicle into gear and headed for the on ramp.

Valerie's apartment was on Cole Street, not far from Haight, the first floor of an old three-story brick building. When he arrived, it was almost two; her windows, like most of the neighborhood, were dark. She had probably worked late and come home to a lonely dinner, he thought with a vicious flare of guilt.

He still had a set of keys; as his fingers fumbled with them, opening the iron gate in front of the building's stairs, he realized for the first time that her not asking for their return was not an oversight. Valerie never forgot anything. The only explanation was that she still hoped he would come back—but not, he thought wearily, like this.

His physical pain had mounted steadily during the drive, abetted by the truck's rough ride, and he had finally stopped at a late-night grocery store in Marin to buy a pint of whiskey. He had then discovered that his swollen jaw made swallowing next to impossible; in the rushing wind of the open window, the liquor had run out of his mouth and streamed down the side of his face, giving rise to a burst of insane laughter. But after a few tries, he managed to get his swallowing mechanism working, and by the time he reached the Golden Gate Bridge, he had achieved a state of numbness, careless even of the night in jail that awaited him if he attracted the attention of the Highway Patrol.

He closed the gate quietly behind him and made his way, lurching a little, up the stairs. At her door, he hesitated, key in hand. At least he should have called.

He gave three sharp taps, then slumped onto the stoop, his back against the door.

What seemed like a long time passed. He sipped from the pint, deciding she had not heard. But when he thought of trying again, he found that he was content as he was—even grateful. A delicious drowsy peace was rising around him; he began to drift into a half-sleep. He would doze for a few moments, he decided dreamily, really rest at last; then rise and slink away from this mistake he had been on the verge of making.

Mistake, yes: another one. Selena's face refused to leave his mind; she floated before him, caught with that look of gentle imploring he had seen—or had he only

165

imagined it?—in the instant before the brutal reality set in. None of it made any sense, but who had ever said it had to?

When the porch light came on he blinked, torn from his fantasy, and did not sit up fast enough to avoid falling backward with the opening door—only to cry out as it stopped short, caught by a chain, jolting his savaged ribs.

"Who are you?" Valerie's voice demanded, low and enraged. "How dare you sleep on my porch? Leave this instant, or I'll call the police."

He scrabbled free of the door and pulled himself to his knees.

Val," he rasped, turning into the light.

He could just see her face through the crack in the doorway. It was tense and pale with anger—then, suddenly, disbelieving. For seconds, she stared at him.

Then, with the brisk professional manner he knew so well, she said, "Wait." She pushed the door closed and unhooked the chain. He stumbled into the familiar living room and stood blinking, while she turned out the porch light and rechained the door.

She came to him and laid a finger on his cheek. He drew back, wincing.

"What in the world?" she said wonderingly.

He stared at her in misery, trying to say, *Val, it's all a mistake, I shouldn't have come here.* But her face had gone, soft with concern, her touch was light and caressing, her skin smelled sweetly of sleep; and as she leaned toward him, her robe fell open, revealing a shadowy glimpse of her breasts.

"I kind of went into the wrong bar," he said, trying to smile, but hearing his voice nasal and cracked.

Her mouth tightened, but the softness stayed in her eyes.

"Do you need to go to the ER?" He shook his head. "Then get undressed. I'm going to run you a bath."

She came in with codeine tablets and cognac, then sat on the edge of the steaming tub with her robe tucked around her thighs and washed him, her fingers silently enumerating his bruises and contusions. She dried him with a large fluffy towel and eased him into bed, helping him find a position acceptable to his tortured ribs.

And then, with that same professional competence, blew him.

"You're not a woman," he mumbled, taking her face in his hands. "You're an angel."

"Sleep now," she said, and kissed him lightly. "We'll talk tomorrow."

No, he thought, drowsy with the codeine: it had not been a mistake after all. This was the right woman, loving him and caring for him even after his transgression. This was what true, mature love was all about. He touched her hair and felt her turn so her breath was warm on his shoulder, and then the blackness of sleep dragged him down.

NINE

Roy Lutey pushed back from the breakfast table and brought his coffee cup down on it just loudly enough to make Dora jump. Hurriedly, she rinsed soapy dishwater off her hands and went to fill the empty cup. That done, she cleared away his plate, gummy with yellow egg yolk and toast scraps. Although he ate like a mule–three eggs and a fistful of bacon every morning, two thick sandwiches for lunch, and a dinner that would have fed her for a week, besides the six-pack or two of beer he consumed each night–his body remained as lean and rangy as when he was a teenager. The sleeves of his work shirt were rolled up to reveal knotty forearms; his jeans were tight over his muscled thighs. His strong lantern jaw, long sideburns, and combed-back hair gave him the look of an old time country-western singer. All in all, he was a handsome man, even if Dora had sometimes thought secretly that his eyes were a little too close together.

"Got to get that sulfur spray rig running," he said, more to the air than her. "God damn pump's clogged up, ain't been cleaned since last year." He watched her wince at the curse, then leisurely shook a Marlboro from a pack and lit it. Dora sighed inwardly. It was wrong, she knew, but she wished he would go. During the mornings and afternoons, when the house was hers—hers and the Lord's, she corrected herself—her mood lightened; but when Roy was around, there was the sense of being in a cage with a not-quite-tame beast. It seemed that if anything, he had been growing more sullen lately, as if some deep, secret source of anger was gnawing at him. She busied herself with the dishes, not daring to allow her impatience to show, let alone to voice it.

At last coffee and cigarette were finished, along with his morning litany of disparaging remarks about his coworkers, sung increasingly to the tune that all the real responsibility of running the winery fell on his shoulders. As he reached the door, she called after him:

"Praise the Lord."

"Praise the Lord," he muttered in reply, and let the screen door bang behind him, signifying the end of the ritual. Dora sagged against the sink with relief. As always, she had been up since five-thirty, getting a bite of breakfast for herself and Rosalie, then sending the girl off to play—and getting her out of the house so she would not become the target of one of Roy's unpredictable bad moods. Now, at last, she could take a moment to rest. Dishes finished, she poured herself a cup of coffee and carried it outside onto the porch.

This was the best time of her day, before the heat began, before she had to worry about lunch, dinner, and the thousand other chores that cropped up so endlessly.

She sat overlooking the forest and cliffs, and thanked Jesus for this little patch of promised land He had led them to. Only a glance at the big house disturbed her tranquility.

Two weeks ago, Selena had stayed out all one night, and Dora had seen her come in early next morning, dressed like a harlot in skin-tight crimson pants. Later that day, she had tried to talk to Selena again, to tell her about Jesus's love for sinners, about the certain damnation she herself and Roy had escaped, about the Reverend Harner's concern for all lost souls.

But the girl had turned on her with anger of frightening intensity, and warned Dora that if she raised the subject once more, her cleaning job was gone: she would never again be allowed to set foot in the house. When Dora reported this to the Reverend Harner, he had stroked his jaw thoughtfully, then cautioned her to keep a close eye on Selena. Someone so violently opposed to hearing the word of Christ might well be possessed by Satan.

The idea had made Dora weak with terror, and she had avoided the big house for days, praying fervently each night for her family's protection from evil spirits. She had not dared tell Roy, for fear of what he might have done. It was one more burden she carried in silence and solitude, lightened only when she reminded herself that Jesus, with His bleeding hands and crown of thorns, suffered beside her.

But the appointed day had come to clean, and when she made her way, pale with trepidation, up the hill, Selena greeted her warmly and cheerfully as if nothing had happened—as if she had forgotten all about the incident—and by the time Dora left for home, she again felt strong, brave, recharged by the younger woman's mysterious vitality and humor. Could that be a result of possession? Dora knew that the Devil was full of tricks, that one of his prime occupations was clothing evil in the guise of good, but it was hard to imagine that a woman as independent as Selena was under the control of anything but herself.

It was very confusing, and there was nothing to do but wait. There seemed no immediate danger, and, as Ecclesiastes taught, to every thing there was a season, and a time to every purpose under heaven.

Only—more than once, in the heat of the afternoon when she was alone in the kitchen, she had gotten the distinct sense that she was not alone at all. It was impossible to explain or even describe; just the feeling that there was someone, or something, watching her.

Two or three times, she had come back to the room to find that some object, a pan or plate, had moved slightly, or at least she *thought* it had—she was never absolutely sure. She had glimpsed shadows, from the corner of her eye, that seemed more than shadows during the instant before they appeared. The day before yesterday, a glass had fallen from a shelf, shattering, making her whirl around with a squeal of terror. It must have been jarred loose by vibration, she told herself, even though it had been sitting on a level surface several inches from the edge. Perhaps there had been a tiny earthquake. Even though nothing else had moved.

171

But that was not the worst. Twice now, in the dusk, when she had stepped outside to do some chore or just to be alone for a minute, with Roy in front of the television and Rosalie in her room with her Bible picture books, she had thought she heard a baby crying. It was a soft, distant, barely audible sound, but there was no mistaking its tone: not fretting or hunger, but terror. Dora had searched frantically for its source, but it seemed to come from all around her, or from nowhere, remaining the same no matter which way she turned; and then, as suddenly as it had begun, it would be gone. The first time, she had hurried down to the Vasquez's house, making up an errand; but Estrelita's baby, the only one on the estate, was home and fine.

She was hearing things, Dora decided; perhaps it had something to do with her nervousness about Selena, or perhaps she was being punished for the vile pleasure she took during those sinful moments with Roy.

Or perhaps, she thought with a thrill of fear, the Reverend Harner was right: Satan had come into her life, to tempt and test her allegiance to Christ. There must be no more yielding. She must be righteous and strong.

"I want to be one of Your soldiers," she whispered. "I want to sit by Your right hand on Judgment Day. Forgive me, Lord, I won't let him do it again."

But even as she spoke the words, she could feel Roy's restlessness beside her in the dark, feel him finally turn toward her, smell his beery breath as his rough hand reached, with that odd awkward tenderness, beneath her gown, and she knew that she would do as she always did:

submit, and bum with shame as the moans of pleasure she was unable to suppress broke from her lips.

Her reverie was interrupted by the sight of a figure walking up the road toward her. She immediately identified Estrelita, wearing a flowered house dress. On her back, the baby, eleven-month-old Roberto, was slung in a shawl; in her arms, she carried a basket, probably filled with flowers from her garden, a gift she often brought. She was a round, nut-brown woman with snappy black eyes, who after seven children looked closer to forty years than her twenty-eight. She panted up the porch steps and sat heavily in a chair. Dora wondered suddenly, with a touch of envy, if she was pregnant again.

"For ju," Estrelita said, offering the flowers. She understood a little English but spoke almost none, and Dora knew almost no Spanish; much of their communication was done through gestures. It did not allow for discussion of weighty topics, which was just as well, considering Estrelita's allegiance to the church the Reverend Harner called the Scarlet Woman. Dora prayed for her frequently. But talk was less important than simple companionship: they were stuck here, several miles from town, alone together.

Dora peered into the basket, exclaiming with delight. There were marigolds, petunias, and daisies, all still glistening with dew.

"You always bring me such pretty flowers," she said. Her own garden was devoted mainly to more practical vegetables, and she would send Estrelita home with a basketful of them, welcome help in feeding the many mouths. Estrelita was unslinging the baby, knowing without asking that Dora craved to hold him.

"*Has visto el perillo?*" she said, as she handed the lively, warm, surprisingly solid little bundle into Dora's arms. At Dora's puzzled look, she went, "Woof, woof," then hung her hands like paws and panted.

Dora kissed Roberto's slobbering cheek, thinking. A puppy, yes, she remembered it now; a cute, floppy-eared mutt of perhaps twelve weeks, trailing after Rosalie and the Vasquez kids on the way to their endless games.

"I saw it a couple days ago," she said, unable to remember just when. "Did it run away?"

Estrelita nodded. "Emilio, he don' stop cry." She made the motion of knuckling her eyes.

Dora clucked her tongue sympathetically, making a face at the baby, but thinking about the band of coyotes in the nearby hills. Sometimes late at night she would hear their insane, blood-chilling yelps, making her skin crawl until she clung to Roy's back for comfort. He refused to hunt or trap them, since they killed varmints that might injure the young grapevines. Surely a puppy would be a toothsome snack for them. Even a hawk or owl could have made off with dog that size, as they did with the endless succession of feral kittens around the place. She started to say so, but caught herself. It would not have seemed polite.

And then, for the first time, she realized that she had hardly seen the children for the past couple of weeks. The thought stunned her. Always before, they had been such a noisy, pervasive presence, constantly playing around the house and having to be shooed out of it, that she had become oblivious to them. But now, it was like a loud engine, so long annoying it had become part of the background, suddenly turned off.

"I'll watch out for that puppy," she told Estrelita, tickling Roberto until he crowed with delight. "You put out some food, maybe he'll get hungry and come home."

She gave the baby back and got coffee, and the two chatted in their half-understood way for a few more minutes, then toured Dora's garden, pruning it of tomatoes, squash, and greens on the verge of overripeness. The heat of the day had begun, and Estrelita's sandaled feet raised puffs of dust as she trudged back down the road. The baby's little arms moved as if he were waving, and Dora waved back, thinking with pity of poor Emilio, crying over his lost puppy–

And remembering Rosalie's odd conversation with the boy about the imaginary Mister Asthma-Day.

Wasn't that just about the time the children had stopped playing around the house? Did it seem that Rosalie had become unusually quiet at home? Or was it all just another trick of her imagination, a crack in her faith that the Devil was trying to worm his way through?

Her eyes searched the woods. The foliage was beginning to take on its thick, hot, slightly malignant midday glaze.

The emergency room had been quiet most of the afternoon, when a radio call came that the sheriff's department was bringing in a robbery suspect who'd been injured in a car chase. Excitement rose a notch as the technicians and nurses prepared. Gene Farrell checked on his other patients—an elderly man with a mild heart attack who was now stabilized; a young woman with a toe broken by kicking what she stubbornly maintained was a bowling ball, in spite of her swelling black eye and sullen boyfriend; the usual assortment of children with stomach aches and anxious parents—then stepped into the physicians' private room, to spend a minute anticipating the problems the new arrival might bring. He wanted to be swift and sure in dealing with them. In the ER, he did not like surprises.

The information they had gotten over the radio indicated that the injuries were not serious; the sheriffs had declined the offer of an ambulance and paramedics, which meant that the hospital visit was largely a legal formality—so a defense attorney couldn't claim that the client had been denied proper medical care. Still, there was always the possibility of hidden internal injury, and Farrell wanted to be sure he missed nothing. Malpractice paranoia was in the air, and he was well aware that convicts had little better to do than pursue litigation.

He flexed his right hand; two weeks after his adventure in Foolie's, the sprain was healing well, but muscles and tendons were still stiff. Pain remained in his ribs when he inhaled deeply, but that too was dulling. The sensation brought back the beating and all that had gone before and after. He was still remembering when a tap came at the door.

"They're *heeeere*," sang one of the nurses. Resisting the urge to grin, he went out to meet his patient.

The man was brought in, still handcuffed, in a wheelchair—another obligatory precaution. His last name was

Wiesel, and Farrell could not help imagining a resemblance: in his early twenties, he was skinny and feral looking, with thin shoulder-length hair and shifty but defiant eyes. Dope, Farrell thought immediately: coke, maybe even crack.

The only obvious injuries were facial lacerations, which Farrell saw at a glance were not serious. Of more concern was possible damage to internal organs; he had crashed the car against a tree, and had been still in it, stunned, when he was apprehended.

"Uncuff him, please," Farrell said. The senior sheriff's deputy was a hard-faced, swarthy man named Pavlacek, whom Farrell had encountered several times before on similar occasions. He nodded to his younger partner; as the deputy undid the cuffs, Pavlacek leaned close to Wiesel's face and said softly, "Twitch the wrong way, kid, I'll give you a real reason for being here."

While Wiesel stared back with not very convincing menace, Farrell cautiously probed his torso.

"Hurt?" he said, wincing inwardly at the thought of his own tender ribs.

"I didn't do nothin', man," Wiesel muttered. The older cop grinned wolfishly.

"Let's get him on the X-ray table," Farrell said. "Then I'll clean him up."

Over the next half hour, Farrell examined and pronounced clear the X-rays, received a bloodless urine sample, and treated the facial cuts, closing the worst ones with butterfly stitches. As he worked, an idea came.

"I think he's fine," he told Pavlacek when he had finished, "but why don't you leave him here an hour or two for observation."

Pavlacek shrugged. "I'm in no hurry to hit the bricks again. One car chase a day is plenty." He turned to the deputy and said, "Call it in, huh?"

While the deputy spoke on the radio, Farrell caught Pavlacek's eye and motioned him aside.

"Actually, I wanted to talk to you a minute. How about a cup of coffee?"

The sheriff's eyebrow rose: a look of professional assessment. "If you're buying."

"You got the wrong dude, man," Wiesel called after them hoarsely. His wrist was cuffed to the iron bed. "I'm gonna sue your ass!"

Pavlacek sighed. "'The stupid cocksucker. He's robbed three Seven-Elevens in the last two weeks. Not only is he on video, he's come away with less than a hundred bucks every time. I mean, for Christ's sake."

Wiesel's jumpiness, rapidly shifting eyes, and inflamed nasal passages had deepened Farrell's suspicion. Blood test results would confirm it.

"Nobody ever said crack made you smarter."

"For truth. It's one thing when they're crazy *or* dumb, but when they're both—" He shook his head. "I've been a cop a couple weeks, and I've never seen anything like the way it's getting. And it isn't just New York and L.A. any more, believe me."

They reached the cafeteria door. "Are you good for some information?" Farrell said.

"I'm on the clock," said Pavlacek.

178

Farrell's shift ended at 8:00 PM. After briefing his relief on the remaining patients and spending an hour bringing up his charts, he drove home and distractedly filled a glass with ice and Tanqueray. In a routine that was becoming increasingly familiar, he carried it to the darkening living room, sat on the couch, and stared out over the empty field.

"Ever hear of a character named Icepick?" he had asked Pavlacek.

The sheriff's heavy-lidded eyes opened all the way, and he glanced at the elastic bandage on Farrell's wrist.

"You saying what I think you're saying?"

"Not him. One of his pals."

Pavlacek carefully mixed a packet of artificial sweetener into his styrofoam cup of thin cafeteria coffee.

"That may be the only reason you're still alive."

"That bad?"

"Way, way worse. How'd you run into these gents?"

"I had a drink in a place called Foolie's."

"Good idea," Pavlacek said approvingly. "Did you wear your 'Bikers are faggots' T-shirt?"

"Okay, I get it. It won't happen again. I'm just curious about what I stepped in."

"What you stepped in," Pavlacek said, "is some of the evilest shit in this part of the country." He added a packet of nondairy creamer and continued to stir. "One Phillip Joseph Grabowski, a.k.a. Icepick Phil. Got the name in prison, I'll let you guess how. He was sort of a child prodigy; had a yard-long sheet by the time he was eighteen, and spent five of the next seven years in the joint, including a hitch in San Quentin."

179

"'The tears,'" Farrell said.

Pavlacek nodded. "In Q, he met some professionals and started wising up. In other words, learning how to get other people to do the mule work—and take the falls. When he got out, he started his own operation. Guaranteed success formula for your garden-variety gang: a bunch of mean dumb fucks and a few mean smart ones.

"These guys are not affiliated with any motorcycle club. The biker stuff is a hobby for some of them, a cover for others. What they are is serious criminals. Mainly dope, including several speed labs, and probably the crack our pal Wiesel was so anxious to get his hands on. The stuff also has a way of trickling down to the schools and playgrounds, which puts a particularly pretty edge on it."

"I see those kids in here," Farrell murmured.

Pavlacek cautiously sipped the grayish brew in his cup. "Yeah," he said. "I guess you do.

"Well, besides throwing you that particular bit of business, your pals also dabble in just about any other profitable sideline: blackmail, extortion, guns. Murder. Sometimes they combine the whole routine, a sort of multimedia event. About two years ago, for instance, there was an incident where one of their dealers decided he wanted out. There's a problem there: once you're in with those people, you don't *get* out. This individual refused to accept that. Persons unknown went into his house one night, tied him in a chair, shotgunned his old lady and infant daughter in front of him, then set the place on fire, with him still alive.

"The word went out that it was a 'lesson' murder. It taught some people something, that's for sure. We never even picked up a suspect, that's how scared all our snitches were."

Farrell swallowed, feeling slightly nauseous. "I can't believe there are people who'd do something like that for money."

"Are you shitting me? There's people who'll do it for the fun of it." The deputy leaned back, throwing an arm over the back of his chair. His khaki uniform was sweat-stained at the armpits, his face lined with cynicism. "All of which is by way of saying, you're way out of your league, Doc. Piss those people off enough and you're dead, and I mean fucking *dead*. And none of them will ever see the inside of a jail."

"Like I said, it won't happen again."

Pavlacek grunted noncommittally. "Foolie's isn't all that hard to stay out of. In fact, it's not all that easy to find. How'd you happen in there?"

"Looking for somebody," Farrell said, feeling his face warm.

"Yeah? Well, if it's coke you're after, I suggest you develop new contacts. Not that I'm saying I approve, you understand. But you're getting a rep in the department as a decent croaker to work with, and I don't want to find you in a dumpster some night."

"It's not coke."

"I'm glad to hear that." Pavlacek finished his coffee and stood. "I'll just add that if it's a broad, there's better places to find them, too."

Farrell nodded, as much to himself as to Pavlacek.

After the deputies and their charge left, Farrell had put the matter out of his mind, an easy enough thing to do in the tension of the ER. But in the lonely darkness of his living room, he felt an ache that he traced to a combination of emotions: regret at his own ineffectualness that night, anger at Selena, fear for what might have happened to him—and the simple pain of having cared for a woman, however absurd it might have been, who rejected him utterly.

But mostly, what he felt was unhappiness that he could do nothing to help her. It was an adolescent white knight fantasy, perhaps, but mixed with a genuine concern for this young woman who seemed not to understand the company she was keeping, or the kind of consequences that were certain to ensue. Or worse, who was burdened with a sickness he had run into before: a need not just to be dominated, but abused, by men who were nowhere near her worth.

He shrugged and stood to refill his glass. Well, there had been one positive outcome: he had come to his senses in realizing that Valerie was the woman he both wanted and needed. He had spent five days with her, recuperating; he remembered again her tenderness to him, and how easily the two of them had fallen back into being together. She had not once mentioned the subject of his returning to the surgery residency. For his part, her steadiness, instead of irritating him; now seemed like a pillar to cling to in a stormy sea. It was as if the beating had knocked out of him some false conception of a romantic adventure that had no basis in reality.

Reality, he thought, was Valerie's domain, and she was right: he belonged there with her. He had not told her of his reason for being in the bar, but said that he had only happened in. Someday, perhaps, he'd share with her the truth in all its preposterousness.

He picked up the phone and dialed Val's number, hungry for the sound of her calm voice to fill the ache that deputy Pavlacek's information had opened.

But even as the phone began to ring, his mind fixed on the instant when he had imagined he saw anguish, pleading, on Selena's face. *Had* he only imagined it?

Val's answering machine came on. He hung up without leaving a message. Pavlacek's information was sinking deeper in, making him realize the seriousness of the situation. It had not just been a barroom brawl, as he had been tacitly assuming. He had been in real danger of maiming or death—had walked into the lair of extremely dangerous, powerful men, insulted the leader, and made a fool of the number-one heavy. Why had he gotten off so easily?

He had started to wonder if Selena had intervened.

The score was three to two in the seventh, Dodgers and Giants, a situation which normally would have held Roy Lutey riveted to the TV; but tonight, he was feeling restless. When Hershiser retired the side and the usual stream of commercials began, he got a fresh Coors from the kitchen and stepped out onto the porch.

It was after nine, and full dark. The nightly sea breeze that kept the heat from being unbearable was rising, carrying the sweet mysterious scent of the world in bloom, making the transition from the freshness of early summer to the overripeness, laced with decay, of late July. A glance at the house's upstairs showed the lighted bedroom windows where Dora sat mending clothes and praying. Roy turned his back deliberately, sidearmed the Coors can into the brush, and stalked to the toolroom, where he kept a bottle of Old Crow. There were times when beer just did not cut it.

The truth was, he had had about enough of praying. He had bought in wholeheartedly at first, during a time of desperation, on the run from bills and outstanding warrants and a violent streak he just could not seem to control. Jesus had offered the answer, and for the first time in his life, Roy Lutey had gone down on his knees and begged for something: forgiveness, salvation, a life that was not an accelerating spiral toward certain disaster. And it seemed that his prayers had been answered: this house, this job, situations where people left him alone and there were few of the irritations and temptations of his former life.

But gradually, another aspect had begun to dawn on him. One of the reasons he had things his way up here was that the pay was hardly better than subsistence. Of that, he gave a chunk of every dollar to the government and another twenty cents to the church—most of which, he'd come to realize, went to line the Reverend Harner's pockets. Harner bought a brand new Cadillac every year, wore more gold than a Turkish princess, and owned a dozen pairs of fifteen hundred dollar ostrich-skin boots.

But the Reverend Harner had a lot of connections in the business community. What it really came down to,

Roy had finally figured out, was that he was more or less the equivalent of the Mexican body brokers who farmed out the migrant workers. He set up desperate congregationers in some shithouse situation with the small-time phony landowners and businessmen who came to church and prayed so piously on Sunday but were really only in for the cheap labor, then took twenty percent of their wages under the guise of it being for Jesus, and probably got a kickback from the employers too. And while it was never stated, it was understood that if you left the Church of the Most Holy Goddamned Redemption, that was the end of the job.

All of which was just fine for Reverend Harner, but it left a man like Roy Lutey essentially a slave, working his life away out here in the tule-dongs, with a wife he practically had to take a crowbar to to pry her legs apart. Even that, Jesus had ruined. In fact, about all he could see that Jesus had done for him was to stick him in a cage a little softer than the one he used to be in.

Softer, and a hell of a lot less interesting.

He drank again, wiped his mouth with the back of his hand, and turned his moody gaze up to the big house. The windows were bright, and the silver car gleamed in the moonlight. The little rich bitch was home. Christ, twenty-one years old and worth more money than he would ever see in his life. There was no denying that that was a lot of what was eating at him. Things had been dull, but pretty much all right, until she showed up. From then on, the comparison of the little he worked so hard for to the much she had simply been given was like a kick in the balls every time he thought about it.

185

That, and the body she flaunted in his face. Which he had never gotten more than a glimpse of in spite of many hours of trying.

It had started not long after her arrival, when he had seen her dressed in a terry-cloth robe, carrying a towel up to the waterfall. He had been unable to get her out of his mind, and a half hour later, had found an excuse to climb a ridge that looked down over the little pool. When he reached his vantage point, he had stopped short and let out his breath in a long slow hiss. She was stretched on her belly nude, leisurely turning the pages of a book: the soft weight of her peach-sized breasts kissing the sun-warmed granite, the high round arch of her buttocks like a kingdom to be conquered.

But as if she had sensed his presence—impossible, since he was nearly a quarter mile away, hidden in thick brush—she had reached unhurriedly for her robe and draped it over herself; and although he had waited in an agony of anticipation for another half hour, until he had to go back to work, she had not uncovered herself again.

Since then, he had sat numerous times with his binoculars and studied her as she sunned beside the pool or on the deck outside her bedroom; but each time, with that same uncanny radar, she managed to give him only tantalizing glimpses before covering herself, or changing position, or leaving.

It was maddening, and more maddening because it seemed clear that that was as close as he was ever going to get. He was not accustomed to behaving like a gentleman, but had been unfailingly polite to her—moreso than to any other woman he had ever known. But in return, she treated him exactly like the hired hand he was.

What did she do in that huge house all by herself, besides lie in the sun and read her endless books? What was she doing up there right now? He had expected a steady stream of boyfriends, but there had been none, at least none that had stayed the night. He wanted to believe that she was insatiable, a shameless whore, a nympho; but if she was getting it, she was getting it someplace else. And she wasn't getting much of it. She had only stayed out all night twice. His lips tightened. The truth was that she was really only nothing but a cock teaser.

He hid the whiskey under the steps and walked a few yards away from the house to piss. His pecker tingled, half-hard, in his hand. Hell, he hadn't used it for anything *but* pissing in a week. He continued to hold it after he finished, standing there in the dark, imagining his callused palms on those firm young breasts he had never quite seen, the taste of her rich nipples–were they red, or brown, or pink?–the straining of her tight buttocks as she fought and clawed until his thick cock, forced in her to the hilt, changed those struggles to sobbing gratitude.

Angrily, he stuffed his now full erection into his jeans and zipped up. It was a hell of a state for a grown man to be in, made to slink around like a dog following a bitch in heat, by a woman who was hardly more than a girl.

He glanced again at the house, where Dora waited with her endless "thou-shalt-nots," and considered going back inside for the too-familiar ritual of finding a pretext to start an argument, slapping her until she fell sobbing on the bed, then working off his hard-on while she pretended not to like it.

But that was not what he wanted, and he growled, "The hell with it," already moving. It was Selena he needed to see: to immerse himself in the excitement and misery she caused him.

Silently, staying in the shadows, he climbed the hill. The moon was full, but his clothing was dark, and he knew how to move in these woods. He quickly circled the house, peering into the first floor windows, and realized she must be upstairs. The lights in the master bedroom were on–and he just happened to know of an easy-to-climb oak tree, thick with leaves, and hardly ten yards from the wall. There would be no need for the binoculars tonight.

Tense with excitement, he climbed the tree, staying on the back side, his powerful limbs hauling him up until he rested in a crotch. He cautiously parted the foliage that shielded his face from view. The French doors onto the balcony were thrown wide open, giving him a clear look into the bedroom. He was close enough to read the time on her alarm clock. But of Selena, there was no sign.

For minutes, nothing happened. Roy was beginning to curse beneath his breath, hearing the whine of questing mosquitoes, wondering if this foray, like all the others, would go unrewarded. If she was not downstairs or in the bedroom, then where was she? Sitting in the dark?

Abruptly, the door opened, and she walked into the room. Breath held, he watched.

She was wearing a sleeveless lemon yellow top and a short stone-washed denim skirt. Without pausing in her stride, she unzipped it and let it fall, causing Roy to suck in his breath and dig his fingers into the tree: Lord God, not a stitch underneath, just as he had always suspected. She disappeared from view into the adjoining bathroom. The translucent curtains over its window allowed a tantalizing view of her flesh-colored silhouette. She bent over the tub. There came the sound of running water. Then she straightened, pulled the blouse over her head, and tossed it aside. Roy groaned softly.

Selena reappeared, giving him a glimpse of her sun-browned flank as she crossed the room to a vanity. She seated herself, back to him, and began brushing her hair with long even strokes. His hungry eyes caressed the hourglass shape of her back, the luxuriant dark mane that came halfway down it. He could see her face reflected in the three-sided mirror, and once, when her gaze shifted slightly and seemed to meet his, an instant of odd certainty that she was staring back at him brought him close to panic. But it was impossible. She looked away, and he relaxed, becoming almost hypnotized by the slow rhythmic strokes of the brush.

At last she stood, pinning her hair up into a loose knot. This done, she turned so suddenly that he ducked, missing her as she walked back into the bathroom. He groaned again, a sound of genuine desperation. He had blown what might have been his only chance. What if she came out wrapped in a towel or robe? He stared at her silhouette bent over the tub, turning off the water. His hard-on ached and his lips moved in the most fervent prayer in years, that she would open those bathroom curtains.

But she did not. With frustration growing into rage, he watched her blurred shape slide into the bath. A slender calf rose into the air.

Maybe, he thought grimly, it was time to quit fucking around: time to stalk into the house and drag her wet and struggling from the bath and take her right there on the floor. It was what she wanted, really: what all of them wanted, even if they wouldn't at first admit it. How the hell did she think she could get away with driving a man half crazy, then shutting him off like a water tap?

The law might not see it that way, a voice in his mind whispered.

The hell with the law, he thought angrily. She would like it: he'd make sure of that. Besides, how could the law fault a man for giving a woman what she was so clearly begging for? What was he supposed to do with his aching cock, jack off like a schoolboy?

He was nerving himself to push out of the tree and start his descent, when Selena's silhouette rose from the tub. This time, without hesitating, she left the bathroom and walked onto the balcony, straight toward him, as if she were stepping into his arms.

She stopped at the railing, hardly ten yards away, outlined against the light of the room behind. Her sheer animal loveliness was so intense it seemed to shimmer. Roy remained frozen, his mouth stupidly open, staring at her skin glowing through the thousand droplets of clear water, at the deep rich red of her nipples, at the luxuriant dark fleece between her thighs. She stared back as if she could see through the darkness and barrier of foliage into his face: into his heart. For perhaps thirty seconds, she remained motionless. He was dimly aware that the forest around him had gone silent, as if even the crickets were hushed by her splendor.

Then something bit him on the neck. He tensed, not daring to move and slap it. But the irritation rose swiftly to real pain. It was not a mere mosquito or even a wasp, but something, he realized, with teeth, biting hard, breaking skin, chewing into his flesh. Abruptly, there was another on his arm, and then his thigh, and then, Christ! his rapidly shrinking cock.

Within instants, a swarm of them was burrowing in, rending his flesh in a frenzy. He yelped, then howled, slapping with one hand and clinging to the tree with the other, until his desperate body, in its confusion, let go with both hands at once, and he plunged through the branches to the ground. His ankle hit something uneven and turned. A tearing pain shot up his leg. The tiny teeth ripped and tore. Shrieking, dragging his leg, he half-crawled, half-ran back down the hill to home.

At exactly what point the biting stopped, he wasn't afterward sure; it was over by the time he reached his porch. Trembling, he pulled himself onto the steps and reached for the whiskey. As he raised it, he heard Dora's footsteps approaching. He swiveled, hiding the bottle against his chest.

"Roy, honey, are you okay?" she said anxiously, pushing open the screen door. "I heard some yellin'–"

191

"Yeah, I'm okay," he said viciously. "I run off a stray dog and twisted my ankle. Now get the hell back inside and leave me alone!"

The door closed quietly, and his shaking hand raised the bottle to his lips. What in Christ's name could the things have been? He took a long drink, then another, before summoning the courage to examine himself for the damage the furious teeth had done.

A minute later, feeling weak, he drank again. There was not a mark on him.

And he realized that his frantically slapping hands had never touched a single thing.

Bony fist clutched around the bottle, he sat staring out into the night, remembering his last glimpse of her, standing like a nude goddess at the balcony railing.

Was it just another figment of his whiskied imagination, or had she been smiling faintly as he crashed out of the tree?

Selena watched with grim amusement as the howling, limping man slunk off through the brush. She had been enjoying the night air through the open doors, until she realized he was spying yet again. At that point she simply lost her temper, and in a burst of rage, unleashed the companions.

She had had enough of vile men.

So, Selena, even though you starve us, you do not hesitate to call us to your bidding. What a fine friend you are! Tenderhearted to humans, but mistreating those who serve you.

She exhaled in exasperation. "You can count as well as I can, Hasmoday. In a few days, you will feed."

The imp smiled ferociously. *Feed? It will be even less than last time. This one has a heart like a pebble to begin with, tiny and hard, and our brother who rides him takes what little remains. We cannot draw blood from a stone.*

"Tighten your belts, then," she said angrily, "and spare me your tales of woe. Two men in two months: more than I have ever given. It is not your need, but your greed that has grown."

Hasmoday clasped his hands in false, exaggerated sorrow. *I try to reason, to warn you for your own good. You refuse to listen. You have ignored our mistress's demand; her rage mounts.*

Selena, do you think this is one of your schoolgirl games? Do you not understand the import of what I say? You flirt with danger beyond human dreams, although safety and reward lie within your grasp. Give her the man she craves! He is a fool, but a brave one. What a fine feast he will make!

How much easier to endure the embrace of one like him than the reptile you so recently bedded! And there need be only a few more strong souls before you will be free of them forever. The deluge is coming soon, Selena. After that, the cattle will sacrifice each other gladly as they did in the past, as they were meant to—and you, as priestess, will be inviolable.

Go to him, before it is too late! You have only to smile on him; he will do the rest.

"I will choose the men I please," she said defiantly.

The imp drew himself up. His gaze was contemptuous, and for the first time ever, his tone to her was not politely mocking, but underlain with cold, thinly veiled threat.

You have demanded a task of us this night, but you refuse to reward us properly. This bursts another link in our bonds of servitude. We are no longer the beggars we were.

I warn you once more: obey our mistress's wishes, or face the consequences.

As he faded, she forced herself to ignore him. But her fists were clenched and her heart beating fast.

How was it possible that she had never before realized what was suddenly as clear as if it burned with fire in her mind? The imp was not, never had been, her friend or even companion.

He had been her slave.

Beneath his seeming charm lay years of resentment and fury at having been bound by unknown rules to serve her, instead of running free; at being forced to subsist on the provender she gave him, instead of the far more toothsome children he preferred.

And now, like any slave who gained strength, the humiliation he had endured was rising to the fore in a show of vengefulness.

Was it only that—the desire to torment her—that lay behind his demand? Or did he, in fact, speak with the goddess's authority?

Of this there was no doubt: he had never before exhibited such force and insolence.

She wheeled and reentered the house, throwing closed the French doors. Quickly, she pulled on a robe, then hurried downstairs and poured cognac into a snifter. She started to put on music, but there was nothing to suit her mood. Instead, she paced, arms folded tightly across her breasts.

A brave fool, yes: an apt description of Farrell the night he had thought to come to her rescue. Doubtless more the latter than the former. Brash, stupid—

And yet, oddly entertaining. Even thrilling.

She shook her head impatiently. Until that night, she had not slept with the biker—had managed to intrigue him enough, with her aura of class and mystery, to fend him off. But as Farrell had fallen under the boots, she had understood it was the only way to save him. She had whispered an urgent promise to Icepick, and he had turned his hypnotic gaze on her, measuring the intent of her words; then nodded, issued a curt command, and led her out the door.

The night had been one of the worst. But upstairs in her china closet now rested a silver cocaine vial. The white powder that had filled it had been a gift from him to her. That was gone; now it was filled with drying blood. She took more than the usual satisfaction in knowing that when the moon reached its nadir of darkness in two weeks, his own eyes would give birth to the horror that was her gift to *him*.

Could it be true that her control over the imps was ebbing?

She finished the cognac and began to climb the empty staircase. Her imagination was suddenly all too vivid as to what might await her in the goddess's dark realm: as if the imps were whispering the awful secrets they knew, painting horrifying pictures, dwelling with lascivious cruelty on the worst her mind could conceive of, and assuring her it was nothing compared to the neverending reality.

Surrender Farrell? Turn traitor on all the innocents she had sacrificed so much to protect?

She turned to her lonely bedroom, there to toss fretfully until rising birdsong announced the coming of dawn.

TEN

It was Saturday night, and as the evening deepened, Farrell braced himself for the onslaught that police and ER doctors expected, and often shared. He was not disappointed. By eleven-thirty, he had seen a gunshot wound, several vehicle casualties, and a weeping young teen girl who had been engaging in sexual exploration with a phallus-shaped perfume bottle and gotten it lodged firmly inside herself, whereupon fear and pain had tightened her muscles so much that he was unable to extract it. He had given her a mild sedative and had the nurses put her to bed, to wait for morning and a gynecologist. What a wonderful way to be introduced to sex, he thought darkly, stalking to the cafeteria to bolt a cup of coffee before the next nightmare came through the door.

He had just taken his first sip—sitting at a table, stretching to ease the tension in his neck and back, and after his quarter-hour of probing the unfortunate girl, numb to the smile of an attractive nurse—when the intercom clicked on:

"Doctor Farrell, please report to the emergency room."

"Son of a bitch," he said, slamming the cup on the table, already up and striding past the startled nurse.

When he arrived, the head nurse on duty, Janet Black, was sitting attentively at the radio monitor. She was a stocky woman in her late thirties, with fifteen years experience in the ER; he relied heavily on her competence and judgment.

"Somebody reported a motorcycle going off a cliff on Trinity Road," she said without looking up. Farrell closed his eyes. Of all the ways to finish out the night, several frantic hours trying to keep the spark of life going in a motorcycle wreck victim, with the likely outcome of gaining him some years as a vegetable on life-support, was the ugliest one he could imagine.

"The sheriffs and paramedics are on their way," she said. "Chances are he's dead, but you'd better be here to talk to the paras."

He nodded. "Any more information?"

"None yet. The caller was a woman; apparently she was in a car a couple of switchbacks up and saw it happen, but when she got there and looked over the cliff she couldn't even see the bike. She decided the best thing to do was get to a phone."

"Is she sure she saw him at all?"

'We'll find out," Janet said.

"How long have we got?" Trinity Road was steep and tortuous, its center stretch about as far as it was possible to get from a main highway.

"Maybe twenty minutes."

Farrell sighed. "Okay. Why don't you stay here; I'll make a quick round, try to get this zoo under control. Call me as soon as you hear something."

As he checked the occupied beds, giving a few words of reassurance to those who were conscious, monitoring vital signs indicators, administering a shot of Demerol to the moaning possessor of a leg broken in a car wreck, he tried to brace himself for the ordeal to come. If the description of the scene was accurate, then Janet was correct: the rider was probably dead. But there was always the chance of major CNS injury, with a victim who might emerge crippled but alive; or trying to determine which vital organs might be saved for transplants. Even the relatively straightforward job of pronouncing a corpse dead was hardly appealing, especially when it came in looking like it had been run through a trash compactor.

A few minutes later, the sheriffs arrived at the scene. Farrell took the radio monitor from Janet, while she went to tell the triage nurse that all but genuinely critical situations were to be kept in the waiting room for the next few minutes. Impatiently, he followed the flat, static-filled dialogue, his imagination supplying the details. The frightened housewife had pointed out the place where she thought she had seen the ghostly rider make his plunge; the sheriffs were unable to find any skid marks, and a tone of skepticism, clear even through the electronics, was creeping into the voices. Two deputies with flashlights were working their way down the hillside; its steepness did not improve their moods, nor did the fact that the brush was thick with poison oak.

Then there came a pause, and one of them spoke again, his tone changed.

"Yeah, okay, we got something." Farrell leaned forward, listening intently. There was more silence, punctuated by static. "Looks like, ah, a white male, and I'd say he's pretty definitely, ah, deceased. Let's get the medics down here."

"They're on their way," came the answer from the top of the hill. "Any other victims?"

"I think that's, uh, negative, but we'll keep checking." Then he said, with something like awe, "Jesus Christ, he must have been moving. I've got to be a good hundred yards from you guys. Like he took off on a ski jump."

Farrell waited with sick impatience while the two paramedics made their way to the victim.

"No doubt about it, Doc," the leader finally said. "Massive contusions to head and body, and I'm sure his neck's broken. He was dead on impact."

Farrell slumped, both discouraged and relieved.

"Helmet?" he asked, not that it made any difference.

"Nope. Looks like a biker. The machine's a chopped Harley, what's left of it, I mean."

"Okay, bring him in. I'll pronounce him."

"Will do. It's gonna take us a while to get him out of here."

"I've got all night," Farrell said. He replaced the microphone and sat back, staring dully at the radio set. A biker, no doubt stoned out of his skull on some combination of shit. Still, it was hard to imagine an experienced rider coming around a curve on a road like that and not even hitting the brakes before taking his final fight.

But that sort of speculation was the police's work. All that mattered to Farrell was that he was dead. And while he was feeling less than fond of bikers these days, a life was a life.

After a moment, he roused himself and stood. "Mrs. Black, tell triage I'm available," he called, and went to see what new crises the last ten minutes might have brought.

When the body was wheeled in on a gurney, Farrell drew the cover off the face. He was still staring while a deputy recited offhandedly, the information they had gleaned.

"Mortal remains of one Phillip Grabowski, better known as Icepick Phil. The department's been familiar with him a long time. No known family. We called the place he hangs out; somebody's on their way here to make a positive I.D."

Farrell nodded, then, slowly, began the task of determining an official cause of death.

Within an hour, two bikers had arrived from Foolie's. As Farrell had half-expected, one was the thick-set bodyguard. A flicker of recognition appeared in his eyes, but was fast replaced by stone-faced impassivity.

Farrell led them to the morgue and raised the sheet, displaying the lacerations and grotesquely twisted neck. The bodyguard glanced, nodded, and walked stolidly back to the ER. There he stood with folded arms, his face grim and heavy, as the sheriffs questioned him.

His own name, he gave as Edward Mulroney. "Hogface," one of the deputies murmured knowingly, and Farrell glanced again at his bristly hair, massive frame, and porcine nose, still looking slightly swollen. He spoke in a monotone, volunteering no information except what was directly requested: a habit doubtless learned from previous questionings.

The other biker, a younger man whose forearms writhed with tattoos–perhaps to cover track marks–was staying clear of the interrogation. Farrell caught his eye and motioned him out into the hall.

"Was he doing dope?" Farrell said.

The biker shrugged elaborately, his face a mask of cool.

"The autopsy will tell us," Farrell said. "I'm just wondering if you have any notion why a guy who's been riding a Harley twenty years all of a sudden guns it off a cliff one night."

"No idea, man. Whatever Icepick did was his own business."

"Okay," Farrell said. "But if there's anybody else getting their nose in the same shit, you might pass the word."

"I'll keep that in mind."

Farrell hesitated, then said, "What do you know about that girl he was hanging out with?"

The biker stared at him, then, abruptly, grinned, exposing several missing teeth.

"That was you that night, huh. I got to say, that was pretty slick, the move you put down on Hoggy. He was

202

pissed, man. Hadn't been for the chick, he'd of ripped your head off."

"What do you mean, 'hadn't been for the chick'?"

"She got Icepick to call it off. She saved your ass."

Farrell turned away, staring down the empty hallway.

So. It was true.

"How'd she get hooked up with Icepick?" Farrell said, turning back.

The biker grimaced and twisted. "My back's really giving me trouble, Doc," he said. "Little spill I took a while ago. I can't remember too good when it hurts, you know what I mean?"

Farrell gauged the words, then glanced again up and down the hallway. There was no one around. A quick vision of his medical degree and the Hippocratic oath bursting into flame together flashed through his mind.

"Come on," he said, and stalked tight-lipped to the doctors' private room. He unlocked a drawer, yanked it open, and took out his triplicate pad.

"I diagnose you as suffering from severe muscle strain," he said, scribbling a prescription for twenty Percodans. He ripped the top sheet off and slapped it into the grinning biker's palm. "Just don't fill it here in town, okay?"

"Gotcha, Doc." The paper disappeared into a greasy leather pouch on his belt. "Now what was it I was trying to remember?"

"The girl. How Icepick met her."

"Oh, yeah." He shrugged. "They were riding down the street in Santa Rosa, Icepick and Hogface, and they see this chick coming, like, out of a shopping mall, and son of a bitch if she doesn't wave them over and ask for a ride. They couldn't believe it, man." He shook a cigarette out of a pack and cupped a match in his hands. "Weird thing was," he said, blowing smoke, "she'd never tell him where she lived or nothing. Weirder thing was, he went for it. Man, Icepick took no shit from nobody, not broads, not cops, no one." He shrugged. "Guess it don't matter now."

"Was she with him tonight?" Farrell asked carefully.

The biker frowned and dragged on his cigarette.

"Come to think of it, I haven't seen her for a couple weeks. Didn't see much of Icepick lately, either. You know her, huh?"

"Not really," Farrell said.

"Yeah, well, she's some smoke, no doubt." He shifted restlessly, stretching his shoulders. "I better find Hoggy."

By the time they had returned to the ER, the biker's face bad changed back to two-edged coolness. The deputies were off to the side, consulting with each other. Hogface walked slowly to Farrell and stopped. His eyes were liquid with hatred.

"Come on back down to FooIie's some time," he said softly. "We got unfinished business."

"I already saw your side of the street," Farrell snapped. "'You want to talk more business, come on in here like Icepick did and find out about mine." He swept his hand at the array of surgical equipment, looping IV tubes, and electronic monitors that lined the room.

Hogface turned his back and stalked away, looking like an oil drum on legs. The other biker glanced at

Farrell with what might have have been grudging respect, and followed.

"Ride careful, gents," Farrell called after them. "Accidents happen, know what I mean?"

As he turned away, he realized he was shaking, with rage, fear, adrenaline—

And just maybe, the information that it was, in fact, Selena who had saved him, for whatever reasons, from the tender mercies of Hogface.

He stepped back into his room and drank a glass of water, forcing his mind to set his emotions aside—something he had learned well over the past years. When he felt in control, he reentered the ER and checked with triage. In the next quarter-hour he admitted for observation an elderly woman with stomach pains, and was preparing to give an antibiotic to a baby with an earache, when he noticed a man in street clothes waiting in the doorway, trying to catch his eye. It was the sheriff's deputy, Pavlacek. He held up fingers to signify five minutes, and forced himself to be gently patient with the screaming infant.

Finished, he stepped out into the hall where Pavlacek waited.

"Don't you ever get off duty?" he said.

"'I just happened to have my radio on and heard the news," Pavlacek said. "Didn't have anything else to do, so I stopped by the station to see what they had. Thought you might be interested. They checked out Icepick's place. Somebody, presumably him, went through it on a rampage."

Farrell shook his head. "Bad dope is all I can think."

"We're having a hard time with that," the deputy said. "This was one very careful individual."

"Then what?"

"No idea, Doc. If you figure it out, tell us. All I'm sure of is, we're not going to miss him." He turned to go, then glanced back. "Oh, I almost forgot the really weird thing. He smashed all the mirrors."

Farrell stood motionless until Pavlacek was gone. Then he strode to the morgue, shut the door hard behind him, yanked the cover off Icepick's face, and urgently pried open one of the eyelids he had closed an hour before. For perhaps half a minute, he stared. Then he did the same with the other eye.

In the main, they held a look he had seen many times, which he equated with the recognition of death and the fear that accompanied it.

But deep in each pupil, so far back he could not quite make it out, was an image–tiny, irregular in shape, and absolutely black. He flicked on his flashlight and bent close, but it disappeared under the beam. The image stood forth most dearly in lighting that approximated dusk.

Then he straightened, gazing blankly at the empty wall before him, feeling the bristling of the hairs on the nape of his neck. The closest he could come was that it looked something like a coiled serpent, and it seemed imbedded in the tissue: not like an image the eye might have recorded at the moment of death, but as if it were actually *in* the pupils, looking out.

He shook his head hard. You are seeing things, Farrell, he told himself grimly, closing the eyes and covering the face. You are making connections that do not exist. There are a thousand natural explanations for marks in the eyes, from birth anomalies to loa loa worms. Go back to work and demonstrate that you are still a rational, even useful, member of the human race.

He made another round of the emergency room, hoping to get everything stabilized before the inevitable second wave began when the bars closed at 2.:00 AM. But as he worked, phrases played like a tape in his mind: *apparently they found blood and, you know, tissue under his nails . . . bad luck seems to follow her . . .*

Perhaps half an hour later, he stepped out of a cubicle to find Janet Black waiting for him. The expression on her face puzzled him. Arch, he decided, was the closest he could come to describing it.

"You have a visitor, Doctor."

"Another cop?" he said, exasperated.

"I don't think so."

"Well, if it's not that or a patient, tell them to call me tomorrow. I'm busy as a one-legged man in an ass-kicking contest, and it's about to get worse."

"I think you'd better come see this one," she said. She was smiling slightly now. He started to protest further, but she crooked a finger and started toward the lobby.

Where, amid the covert glances of hospital personnel and patients alike, stood Selena Clermont, looking like a goddess who had descended to a battlefield.

"I came to see him," she said. She was wearing a simple black dress and a string of pearls, with only a trace of makeup and her hair done in a French braid. She looked as if she might have been out for dinner at a fashionable restaurant—a far cry from her appearance the last time he had seen her.

He had thought nothing more could surprise him tonight, but it took him a conscious effort to keep his jaw from dropping. Numbly, he shook his head.

"He's not viewable."

"Why? Because I'm not family?"

"Because he looks like he's been worked over with a framing hammer."

"I'm not afraid of blood."

"So I've learned," he said. Her face turned sharp with anger, and he regretted the words, remembering that he probably owed his life to her. He exhaled, and then, more to make up for his rudeness than because it was a good idea, said, "Come on."

He led her to the morgue and once again lifted the cover from Icepick's damaged face. For thirty seconds, she gazed at it, unwavering.

"Enough?" he said. She nodded, and waited by the door, arms folded across her chest in the room's cold, while he covered the corpse once more.

He followed her to the ER, helpless for anything to say, and finally fell back on the time-honored words:

"I'm sorry:"

Her shrug suggested harshness. "Don't be," she said without turning, then added, "even if you meant it."

Perplexed, he said, "Wasn't he your, ah—"

"Lover?" She turned, with a faint, mocking smile. "He was a loathsome human being. And yes, he was my lover, or more accurately, I fucked him. Once."

Confusion destroyed the facade he had tried to maintain. How was it that she always seemed to know more about what was going on than he, was always several steps ahead of him in whatever game they were playing?

"My compliments on your taste," he said, trying to put sting into the words.

"My taste is nobody's concern but mine."

"He must have ridden that road a million times," Farrell said, his anger beginning to rise. "Why do you figure he goes into orbit without ever touching the brakes, right after he starts seeing you?"

"Everybody makes mistakes," she said. "You ought to know."

"Yeah, and how about Lyle Randolph? Did he make a mistake too? You must keep those widow's weeds right at the front of your closet."

She wheeled and stalked out. Farrell hurried after and caught her at the main door, gripping her arm. She looked steadily into his face, her eyes unreadable.

"I heard you stopped the party the other night," he said. "I owe you."

She did not speak. but made a gesture that was half-nod, half-shrug, that could have meant, *yes, you do,* or *you're wrong,* or simply, *I don't care.* Then she pulled free of his hand, turned her back deliberately, and strode off, heels clicking on the pavement.

"How did you know he was dead?" Farrell shouted.

He walked slowly back into the emergency room, past the curious gazes of the nurses, wondering dully how he was going to survive the long remaining hours of his shift.

PART THREE

August 1988

ELEVEN

"This afternoon," Rosalie was saying to Emilio. "It has to be this afternoon, while your mother's out. You can say you fell asleep, and when you woke up, he was gone." Her voice was tense with excitement.

Holding her breath, eye pressed to a gap in the siding of a shed, Dora listened. Exactly what Rosalie was talking about, she did not know, but neither the girl's words nor her tone fit the picture of a children's conversation.

Then Emilio turned so that his face came within view, and it startled her so much her mouth opened. Never had she imagined such terror in a child's heart. His eyes were wet with, tears, his mouth twisted with an all-too-adult anguish.

Shaking his head, he whispered, "*No es possible.*" Then, as if it explained everything, "Ees my *brawther.*"

"Yes," Rosalie said, nodding emphatically. "You *have* to." She paused, then added, with answering fear in her own voice, "Remember what happened to the puppy. If you don't bring the baby, it'll be you instead. They told me so."

Snuffling, Emilio turned and hurried off toward home. "This afternoon," Rosalie called. "You better be there." She watched the boy until he disappeared, then turned and scanned her surroundings with furtive eyes before walking quickly away.

Dora leaned back against the shed wall.

The puppy?

The *baby?!*

Who were *they,* what had they done—and what were they *about* to do?

"Help me, Jesus," she whispered. As she prayed, she began to find strength, knowing that He would not desert her in her moment of need. He had not come to save the just, she reminded herself, but wretched sinners like her.

And as if He had answered her call and was there in the still center of her heart, she grew calmer, and began to think.

The mysterious games in the woods had been going on for weeks, far longer than she had expected, far longer than the usual attention span of children that age.

As usual, Dora had been too busy to worry over-much. It had actually been a relief not having the children underfoot. The only really sinister possibility, she had decided, was sexual exploration; but at ten, Rosalie was the oldest of the group, and it seemed un-likely that the boys would be able to do her any damage, even if they were interested.

It'll be you instead. You better be there.

She realized that her fear was turning to anger: the Lord's righteous wrath was blossoming in her heart. She wasn't yet sure who to be angry *at;* maybe the hairy-legged, bagpipe-playing strangers were really older children, coming from Lord knew where, teaching sinful games to her own.

But whatever this was, it had gone far enough, and whether or not Emilio appeared, *she* would. Some kids were going to get a lesson today they would not soon forget. She started grimly back to the house, determined to follow, unseen, when Rosalie left for the woods after lunch.

But at the door, she paused, remembering the terror in the little boy's eyes–

And suddenly she imagined that mixed with the fear in her daughter's face at that moment, there had been a touch of cunning, even of triumph.

A chill swept through her, weakening her knees. Was there more to this than Rosalie's somehow being the victim of unidentified ruffians? She had always been a good girl, and Jesus knew how hard Dora had striven to raise her in His ways. But for seconds, panic hovered over her. Was it possible that Dora's own sinfulness was coming home in the form of evil seed? That the Devil had taken up residence in her house, in her heart, troubling her with the presences she continued to sense around her? And now, as if that evil was a germ that others could somehow catch, was he beginning to do his work on the flesh of her flesh?

Abruptly, she remembered the Reverend Harner's suspicion that Selena might be possessed.

Could *that* be the source of this trouble?

Praying fervently against her confusion and fear, she hurried inside. The Lord was with her, she knew that.

Wretched sinner though she was, He would not abandon her now, when her life had finally settled into a semblance of peace.

But as she fixed lunch, she marveled at the blandness in the face of the child she had seen, only minutes ago, looking like a fallen angel.

The heat in the woods was so intense it made Dora feel faint, and she paused, panting, wishing for water. She had given Rosalie a hundred yards' head start, could no longer hear or see her, and was getting worried that she would lose the girl–even get lost herself. In her five years here, she had never ventured this far into the forest. Her world was the small civilization of house and yard. There was something pagan, even demonic, about this lush sweltering jungle.

The deer trail she followed was narrow, with thick vegetation brushing and scratching her, occasionally coming together overhead to form a tunnel, shutting out the sun and forcing her to duck. She imagined swarms of ticks creeping beneath her clothes toward the warm pulsing areas of armpit and groin, there to swell up into vile pinkish bubbles, fat with her blood, filling her with horrifying diseases. The menacing oily sheen of three leaved poison oak was everywhere, disguised, woven in with more innocent foliage.

Or rattlesnakes, Lord have mercy. The thought made her freeze, skin crawling, breath stopped in her throat. Roy killed several every year. Suddenly every stick beside the trail writhed with malignant life, every rock and dead log harbored coiled menace beneath, waiting to strike death into her passing ankles.

She collapsed against a tree, on the edge of turning back. Surely this could not be important after all; it was only a childish fantasy, and the best way of dealing with it would be to sit Rosalie down tonight and make her explain.

But she remembered again the girl's face after giving Emilio his instructions—no, after *threatening* him—and the stealthy way she had slipped into the woods after lunch, not knowing that her mother was watching. Dora pushed damp hair out of her eyes and hurried on.

The trail descended gradually, the glades becoming darker. She guessed she had gone over a mile when she came to another trail crossing the first. She stopped again, panting, drenched with perspiration. Both looked equally used. Which was right? The hot dead stillness seemed to shimmer around her, the only sound the low drone of busy insects.

Then she heard the music.

She held her breath, listening in disbelief. The melody was faint, faraway, rising and then falling off until her straining ears lost it and she was sure she had imagined it, only to return, distinct and unmistakable. It sounded like a flute. She swiveled her head, trying to get a fix on her location, wondering if she could somehow have gotten turned around and come near a road or house. But no: she could see the cliffs to the west, and she knew that she had been paralleling them into the deepest part of the woods.

It had to be the children, then. Perhaps one of them had a toy flute, or a radio or tape recorder. At least the sound would give her something to aim for. She walked on, taking care now to be quiet.

By the time she could hear the music clearly, she was sure of this: it was not being played by any child. On its surface, the melody was pretty, lilting, and happy; but beneath that was woven a subtle, complex, haunting strain that seemed to become more sinister by the moment. It sounded like the work of several flutes rather than one. She had never heard anything like it, and she was trying to imagine how children that age might have stumbled on such a bizarre recording, when she heard the sound of voices. Cautiously, she eased off the trail and burrowed through the thick brush, pausing every few feet to look and listen. At last, she peered around a tree and glimpsed moving figures. She rubbed her sleeve across her blurred eyes, squinting.

And stared, not believing what her gaze told her.

The glade was as dark as if it were twilight, shaded by thick spreading oaks and laurels. Seated on a rock outcropping at the far edge was a creature that made her mouth form into an O. From the waist up, it was a man about Rosalie's size, but of powerful build, with naked, sinewy chest and arms.

From the waist down, he had the legs of a goat, covered with coarse brown fur, ending in cloven hooves.

His bearded face was playful, and he smiled charmingly as his lips danced on the reed pipes he held. But there was a sinister hint in the slant of his almond-shaped eyes; and as Dora's heart began to beat hard and fast, she was sure she saw the stubs of small horns protruding up through his wild, curly hair.

In the center of the glade, Rosalie and her playmates were dancing in a circle with their arms linked. They moved clumsily and with obvious reluctance. Around them cavorted a number of creatures similar to the pipe player, leaping, turning somersaults, their merriment contrasting grotesquely with the children's frightened faces.

The music stopped. The pipe player raised his head as if listening, and then Dora heard it too.

The sound of a baby crying–the sound she had been hearing for weeks in her mind, as if prefigured by some impossible warp of time.

The creature began to play again, and this time the dark strain no longer lay half-hidden beneath the melody but emerged to overpower it. The glade seemed to darken further, the air to take on a thick dank quality, as if a cloud had swallowed the sun. The children, moving as if to unheard instructions, stopped the dance and broke the circle, revealing a small rock-ringed fire burning in its center. Dora's gaze fixed in horror on. a small charred shape in the ashes at the fire's edge. From it protruded the unmistakable white of bones.

The puppy.

Slowly, looking terrified and pale beneath his dark skin, Emilio Vasquez entered the glade. In his arms was a blanket-wrapped bundle. Its cries were inaudible over the quickening music, but Dora could see the waving of a tiny fist. The faunlike creatures leaped about in a frenzy as Emilio carried the baby toward the fire. Rosalie met

219

him, solemn as a high priestess, and extended her arms. Emilio hesitated, clutching the bundle tighter, looking desperately from side to side, and Dora, hands clutching at her face, screamed silently, *Yes, run!*

But with a sudden, violent motion, he surrendered the baby to Rosalie and stumbled back, knuckling his eyes. As the girl turned to the fire, Dora again saw that terrible furtive gleam in her eyes: the look of someone insane, someone who had been possessed by the Devil himself. Jesus, Jesus, this cannot be happening, she prayed, but Rosalie was unwrapping the infant, exposing its tiny naked limbs and squalling face. Some distant part of Dora knew she must act instantly, put a stop to this horror, but she stayed crouched, paralyzed, nails digging into her cheeks.

Then a shout came, and the music faltered, and once again died.

Into the clearing strode Selena Clermont. She was wearing a dress that was torn and dirty, her hair was a tangled mess, and she was barefoot, as if she had kicked off her shoes. Her face was white with fury. She hurried forward and snatched the baby from Rosalie's arms, then wheeled to face the pipe player, who had risen and was advancing menacingly toward her with obscene crook-legged hopping.

His playful smile was gone, and his face began to change before Dora's eyes, the features sharpening into a mask of naked, enraged evil. The other creatures too were metamorphosing into grotesque figures, resembling things she had seen in old artists' paintings of hell, with clawlike limbs, misshapen and swollen parts, eyes in bellies and leering malignant faces. They surrounded Selena, leaping and gesticulating furiously, rising in the air to hover, and making ineffective grabs for the child.

The pipe player held out his arms demandingly. No sound emerged from his mouth—and yet there echoed in Dora's brain the vague impression of something like the sibilant hissing of a snake.

Clutching the baby, Selena shouted back in a voice that was altogether human, in words that were too clear in their import:

"By *no* right do you dare to claim him! It is I who command!"

The creature rose suddenly into the air and flew at her, but stopped just short of touching her, hovering in menace. The tension of violent rage mounted until the sheer force of it started spots flickering before Dora's eyes.

But Selena stared at him without flinching. "You will obey me," she repeated forcefully, "as you always have."

Snarling, lips writhing in clear threat, he began to retreat. The other creatures went with him, yelping and dancing their rage. As the company faded off into the woods, Dora could not be sure whether they disappeared into the brush—or simply disappeared.

For a long time afterward—after Selena had gathered the awestruck children around her, and, kneeling, explained to them patiently but severely that what they had done was very bad, and that they must never come here, or have anything to do with Mister Asthma-Day, again; after they had dispersed, Emilio, with the baby in his arms, like a condemned man miraculously reprieved:

after Selena had collapsed to sit for several moments with her face in her hands, then, looking weary and heartsick, put out the fire, pausing to cover the charred bundle of flesh, and started her own way home—Dora remained crouched, clinging to the tree that had supported her during the ordeal.

When at last she tried to rise, her numb legs buckled under her, causing her to cry out in pain: a cry she immediately stifled for fear that *they* might still be lurking nearby. It took minutes of agonized rubbing of the limbs before circulation returned and she was able to stumble back down the trail, head swiveling fearfully to right and left, pausing every few steps to listen, and praying without cease.

The sun was getting low when she emerged from the woods, and the pickup truck was parked beside the house; Roy was home, and he would be angry, wanting to know where his dinner was.

But tonight, that was the least of her worries. Her terror was too huge to keep bottled inside. Tonight, she was going to have to tell Roy, and the Reverend Harner, everything that had happened.

Selena had been aware of the succession of cars and pickup trucks coming up the road through the evening, gathering at the Luteys' house below; but not until she heard the rising chorus of angry voices, and saw the flicker of a bonfire, did she admit what she feared. Her game with Roy Lutey had been a mistake; doubtless, he had told all the assembled men by now about the little teeth—although he had probably not mentioned what he was up to at the time. For that, she could blame herself.

But alone, it could not account for this. One of the children must have told about the companions. And for that, she could hardly blame *them*.

She stood on the second-floor balcony, gazing down at the moving shapes silhouetted by the flames. One voice stood out above the others, strident, righteous, accustomed to command: no doubt the preacher who had his hooks so firmly into Dora. The word "witch" rose clearly, drowned by shouts of affirmation. Her lips tightened with contempt. They were like savages, dancing around a fire to work up their courage.

Hugging herself, she walked back inside. There was no telling how far such a mob would go. This was not the Middle Ages; but the men were under the influence of the charismatic Harner, and she could see the glint of liquor bottles being passed from hand to hand, and it was nighttime in an isolated spot.

Well: there was nothing to do but wait. If the threat became real, she would have to unleash the companions again. It would be the end of any pretense—would affirm their primitive ideas of witchcraft and Satanism—and the end of her residency in this place where she had hoped to find peace. But she was not prepared to suffer at the hands of rabble. By the time they had recovered sufficiently to seek her out again—if they even dared—she would be long gone to Europe or South America.

She formed the mental summons that would bring the companions to her. The familiar shapes began to gather.

What temerity, Selena. You steal the very food from our mouths, yet do not hesitate to call us in need. The imp's face did not bear its usual smile, but a malicious sneer, and his tone was cold and ugly.

Her reply was equally curt. "Spare me your whining, Hasmoday. Keep watch on those men. If they come here intending harm, drive them away. And don't be overly gentle about it."

Certainly, came the reply. *For the stated price.*

"What is this talk of price?" she said angrily.

Feigning ignorance does not become you, Selena. We have made it abundantly clear: men such as our mistress desires, not rotting husks.

"You will make do with the men I choose."

No more. Today, when you robbed us, the scales of justice tipped at last in our favor; our final bonds were broken. We are no longer compelled to serve you. Henceforth, we will work only for hire—and we will set the terms.

"Enough of your insolence! Go, at once!"

The imp folded his arms and regarded her contemptuously. *What a pity, Selena. Look upon them, filling their bellies with drink and their minds with idiocy. They are worse than beasts. And yet, in the interest of saving their kind, you will let them murder you.*

"This is not possible," she whispered. "You are lying again, Hasmoday."

As you wish, Selena. But see: I make no move to obey.

"Then leave me. I will save myself."

Indeed? came the mocking reply. *You had best look to it, for they will soon be here. You will need all your cleverness, too; they have blocked the road, and one of their number is concealed nearby, watching in case you should decide to flee on foot.*

Go ahead, Selena: run. They will hunt you down like a dog. You will enjoy the embraces of men for one final time, in a fashion that will make your worst memories seem tender.

Then they will dispatch you to learn whether I have lied about an eternity of our mistress's wrath–while my little brothers and I will again be free to prowl the wind, and feed to our heart's content, as we were meant to from time's beginning. Our first feast will be tonight, Selena, as you burn. There is no sweeter taste to slaves than the agony of those they were forced to serve.

As if to punctuate his words, the companions converged into a sudden swarm around her head, leering, swirling so close as to almost brush her with their grotesquely sprouting parts. *Now you see,* came a final malicious whisper as they faded, *what it is to be a mortal, helpless in the face of danger.*

Farewell, Selena.

She whirled and strode back to the window. New vehicles had arrived; the number of men was swelling, the voices rising. Stunned by this event she had never dreamed of–like being stripped of a weapon one had always taken for granted, then thrown into the heat of a battle–she tried to understand what to do next. She could call police–but tell them what? The gathering below would appear innocent, a drunken party–until the mo-

225

ment it began to move up the hill. Then it would be too late.

That left only escape.

They have blocked the road, and one of their number is concealed nearby.

She hurried down the stairs, scooping her purse from the table. At the edge of the driveway, she stopped, staring down at the fire. Her stomach twisted with fear. Several cars and trucks were positioned, deliberately or not, so as to block the road. There was no possibility of going around; it was cut into the hillside, with a sheer wall of earth on one side and a steep drop on the other. Nor was there any back exit.

Was it true, too, that an unseen watcher was even now monitoring her moves, ready to sound the alarm?

They will hunt you down like a dog. You will enjoy the embraces of men for one final time–

For half a minute, she stood still, suddenly almost weary enough to simply give up: let this whole evil drama come to its final conclusion.

Then they will dispatch you to learn whether I have lied about an eternity of our mistress's wrath.

Down the hill an ember exploded in the fire, sending up a shower of sparks, bringing a roar from the gathered men.

As if that triggered some atavistic set of memories, her mind abruptly flared with vivid images of torment. Horrified, unable to escape, she seemed to hover over an endless plain of dark fire, watching a kaleidoscope of roasting limbs and shrieking mouths, until her nostrils filled with the reek of burning flesh and her own silent screams threatened to burst her skull.

The images ceased and seemed to hang suspended. Doubled over, choking and gagging, she tried to control her panic. All thoughts of dignity had vanished. She would offer a man, she thought wildly: whoever was closest. Roy Lutey, or Harner, or all of them if that was what it took, even if it meant thrashing shamelessly on her back in the dust for all their greedy eyes to see while they came at her one by one: anything to evade what her mind had shown her.

Not them, whispered the familiar voice in her mind. *You know.*

And even as she shook her head, trying to back away, the images of fire and agony exploded in her brain again, driving her to her knees.

"Yes," she finally gasped. "Yes. You shall have him."

Summon him, came the voice, iron hard. *Bring him, now. Prove to us your promise.*

Coughing, retching, she managed to nod. "Only save me," she breathed.

The images ceased. Her mind began to clear. In a moment, she was able to stand. She stumbled inside to a sink and ran water over her wrists.

Then, feeling the eager presences surrounding her, she went to the telephone stand, opened the book, and found the number.

With relief and anguish warring within her, she heard the dial tone; the mob of men had not had the foresight, or the courage, to cut the line. Her fingers hesitated.

Haste! came the imp's impatient voice. *Fear not, he is home. Although he does not know it, he awaits your call.*

"He hates me," she whispered. "He will never come."

No, Selena. He has fallen in love with you. And she knew that it was true, that it had been true from the moment he'd first seen her: that it did not have to have anything to do with making sense. That it was the first time she had ever been genuinely loved by a man she might love in return.

With trembling fingers, she dialed.

The receiver was lifted after three rings. "It's Selena Clermont," she said, distantly astonished at the steadiness of her own voice. "I'm home, at the vineyard. I think some men are coming to kill me."

She hung up and stood with her hand still on the phone. The imp was visible again, his features haughty.

Let there be no more pretence between us, Selena. Henceforth, we shall be equals—

Until the day comes when you will serve me.

He faded. The telephone was ringing with an urgent sound. She ignored it, and climbed numbly to the third story. There she chose for her vantage point a window in a room at the end of the hall. Below, the hillside plunged steeply. She wanted, she realized distractedly, to be as far as physically possible from what she had done.

She thought of when she had seen Farrell last, at the emergency room the night of the biker's death. Never before had she gone to see a man she had marked for doom. Was not the truth that it was Farrell she had gone to see? Yielding to the need to touch, in spite of herself, this new and seductive emotion within her?

Or had she even then known in her heart that this moment must come, and manipulated him, strengthening her hold over him, so that he would willingly serve as victim in her stead?

In years past, only two men had held out as long as one moon before the terror had driven them mad; none for two.

Far below, the bonfire began to separate into sparks as the men thrust torches into it.

Farrell slammed down the phone and redialed for the third time. After the eighth ring, he shouted, "*You motherfucker!*" at it and threw it across the room. He stood half-crouched, breathing deeply, hands wide open and tensed as if about to seize something and tear it in half.

Men coming to kill her?

Kill?

The obvious answer was that it was a hoax, her idea of a joke. She had found some new scumbag boyfriend and was calling for his amusement, so the two of them could laugh their heads off at the thought of Farrell racing up to the winery to play white knight again. If she was in trouble, why didn't she call the police? If she was at her home, why didn't she answer the phone?

Only—something in him was certain that she would not pull such a trick. That there was a great deal about her he did not understand, that she was aloof, hostile, perhaps disturbed—but not capable of something like this.

That she had saved his life in Foolie's.

And that even if it was a hoax, one more instance of making a fool of himself hardly mattered now.

With that thought, he was moving, striding to a closet and tearing out old boots, camping gear, fishing tackle, until his hand closed around the leather case of his only weapon: a twenty-gauge Browning pump shotgun his father had bought him for bird hunting when he was a boy. He had not used it in years, but as he yanked it from the case, his fingers felt the faint film of oil on the barrel. He had always put it away clean. His hands jammed shells into the chamber, remembering the gun as if they had last touched it only yesterday.

Men coming to *kill* her?

He sprinted out the door to his truck.

TWELVE

The Reverend Emmett Tom Harner raised his hand, commanding breathless silence from the crowd, and he paused, marveling at the collection of fools it had been his life's work to gather around him. Firelight glinted off faces gone slack with drink and eyes that were pools of senseless rage. The tension of barely suppressed violence was like a snarling, bristling beast in their midst. Without warning, he was overcome by the urge to laugh out loud, and actually started to titter nervously, but covered it by coughing.

When he spoke, his voice was charged with righteous fury. "Hath not the Lord Jesus Christ said, 'It were better for him that a millstone were hanged about his neck, and he cast into the sea, than he harm one of my little ones?'" A roar answered him, clenched fists shaking in the air, some of them holding crude torches they had hacked from pitchy logs.

"And hath not that woman"—he whirled to point up at the big house on the hill—"that *witch,* corrupted our children, and brought to harm even a baby still at its mother's breast?"

The response was thunderous, deafening. The bottles of cheap whiskey which he himself had brought circulated from hand to clutching hand, while axes and pitchforks were rising in the air along with the torches.

"And is it not written in the Holy Book, 'Thou shalt not suffer a witch to live'?"

This time there was no stopping them. He watched Roy Lutey leap to the crowd's front, his long-jawed, close-eyed Okie face resembling an Elvis Presley who had been squeezed by the forceps at birth. It was Lutey who had arrived with the story, bursting into the church shouting *witch!* Harner had listened with inward cynicism, hearing clearly beneath Lutey's words his lust for the woman: an echo of his own frustrated itch to draw her, and her fortune, into the fold.

The idea of witchcraft was preposterous, of course. Lutey's wife Dora had spouted some garbled nonsense about children and demons, and Roy himself claimed he had been walking past Selena Clermont's house one evening when he was set upon by some sort of invisible teeth. In truth, Dora was gullible enough to believe that the Second Coming of Christ was going to take place right there in the Church of the Most Holy Redemption, with the Reverend Emmett Tom Harner presiding; whereas Roy had doubtless had his nose in a bottle and disturbed a nest of yellow jackets or carpenter ants.

But as Harner had stared into the man's sweating narrow face and listened to the story unfold, it was as if a voice from God Himself had sounded within him, telling him that his long-awaited chance had finally come: that this was his ticket to move from backwater churches and cretinous congregations and small-time scams to the big world of headlines and television–a world that had a nice fat hole in it after the disgraces of Bakker and Swaggart.

And so he had sent Lutey off to gather a collection of men Harner knew could be counted on to act without thinking: men like Lutey, who understood that they had gotten a raw deal from life and that it was never going to get any better, and who ached for a chance to unleash their rage. He himself had pulled out his trusty bibilical concordance–a most useful tool, as reading actual scripture bored him to tears, and he had never taken much trouble to do so–and looked up everything there was on witches. His memory and tongue were both glib; he had had no trouble belting out the words that were powering the crowd up the hill this moment.

Someone was crying out his name. He turned to see Dora Lutey running toward him, her face tearful and anguished.

"Reverend Harner, you ain't going to do nothing to hurt her, are you? Because I told you, she's the one *saved* that baby."

"She consorts with evil spirits," he growled. "She is the Devil's agent, and she must be punished according to the tenets of the Lord."

"But the law–"

"The law? *The law?!* The law of Jesus Christ is the only law I obey, woman. Do you know a higher law than His?"

233

He watched with satisfaction as she fought to find words, then finally lowered her eyes and shook her head. A good-hearted woman, and not uncomely—he had more than once considered persuading her to celebrate a particular form of the Lord's bounty privately with him—but compared to her, her husband was an intellectual giant.

"Back to your house, then," he thundered. "For the province of woman is to obey man, and to be a helpmeet unto him in his time of trial."

Shoulders bowed, she slunk away. He turned back to watch the crowd, rubbing his jaw. Her mention of the law had struck home. But he did not intend for anything to happen to the Clermont girl, not really: a confrontation, at worst a thrashing, but above all, the exposure of the story to the world. He wanted the reputation as a Christian soldier courageous enough to fight the Devil himself. Not Bakker, not Swaggart, not even Oral Roberts, who was genius enough to claim ultimatums received directly from God—not any of these men could declare that they had faced down a witch.

And if things did get out of band, well, he himself had not so much as touched a torch.

He hurried after the crowd, shouting, "Make way! Make way, you foul fiends and spirits of hell! Yield to the army of Christ!"

Rage, guilt, and confusion warred with fear when Selena saw the torches begin moving up the hill. She gripped the windowsill, deliberately forcing anger to the fore. She would need it—all the fury at men she could muster—when it came around to doing Farrell.

By the time he arrived, the companions would have attacked, and the mob would have fled. He would not have time to wonder why, she thought unhappily, for she would fall into his arms as if she were desperately grateful that he had come to her aid–even though it had proved unnecessary. Events would quickly take their course: she would see to that. Then, feigning shyness, she would tell him she needed to be alone, to sort out her feelings.

And while he drove back down the mountain in a euphoric daze, she would pack and disappear into the world, trying to understand what must come next.

Cruel, but unavoidable.

He would not suffer her loss for long.

Another glance at the approaching men made her tingle with fear in spite of herself. Somehow, she had not actually believed it would come to this. But staring down at the angry faces, the truth of the imp's words was clear. There were about two dozen of them, with Roy Lutey in the lead. The torchlight glinted off metal in their hands: pitchforks, axes, shovels.

Her fists tightened: away with whatever compunctions she might have had. If the cost was a man not directly to blame, so be it. Let the guilt fall on the heads of those who had forced her to this moment. Hasmoday was right about that too: they were not worth saving. Along with defeat came relief at embracing the end of her years of struggle.

The mob stopped at the bottom of the hill, some forty yards below the house; there they milled in confused conflict between the rage they had worked up and their fear of coming too close. The torchlight gave the sweating faces a strange ruddy gleam, distorting them, she noted with distant irony, into grotesque, demonlike masks. The preacher was making his way to the front: a heavyset man with long sideburns, cowboy boots, and a string tie. He took three steps forward from the crowd and faced up at her. The angry murmur behind him dropped off into a silence that stretched for most of a minute.

Abruptly, Harner thrust a clenched fist into the air and shouted, "Woman, are you in league with Satan's forces?"

Absurdly, she could not help being amused. She folded her arms and leaned against the window jamb, waiting.

"Is it not true that you set fiends upon our brother Roy?" A murmur of menacing agreement rose from the men. Selena did not move.

"That our Christian children have been corrupted and their very lives threatened by the foul minions you command?" The murmur leaped into angry shouts, with torches being shaken in the air.

"Come down, sister, that I may cleanse the evil from your soul, through the power of Jesus Christ! Come down and kneel before Him, and let me wrestle, in His name, with those devils that possess your heart!"

"Yeah, come down, witch!" Roy Lutey shouted, and among the echoing cries of "Come down," and "Come to Jesus," rose a single voice shrieking, "Burn her!"

Harner held his hand up, and an uneasy muttering stillness returned. "It is written in the Good Book, 'Thou shalt not suffer a witch to live,' he intoned ominously. "If you will not allow the Lord to cleanse the evil from your heart–"

When still she neither moved nor spoke, the voices rose angrily again. This time, several of the men moved forward, and then the whole mob began a wary, step-by-step advance. Roy Lutey's bony fist was clenched around a torch, his shoulders hunched, and his close-set eyes darted from side to side as if he expected attack any instant from the invisible teeth.

This time, my friend, she thought, standing straight and preparing herself, there will be no playful bites to frighten. This time, there will be blood.

"Hasmoday!" she hissed. Instantly, she felt the familiar shapes around her.

Will you stand upon your oath, Selena? Will you deliver the man this night?

She hesitated only an instant before whispering, "Yes."

I congratulate you on your wisdom, slow through it was in coming.

Yes, she thought, he was right: if she had only real-ized it, she would have been spared many years of anguish. Her gaze traveled from face to approaching face, and the dark half of her nature, that part that was of the same essence as the companions, grew hot with an anticipation she could not control.

Take them! she commanded silently. Stop only short of murder. Go!

All in good time, Selena.

She wheeled, staring at the imp's mocking face.

237

We will attack when I see fit. Fear not, we will allow no harm to come to you. A golden era lies before us, with you as its spearpoint.

She clamped shut the protests arising in her mind. This was no time to argue. The mob was within twenty yards of the house now, clearly gaining confidence.

"Stop them!" she cried furiously. Instead, the imp faded, and through her panic, she realized that his malicious smile seemed genuinely amused.

Then, as her frightened gaze swept back across the crowd, she saw a glint of light on a curve of the winery road, perhaps a half-mile away. The light disappeared behind trees, then emerged seconds later.

Headlights. Coming toward the house.

On blind instinct, she leaned out and raised her hand in an imperious gesture. As if she had thrown a grenade, the men stopped short, some stumbling backward.

The headlights paused, then went out, at the blockade of vehicles on the road below.

Fascinated, amazed, Selena stared, straining to see into the black night, The bonfire flickered briefly as if a shape were flitting past.

Aburptly, Roy Lutey howled, "Burn, witch!" and ran forward, hurling his torch at her. It circled high in the air to fall harmlessly short. But others followed, and several of the torches shot beneath and to the sides of where she stood, hitting the wall of the house.

Then came the sound of splintering glass. She whirled to look down, and saw with horror that the draperies had burst into flame.

The men saw too, and the rain of torches stopped. They drew back, suddenly quiet again: confused, as if realizing that what had till now been an absurd if nightmarish fantasy had taken a real and serious turn. The flames climbed the drapes with a swiftness that made her stomach lurch, licking like greedy hot tongues at the window's wooden lintel and jambs.

"Hasmoday!" she screamed.

Remember, Selena, came the mocking voice, *what lies in store if you break your vow.*

Then a figure burst over the top of the hill holding what she recognized, with amazement, as a shotgun. Without hesitation, he jacked the pump and fired into the air, a noise so unexpected and atrociously loud that she fell back against the window jamb, her hands groping futilely for support.

The shotgun sounded again. Men were diving for the ground, scurrying frantically backward,. tumbling down the hill. The newcomer leveled the gun to just above their heads and fired a third time. The sound was like a cannon, and the panicked mob scattered in all directions, running on hands and knees, clawing at the earth and each other to get away, leaving behind a clutter of axes, pitchforks, and torches.

As they disappeared down the hill, she caught a final glimpse of the Reverend Harner's heavy figure, trundling along clumsily in his high-heeled boots, waving his arms and shouting hoarse curses at those who were leaving him behind.

Farrell trotted to below the window where Selena stood.

"We have to stop the fire," she called, and turned as if to go into the house.

Smoke was billowing from the shattered downstairs window, and wisps were already beginning to escape from the second story.

He yelled, "Wait," and hurried over to stare inside. Both drapes and carpet had caught, and now the furniture was going up, turning the room into a chaos of flame. Worse, the stairwell was rapidly becoming impassable.

"Is anybody else in there?" he shouted.

She shook her head.

"You're not going to be able to get down the stairs." He gauged the window's height with his eyes. Even if she hung from its edge, the drop was nearly thirty feet, and she would land on the steep hillside. At best, she would break bones, and there was every possibility of spinal injury or even death. Feeling desperate, he turned in a circle, searching for anything that might help. There was doubtless a rope around somewhere, or even a ladder, but he might spend all night looking. Then his gaze caught a second-story balcony. If she could get back down to there, it would be a comparatively easy drop to the ground.

But flames and deadly fumes would be rising rapidly up the stairwell. He had treated enough fire victims to know that smoke inhalation was quick and merciless; if she went exploring, the danger of her succumbing was great. If she stayed where she was, she could at least breathe.

"I'm going to go in and check it out," he yelled over the rising roar.

She shook her head stubbornly. He could barely hear her words: "That's stupid! I'll just come down."

"No! The smoke might get you. Let me look; if it's okay, I'll tell you, and then you can come down." Otherwise he thought but did not say, you're going to have to jump.

She leaned over the sill, still shaking her head, shouting something back.

"Stay put, goddamn it!" he screamed, and sprinted toward the balcony. He hopped onto the windowsill and leaped back and up, straining to catch the railing's posts. His fingers grazed and missed, and he hit the ground hard and off balance, nearly turning an ankle. Teeth clenched, he got onto the windowsill again, inhaled deeply, and jumped as hard as he could.

This time his fingers caught and wrapped around a post. He grunted with pain as the weight of his body came down, tearing at his healing ribs, and he swung for a moment before gaining the strength to haul himself up.

Panting, he stepped forward to a pair of French doors. They were hung with translucent curtains, and while he could not see flame behind them, he knew that a smoldering room could explode with a sudden rush of air. Feel them, he reminded himself. If they're warm, and you open them, chances are the room goes up and takes you with it. He moved his palms quickly up and down. The glass was cool. He held his breath, twisted the knobs, and jerked the doors toward him, leaping back.

Smoke escaped, but no flame. He stepped into a bedroom, automatically noting the clues that so clearly marked the presence of a woman, that contrasted so distinctly with his own spartan place: a china cabinet filled with trinkets, a dresser top cluttered with makeup and perfume, paintings and weavings and hats decorating the walls. On the open door to the adjoining bathroom hung a robe and a black teddy. In a strange way, it was the most intimate moment he had shared with her, and he had to fight the temptation to linger and examine.

He hurried to the door, beginning to cough from the smoke. Cautiously, trying to gauge where the stairs were, he stepped into the hall just as the house's lights went out. As his eyes adjusted, he saw a deep red glow to the right. He moved quickly toward it. A sound like stage thunder combined with a frenzied crackling grew louder. The smoke came thick, blinding him and taking his breath. He threw his arm across his face, sucked in a lungful of air through his shirt sleeve, and plunged forward long enough to get a look.

The inferno had come halfway up the stairs to the second story. The landing and first few stairs to the third were smoldering; above that, he thought it was clear, although the smoke made it impossible to be certain. He retreated and leaned back against the wall, coughing–and understood that there was no way he was going to tell her to come down those steps alone while he stood safe on the ground.

He raced back into the bedroom and ripped the cover off the bed. With it wrapped around him like a burnoose, he paused to inhale three times, the last time taking in as much air as he could hold. Then he sprinted back down the hall and lunged into the flames.

They writhed like hideous red snakes around his legs, clutching at him, crawling up the bedspread, searing his flesh. His groping feet found the first stair, then the second. As his weight came onto his back foot, it broke through the weakened tread, trapping him. The burning splinters drove into his flesh like red-hot teeth, and he screamed in pain and fear as he tried to wrench the foot free.

At last it came, and he bounded up the next two flaming steps. The smoke remained thick, but he sobbed with relief at the confirmation that the upper stairs had not yet started to burn. When he reached the top landing he stumbled into a hallway, dropping the charred bedspread. He had lost all direction, and he tried to shout her name, but the smoke filled his lungs, and he doubled over, coughing and retching, on the verge of passing out. *Lie down on the floor, fuckhead!* an internal voice shrieked. He pitched forward and turned his face to the side, feeling the hardwood against his cheek. Here, the air was relatively dear. He forced himself to breathe slowly and deeply, until he felt clarity returning.

"Selena," he called out hoarsely, and then louder, "Selena! Where are you?" He filled his lungs, rose into a three-point football crouch, and charged down the hall, throwing open doors and staring into the dark, empty rooms.

As he reached the door at the end, it opened. Farrell caught her in his arms, stopping just in time to keep from knocking her sprawling. She stared wide-eyed into his face, and shouted:

"Who the hell do you think you are, Indiana Jones?"

He glanced behind him. Flames were flickering at the top of the stairwell he had just left. The thunderous sound was rising like the footsteps of an advancing army.

It was now or never: a few-second plunge through the inferno, or a jump, and with it, the possibility of ruined lives, not just for her, but for himself. He turned back toward the flames, hooking his arm around his waist. Her hand grabbed his, pushing it away.

"For Christ's sake, I'm not trying to feel you up," he yelled.

"You shouldn't have–"

He gripped her upper arms, squeezing hard. "We've got maybe thirty seconds," he shouted into her ear. "Let's argue on the ground, okay?"

This time she allowed herself to be led. He hurried forward, trying to shield her with his body. When they reached the smoldering bedspread, he pulled her to the floor.

"Are you sure this is going to work?" she yelled.

"I made it here, didn't I? Shut up and crawl onto my back."

With obvious reluctance, she obeyed, and helped him arrange the bedspread over them.

"Now fill your lungs," he roared.

After several breaths of the relatively smokeless air, he stumbled to his feet. With her arms around his neck and legs wrapped around his waist, he began the descent. Hardly able to see, he groped with his feet for the stairs, staying at the inside edge. Some part of his mind counted steps with childlike, idiotic patience, although he had no idea how many he had come up.

At last, when he thought he could not hold back any longer the scream in his lungs, his foot found the hallway floor. He broke into a lurching, stumbling run to the bedroom. Flames were licking at the doorjamb and furniture. He hurried through, kicked the French doors shut behind him, and let her down. She tossed aside the smoldering bedspread, and both collapsed against the balcony railing, sucking clear air into their starving lungs.

"We're not done yet," he rasped, glancing anxiously up at the smoke billowing from the roof above, suddenly wary of tiles or chunks of flaming wood that might claim what the fire had so far spread. "Give me your hands, and over you go." He gripped her wrists tightly as she climbed over the railing and stood on the deck's lip.

"How come I have to go first?" she said, looking doubtfully at the ground. The drop was not more than twelve feet, but looked farther.

"So I'll have a soft place to land. Just do it, okay?"

He braced his feet and knees against the corner post. Behind him came a sharp explosion and a whoosh of air. The heat on his neck leaped in intensity.

"Keep your knees bent, and roll when you hit," he said. "Now lean back."

She leaned, until she hung suspended by his grip at a forty-five degree angle, as if they were dancing. Then she sank into a crouch, and after hesitating a second longer, let her feet slip from the deck. Braced, Farrell absorbed. her weight, leaning as far over the railing as he could go.

"On three," he said.

When he released her, he watched tensely as her firelit shape fell the last several feet and tumbled. For heart-wrenching seconds, she lay still.

Then she rose to a sitting position and waved weakly. As he slung his own legs over the railing, he allowed himself a glance behind him. The French doors were wreathed in flames, the deck itself now beginning to burn. He realized that is was supported by cantilevered floor joists, and wouldn't that be just right, he thought as he crouched and gripped the posts, if they burned through just about *now* and the whole fiery shitaree came crashing down on top of me.

He hit with a grunt and wasted no time getting to his feet. The house was one huge roaring inferno, with flames as tall as a man shooting out the shattered windows and beginning to lick the edges of the roof. The deck was sagging. Selena's Lotus was rapidly becoming a scorched chunk of metal, its glass melting, its tires pouring out greasy black smoke.

When he turned, she was standing beside him. "Let's get out of here before that car blows up," he said. As they trotted across the drive, a glint of metal caught his eye: the barrel of his shotgun. He paused to scoop it up, then hurried behind her down the hill.

The caretakers' house was dark and looked deserted. The cluster of vehicles that had blocked the road was gone. His own truck was where he had left it, swerved into the hillside in his haste to reach the big house. It appeared unmolested–had probably gone unnoticed in the panic.

"I've got to admit, you know how to show a guy a good time," he panted, opening the driver's door. "I was just going to hang around my place tonight, maybe watch some TV."

She had turned to stare at the flaming house on the hill, as if she were trying to imagine, for the last time, what it had looked like during its years of beauty. The new moon hung over it, a thin crescent hovering distant and aloof over this merely human tragedy.

"You cheated me," she said with quiet venom.

Farrell glanced around uneasily. It was obvious that she was not talking to him, and there was no one else. He cleared his throat.

"I don't mean to interrupt anything personal, but maybe we should, like, tell somebody about this."

She looked at him as if she had forgotten his existence. Then, for just an instant, her face again seemed to take on that strange bemused look he imagined he had seen in Foolie's.

"Only fair, I suppose," she said. "I've been cheating them all these years."

Throat dry, he stared at her, wondering if this were the madness he had half-suspected, finally evidencing itself clearly.

But then her face softened, and she managed a trace of a smile. "Thank you," she said quietly. "I'm sorry to trouble you any more, but if you'll just drop me off at a hotel–"

"Bullshit. You owe me an explanation, lady, and you're coming to the Hotel Farrell to deliver it, just as soon as we're done talking to the fire department."

He stowed the shotgun behind the seats, and then backed the truck out of the hillside. Selena hesitated, then, slowly, got in.

As they started down the road, a heavy *BOOM* filled the air behind them. He glanced in the mirror in time to see the shower of sparks and flying metal that had been the Lotus, cascading onto the grounds like a fireworks display gone amok.

THIRTEEN

Coming back down the road, they passed trucks from the rural fire department, racing to the scene. Farrell swerved to the roadside to flag them down, but she gripped his arm and said:

"Let them go. There's nothing we can do but get in the way."

Astonished, he said, "But you've got to tell the police what happened."

"Tomorrow," she said. "After all this, I just can't face it." She squeezed the arm she held. "Please."

He stared at her, sitting beside him in, the darkness, face unreadable. "All right," he said, "tomorrow," and drove on, distantly amazed at the power of this woman he hardly knew to make him utterly abandon good sense.

Her silence continued until they reached his house; he did not try to breach it. In the kitchen, he took two glasses from a cupboard and poured a generous slug of Glenlivet Scotch into each. He handed one to Selena and drank the other straight down. When he had gotten his breath back, he refilled his glass and gestured her into the living room.

She sat on the couch, looking uncomfortable and tense. He remained standing, the whiskey rising through his brain in a gentle warm explosion, taking the edge off his pain, increasingly making its presence known as adrenaline faded.

"First things first," he said. "Are you burned?" For the first time, he took a close look at her. She was wearing a skirt and thin blouse, but though her arms and legs were smudged with soot, he saw no evidence of anything serious.

She shook her head. "I don't feel anything."

"You'd know by now. Any other injuries? Sprained ankle?"

"No." Then, with an edge to her voice, "You were quite adequately heroic."

He bristled, but ignored the barb. "Then why don't you tell me who those men were, and why they set fire to your house? With you in it?"

Some seconds passed. Then she shrugged. "One was Roy Lutey–the vineyard hand who confronted you when you came to get your jack that day."

Farrell nodded, remembering with grim satisfaction that long-jawed face turn white with panic as he had fired off the shotgun.

"The others are all members of his church. They think I'm a witch."

He choked on a swallow of Scotch, doubling over and swiveling away to keep from spraying it on her. She

250

watched him impassively, her hands clasped around the glass resting on her knees.

When he had regained control, he could think of nothing to say except, "Well, are you?"

"Not exactly."

"But not exactly not?"

"Something like that. Let's say they had some reason for thinking so."

"I don't suppose I could get you to elaborate."

She stood and walked to a window. "I really don't want to go into it."

Farrell stared at her back, again feeling the cold suspicion of insanity creeping around him.

But perhaps because of the vulnerability that suggested, she had never seemed lovelier. Her arms were clasped tightly across her chest, her shoulders hunched forward as if in defense. The dim light glinted off a silver earring, still in place after all that had happened, accentuating the curve of her neck. Unease and yearning rose up in him, making him feel helpless. He walked to her and touched her shoulder. She neither responded nor moved away.

"You don't have to believe me," she said. "It's better if you don't."

"Why'd you call me? Why not the police?"

She exhaled. "What could they have done? They wouldn't have found anything but some men drinking around a fire. I had no idea it would get so serious."

Then she turned to him and quickly kissed him, the briefest brushing of lips.

"Thanks," she said, "for being on my side." She set her drink on a table and walked to the door.

"Where the hell are you going?" he said angrily, striding after her.

She stopped, her hand on the knob. "I owe a debt." Her voice was very quiet. "I have to pay it."

"If the cops can wait till tomorrow, so can that."

"No," she said. "It can't."

She started to pull the door open, but Farrell stepped forward and slammed it shut with the flat of his hand. Glaring down into her face, he held it.

"That's not much of an explanation, lady."

"It's all you're going to get. Let me go."

"Then listen to this one," Farrell said, still holding the door. "You got such a charge out of watching me get the shit beat out of me the first time, you called me up to watch it happen again. Only things got out of hand, and the joke turned on you."

His outthrust arm was brushing her hair, his chest almost touching hers, and he felt the intensity of his own anger as her face softened before it. She lowered her eyes.

"Bingo, huh," he said. He pushed away from the door in disgust and turned his back. "Have you ever been committed?"

Unexpectedly, she laughed, a thin, brittle sound. "That would be the easiest answer, wouldn't it? Especially for a doctor."

"All I know is," he said, "I've almost gotten killed twice hanging around you. The first time was my doing, okay. But not this time. This time you set it up. And I can't help remembering that seems to be a common experience for the men you decide to get interested in."

For thirty seconds, neither moved nor spoke. Then she said, "Your burns need attention."

He shrugged impatiently. "They're not serious."

"You should go to the hospital. I'll drive you. I can call a cab from there."

"Fuck the hospital," he said, turning again, and this time his fury swelled uncontrollably. "Don't tell *me* I need a hospital." Then his hand gripped the front of her blouse, and he jerked her close to him. "I don't know what kind of game you're playing and I don't give a goddamn, but you quit it, understand? Quit pretending all of a sudden you care about me!"

He released her, shoving her back so she hit the door hard, then pulled his keys from his pocket and threw them at her, striking her in the chest.

"Take the truck and get out of here, just call the ER and tell somebody where you left it. Here," he said, tossing his wallet, "there's a hundred bucks in it. Take that too. Disappear."

He wheeled and strode back into the living room, shaking with an intensity of rage, of an urge to hurt, that he had never imagined he could feel toward a woman; understanding distantly that it was the nearest thing to real insanity he had ever experienced.

When she touched his arm, he whirled, his open hand rising to strike her.

But in her eyes was that anguish, and his hand slowed, and gripped her hair, and then he had clamped his mouth over hers, and while she moaned in protest and tried to push him away, she was kissing him back. Blindly, hardly aware of what he was doing, he reached beneath the brief skirt and found her flesh so hot it seemed to burn his hand.

She tried to break free, saying, "No, stop, we can't"– but he pulled her to the floor and pinned her writhing hips and sank into her with such force that she cried out, her head whipping to the side. While her voice continued to whisper, "No, no, no," in a steady sobbing rhythm, her movements changed to match his, her knees rising, ankles locking in the small of his back, and Farrell drove himself into her with that same fury. The world disappeared around him, the hair on the back of his neck stood straight, and as he roared out his spasm, like a madman, like an animal, lights flared and burst behind his eyelids the way he had imagined would occur at the moment a hanged man's neck snapped.

For a long time, they lay quiet. Then Farrell said wonderingly, his voice muffled against her neck:

"My God, I raped you."

He could hardly hear her words: "No. It's I who have done for you."

He rose on an elbow, staring down. Her head was turned to the side, face hidden by her hair.

"What do you mean?" he said hoarsely. He turned her to look at him. Her eyes were soft and wet, her cheeks glistening. Astonished, he repeated, "What?" She said nothing; only shook her head.

"Selena," he said, and paused, and then the words tumbled out of his mouth in a babbling stream, a release echoing the sexual one, of all his trapped emotion. "I'm in love with you, I'm absolutely crazy about you. I want you to love me back. I want to marry you. I want you all to myself forever. I want to hide you in a mountain cave where nobody else can ever look at you again but me."

She was silent again, then, finally, whispered, "We have tonight."

She pushed him off her and sat up, primly pulling down her skirt. "We need to bathe," she said, businesslike now, "and take care of your burns. You go shower first, you're filthy. Then run me a tub."

"You're really not angry?" he said. "About—"

Her head turned to the side, then gave an almost imperceptible shake. "I wanted you, too."

Stupidly happy, he kissed her and got up. "We've got a lot longer than tonight." As he started into the bathroom, he turned, suddenly anxious. "You'll still be here when I come out?"

Kneeling, arms clasped over the end of the couch, she was gazing out the window. After what seemed a long time, she nodded.

Grinning idiotically, he stripped and kicked the pile of sooty clothes aside. The grin disappeared when he glanced in the mirror. He resembled a singed clown in blackface. A great first impression as a lover, he thought ruefully: look like a barbarian and half-rape the girl to boot.

But she had told him she wanted him. The grin returned.

Then, as he reached for the shower faucet, his hand paused. A witch?

Not exactly. But not exactly not.

And even if that was only a joke or game, what about Icepick and Lyle Randolph?

He shrugged, adjusting the water temperature to cooler. There would be time later for the explanation of mysteries.

There had better be time, too, he reminded himself uncomfortably, to talk to the police.

He stepped in, wincing as the stream touched his skin, and making a strangled sound when it found the torn place where his ankle had plunged through the stair tread. The burns were mainly on his legs and the backs of his forearms; none were beyond first degree. Carefully, he washed his body, then lathered his hair. Although the pain remained, it was overcome by the sense of cleansing. Finished, he quickly scrubbed down the tub with Comet, rinsing it clear of the residue of soot, then began to fill it with steaming water.

When all was set, he wrapped a towel around himself and started out. At the door, an instant of heart-wrenching fear made him stop: suppose, in spite of her promise, she was gone?

But she was standing at the window, fingers pressed against the glass, gazing out across the dark grassy field.

"'This is the way they'll come," she said, so softly he hardly heard her.

It was the second time she had talked about *them*. But as he was about to ask who they might be, she turned. Quickly, she unbuttoned the blouse, tossed it aside, and almost in the same motion, stepped out of the skirt. The words died on his lips as he stared. A burning began in the back of his throat. He walked to her, took her in his arms, felt his penis lifting. She allowed herself to be kissed. then pushed him away, saying:

"Find some burn cream, and wait in bed. I won't be long."

Among his medical supplies, he located a tube of Silvadene, then walked into the bedroom, tossed away the towel, and eased himself carefully onto the bed. The touch of the cool night breeze soothed his tender skin. His gaze fell on Valerie's picture. He hesitated, but then turned it away.

Selena kept her promise to be quick. She lathered his burns with the cream, hushing him when he tried to speak. Soon, caresses gave way to searching looks and probing kisses. As the hours of the night passed by, and she straddled him or lay twisting and panting beneath him, he could almost feel something indefinable deep within him slipping away.

At last, utterly drained, he was unable any longer to fend off sleep. As he slipped into a fluid landscape of eerie surreal beauty, he mumbled:

"I want to know everything about you."

Afterward, he was never sure if he heard or dreamed her whispered words:

"When the moon dies, poor love, all your questions will be answered."

FOURTEEN

A sheriff's car was parked at the entrance to the winery, and a deputy flagged Farrell down as his truck approached.

"Place is closed today, sir. There's been a fire."

Farrell handed over a card identifying him as a physician on the hospital staff. "Official business."

The deputy examined it and gave it back. "There's nobody injured up there, Doctor Farrell."

"I know," Farrell said. "I was there when it burned."

The deputy stared, then said, "Wait right here," and went to his radio. His gaze stayed on Farrell as he talked. When he put the receiver back, he returned to the window of the truck and said, "Drive right on up. Lieutenant McIntyre is real anxious to talk to you."

It was late morning. He had awakened in the first light of dawn, his mind filled with the sense of haunting lovely dreams already faded from memory, and reached for Selena.

She was gone.

He had searched the house, calling her name, disbelief giving way to anger, then fear. His keys and truck were gone too. He had called the hospital, and yes, a woman had telephoned in a message: the truck was in the parking lot, the keys under the seat. He had called a cab, hoping there would be a note in the vehicle, some indication of her whereabouts and plans.

But it was empty of any sign of her, as empty as he felt himself. He drove to the winery, because he could not think of anyplace else to go.

His depression deepened as he came in sight of the house. Although the great heaps of ashes were sodden with water, fallen beams and roof sections still smoldered and a haze of smoke hung in the air. The foundation walls looked like remnants left after a bombing raid. Several fire department and sheriff's vehicles were parked in the drive, and men wearing protective clothing prowled the ashes.

One of them, squarely built and balding, turned from the site at the sound of the truck and strode toward it. Although Farrell had never met Detective Lieutenant McIntyre, he was familiar with the man's reputation; he was not known for either pleasantness or sense of humor. But Farrell was feeling too detached to be intimidated by McIntyre's bullish approach. He stepped out of the truck and waited.

"You better believe you're in trouble, Mister," were McIntyre's first words.

"Doctor," Farrell said.

They squared off like fighters trying to stare each other down. "You were here when the place went up?"

McIntyre said. Farrell nodded. "Then why the hell didn't you call us?"

Farrell pointed at what was left of the third story. "The owner was trapped up there. It seemed important to get her down. By the time we did, the house was gone, and there was no phone booth handy."

"Don't get smart with me, you son of a bitch," the cop snapped; but then he turned, gaze following Farrell's pointing finger. "You got her down from there?" Farrell nodded again. "How?"

"Carried her on my back."

McIntyre smiled malignantly. "You're telling me you went into a burning house and played Prince Valiant?"

Farrell rolled up his sleeves, exposing the burns on his arms, then started to unbuckle his belt.

"I've got others. Want to see?"

McIntyre grunted. "The lady in question being Miss Selena Clermont, I take it. Where is she?"

"I wish I knew," Farrell said.

"What's that supposed to mean?"

"I took her down to my house. She left. I don't carry handcuffs."

"Why didn't you call us last night?"

"Somebody already had. We passed fire engines coming up as we were leaving. She was understandably upset and wanted to wait till morning before she dealt with police."

"Then she flew, huh?"

Farrell said nothing, but just returned McIntyre's cynical stare.

"Any idea what started it?"

"There was a mob of men," Farrell said. "Some of them had torches. It looked to me like one of those torches found its way through a window."

McIntyre's bushy eyebrows rose. "A mob of men with torches? Did they know Miss Clermont was in the house?"

Farrell hesitated just an instant, then said, "I don't know, I got here right as the fire started."

"You just happened to be in the neighborhood."

"She called me."

"So she knew there was trouble coming."

Farrell hesitated again. "Yes."

"Why would she call you instead of us?"

"I asked her that. She said the cops would have figured it was just a drunken party, that she was crazy."

"That still doesn't explain why she called you."

Farrell shrugged. "She said she wanted somebody with her. She didn't think it was going to get so rough."

"I see," McIntyre said, making it clear that he did not. "And what happened to this mob?"

"They dispersed."

"At your arrival?"

"Yes."

"So before you climbed the tower and rescued the princess, you ran off the bad guys single-handed?"

"Fuck you," Farrell said. He reached for the door handle of the Datsun.

"Let me remind you, Doctor Farrell," McIntyre said, stepping closer, "that the crime of arson is a felony punishable by up to life in prison, and that failure to cooperate fully in an investigation can be construed as complicity. You're already on my shit list for not checking in last night, and my shit list can get very, very uncomfortable." His stare was hard and even. "I don't know what kind of game you and your girlfriend are playing, with your cute little story about a mob and a rescue, but I don't think it's funny, not at all. I don't like guys who set fires. I've seen buildings destroyed and I've seen people killed. This one could have started the whole goddamned forest going. I suggest you drop into the sheriff's office and make a full statement immediately, and that you contact Miss Clermont and advise her to do the same."

"I told you I don't know where she is," Farrell said, getting into the truck.

McIntyre's thick hand came to rest on the windowsill. "Farrell," he said, "if this is some kind of insurance scam, I will find that out, trust me. Guys who pull that shit go to San Quentin, and middle-class white boys there learn all kinds of new things about race relations and sex practices."

"Okay," Farrell said. "I give up. First I set myself on fire, and then–"

"It's been done."

"Then why the hell would I come back here?"

"You're trying to look innocent. Since she walked on you, you're afraid she got scared and might roll."

Farrell's gaze moved past the policeman's angry face and came to rest on the small house at the foot of the hill, where the vehicles had been parked.

"Have you talked to Roy Lutey?" he said.

McIntyre's grip tightened on the windowsill, as if to hold the truck from taking off.

"You have reason to believe he's implicated?"

"He was in the mob. I saw him."

"Why the hell didn't you tell me that right off?"

Farrell shook his head, too weary for more combat. "It didn't occur to me. Look, I didn't come here expecting any of this. I'm not thinking too clearly."

For the first time, McIntyre's face relaxed slightly. "We tried to find him. Seems him and his wife took off. We're guessing they were in a hurry, since they left everything in the house. Didn't bother to call in the fire, either; that was a Mexican family down the road the other way." He turned away, rubbing his bristly jaw. "We got an APB out," he said. "Doctor Farrell—what the Christ was that mob of men doing, burning a house with a young woman in it?"

"They're fundamentalists," Farrell said. "They decided she was a witch."

McIntyre's eyebrows shot up. "A *witch?*"

"That's what she told me. I was surprised too, believe me, but I can promise you they were carrying torches. Along with the axes and pitchforks you must have found lying on the ground. They were waving them around when I got here—just like *Frankenstein,* Lieutenant."

"Fuck a wild man," McIntyre muttered. He turned to stare at the smoldering ashes. "*If* I believed you, and I'm not saying I do, how'd you scare them off?"

Farrell reached behind the seat for the shotgun and handed it out through the window butt first. McIntyre whistled.

263

"I didn't hit anybody," Farrell said. "At least not on purpose."

McIntyre pulled a handkerchief from his pocket and took the weapon gingerly. "We'll run it through ballistics. Would you recognize any of those men again?"

"Lutey, maybe. I'd seen him once before."

For a moment, McIntyre gazed thoughtfully at nothing, his fingers drumming the windowsill. "Okay, Doctor," he finally said. "Your story's looking stronger. But drop by and make that statement, and stay close to a phone, huh? And if you see your friend, tell her to give us a call."

"Yeah," Farrell said. "Do the same for me."

As he started away, he skirted a large chunk of burned, twisted metal, and realized it was a piece of the Lotus.

He drove slowly out the dirt road, waving at the deputy who still stood guard, remembering that he had a twelve-hour shift to pull at the ER, beginning at 8:00 PM. He was weary, depressed, needing food and rest before he could conscientiously perform his work. But the thought of both repulsed him.

His burns hurt, a bad, sometimes excruciating, constant pain. There was also a strange sharp sting beneath his jaw, a cut he did not remember getting. There had been dried blood on his throat when he awoke.

But all that was inconsequential compared to the void that was already opening in his heart.

Early the next afternoon, Farrell's telephone rang, dragging him from the few hours' restless sleep he had managed after finishing his shift. He lunged for the phone, and with a stab of disappointment heard a man's voice say, "Doctor Farrell?"

It was McIntyre. They had picked up Roy Lutey, and wanted Farrell to identify him. Dully, he agreed. In the mental twilight of too little sleep at the wrong time of day, he showered, shaved, and dressed, holding at bay the constant straining awareness of the empty house and silent telephone. On his way out the door, he had to resist the urge to have a drink.

This time McIntyre was civil if not friendly; though he did not say so, Farrell sensed that his story was no longer in question. The detective led him into a small room empty except for a few chairs and a table.

"Ever done an identification?" he said, gesturing at one of the chairs.

Farrell shook his head.

"The one important thing is to be sure. Think of this as testimony you might be asked to back under oath." He laid on the table a sheet of paper with nine passport-sized photos on it. All the men looked vaguely alike—but there was no mistaking Roy Lutey's hillbilly haircut and close-set eyes.

"That's him," Farrell said immediately. "Number four."

"Be sure."

Farrell closed his eyes, remembering the man's face, angry the day he had gone to get the jack, terrified when he had fired off the shotgun in front of the burning house.

"No doubt about it. I'd swear it in court."

McIntyre nodded. "Okay, that's it." He stood, and they walked down the hall to a glassed-in cubicle containing a couple of steel file cabinets that looked like they dated from World War I, and a matching desk. The green cinder-block walls were hung with crime prevention posters and directives, their texts dutifully recapitulated in Spanish beneath the English, their comers loose and stirring with the breeze from the opening door. McIntyre hung up his jacket, exposing a .38 revolver in a well-worn shoulder holster. He took a pot from a coffee machine and raised it inquisitively.

"Sure," Farrell said. "Black."

"We picked him up this morning," McIntyre said, filling two chipped ceramic mugs. "He just went back home and showed up for work as if nothing had happened. It looks like him and his church buddies got orders from the preacher, who is a pretty slick individual. Nobody's saying anything."

The coffee tasted like a crow had been boiled in it. "Which means?" Farrell said.

"You're not going to want to hear this, but it means, probably, no charges will be filed."

Farrell set the cup down, staring.

McIntyre sighed. "For openers, we can't prove who actually set the fire. We can't even prove who was there, except for this guy Lutey."

"I would think," Farrell said slowly, "that if you gave him the same little pep talk you gave me, about life in San Quentin and race relations and sex practices"–he paused, seeing with grim satisfaction McIntyre's shoulders contract–"and made it clear you were going to put some teeth in it, he might be amenable to chatting with you."

"Chances are you're right, Doctor Farrell. But there's another wrinkle involved." He sat on the edge of the desk and took a slurping drink of coffee. "Jesus," he said, grimacing at the cup. He paused, gazing out the single wired-glass window. Traffic and pedestrians moved along the streets of the town below–oblivious, Farrell thought, as he himself had always been, to what was taking place in this building.

"I don't know what your relationship with Miss Clermont is." McIntyre waited.

Farrell shrugged. "I told you the truth: I hardly know her. I'd met her a few times. I was attracted to her, but she wasn't friendly. That was that.

"Then she called me, out of the blue, and told me some men were coming to kill her. Of course I thought it sounded crazy, but I went up there, and she wasn't kidding. The fire happened just like I said. After we got away, I took her back down to my place–" He paused.

"Go on. It's important."

Farrell exhaled. "We spent the night together. When I woke up, she was gone. She'd driven my truck into town and left it in the hospital parking lot. I haven't heard from her since."

"If it's any consolation, nobody else has either. We've checked everywhere. She's vanished. Nice to have money like that, huh? She could be anywhere by now."

"You said something about a wrinkle."

McIntyre got up off the desk and dumped the rest of his coffee into a wastebasket. "You don't have a cigarette,

267

do you?" Farrell shook his head impatiently. "Good, I'm trying to quit." He walked to the window and stood, back turned, hands in pockets. "Okay, it goes like this. Nobody will talk about the fire, but Lutey's wife has come up with a very entertaining story about what happened first. It seems their daughter took to playing games in the woods. Mrs. Lutey got nervous and finally followed on the sly." He turned back, lips twisted. "She says there was a bunch of kids about to sacrifice a baby. To demons."

Farrell opened his mouth, starting to rise out of his seat, but McIntyre held out his hand for silence, and continued.

"Then who should show up in the nick of time, but Miss Clermont. She reads the demons the riot act, saves the baby, and sends the kids home.

"Okay: obviously, Mrs. Lutey is a little cracked. But I've talked to her very seriously, and I think she actually believes what she's saying. And the little girl backs it up.

"Now, you know as well as I do that a *jury* isn't going to believe it, at least unless it's a jury made up of those church people. But that's not the point. What the point is, we have witnesses that something ugly was going on, something involving kids, and that Miss Clermont is implicated in it. I don't need to tell you that anything within a million miles of child abuse right now is gonna set off a witch hunt, only the real kind–the kind that could put somebody in prison for the rest of her life."

"There is no way," Farrell said emphatically, "that Selena was involved with anything like that."

"I thought you said you didn't know her very well."

Farrell opened his mouth angrily, but McIntyre stopped him with an outstretched palm.

"First thing the D.A. would ask. Let me finish.

"If she wants to press charges about the fire, fine, but here's what's going to happen. That's going to get swept under the rug, and it's going to turn into a trial about what was going on with those kids. Even though the demon stuff is obviously hocus, that's just the kind of thing a child would say to disguise an ugly truth. Any half-assed smart attorney could get those kids on the stand, together with a psychiatrist, and make things very unpleasant for your friend. Especially since she's done this disappearing act."

So that, Farrell thought, was where the witch business came in: the testimony of a child playing a game, blown up by the paranoia of a fundamentalist parent.

"It looks bad for her, Doctor Farrell. Between you and me, it was that preacher who figured this out. He's very cagey, and understands how to cut a deal."

"So they can bum down her house and try to kill her and get away scot free," Farrell said slowly, "even though she's innocent."

"*If* she's innocent. Let's face it, she did jump the boat."

Farrell looked at him sourly. "I thought you guys were supposed to discourage frontier justice."

"We do the best we can, Doc. If you think it's easy, try it."

For a moment, neither spoke. Then McIntyre said, "So you see, the way it breaks down is, we leave things like they are and just quietly stick this case in the back drawer. Our investigation has cleared you and Miss Clermont of any arson suspicion. If she doesn't press charges about the fire, the parents don't beef about the kids. The insurance company's happy, because they don't have to pay unless she shows up to defend her claim, which, in my unofficial estimation, would be a very foolish thing for her to do." He gave Farrell a meaningful look. "Officially, of course, I'd still like to talk to her, but just between us, it might be a good idea for her to stay away from here a while. Like, forever."

I honest to God don't know where she is, Farrell started to say, but only shook his head wearily.

"So this identification was nothing but a dog and pony show."

McIntyre shrugged. "A positive I.D. is never useless, Doctor Farrell. It gives us something on him if anything new turns up. And for sure, it will give him and his buddies something to think about."

Farrell nodded, lips compressed. He pushed the half-full coffee cup away and rose to go.

"Hang on just a minute," McIntyre said. He disappeared down the hall into another room, and returned with Farrell's shotgun. "Fired three times recently," he said. "Nobody's prints on it but yours." For the first time, he offered his hand. Farrell took it, and they shook.

"Sorry about the unpleasantness," McIntyre said. "Just doing my job."

Farrell walked through the lobby, ignoring the stares of the building's personnel at the shotgun in his hand, and started toward his truck. Then he realized that a woman he did not recall ever seeing was hurrying toward him. She was in her mid-thirties, with ginger-colored hair and the kind of lanky weathered looks that might have been attractive if she didn't seem so scared and weary.

"You're her friend, aren't you," she said, speaking in a harsh whisper; glancing over her shoulder as if she feared being overheard. "I seen you come up there that night, with that gun in your hand."

Astonished Farrell said, "Yes."

"She saved that baby; mister," the woman declared. "I tried to tell them. Hadn't been for her, that little boy'd have been burnt alive."

Abruptly comprehending, he stepped forward, gripping her shoulder. "You were there," he said through his teeth. "Tell me what happened."

Cunning entered her eyes. "What're they gonna do with my man?"

"Nothing," Farrell said. "They're going to let him go. Now what happened, really?"

"I told the truth, before the Lord. It was just like I said."

"But she wasn't doing anything to *hurt* the kids. She saved the baby."

"Oh, she's still a witch, don't you worry about that," she whispered, eyes bright with fear again. "Those creatures was talking some language like snakes. And *she was talking back.*"

The woman pulled away, and though he took a step after her and called, "Wait," she hurried quickly around a corner and out of sight.

Slowly, he walked to the truck. It was time for that drink.

FIFTEEN

For Gene Farrell, the next days and nights passed with agonizing slowness. He slept poorly and paid little attention to eating. As his burns healed, he realized that the pain had helped keep his mind off the far worse ache in his heart. He took to running as many miles as he could whenever he had the chance. He was becoming gaunt and hollow-eyed, arousing comment from people at the hospital.

Each time he pulled into the driveway, his gaze searched house and yard for any tiny change that might indicate someone had been by. He could not stop himself from jerking spastically when the telephone rang. He found excuses to call Elaine Ross, on the slender chance that she had heard from Selena, but spoke to no one else outside the immediate needs of work. The sight of happiness, laughter, even sunshine, made him feel physically ill. The thought of seeing Valerie was worse.

In spite of the running and the demands of work, he still found himself with an unbearable weight of time on his hands, and absolutely no interest in anything that might previously have sustained him: or rather, as he was beginning to think of it, that might have sustained the man he once had been. Instead, he spent his free hours sitting on his porch with a drink in his hand, waiting with vicious impatience for the mailman, or staring moodily at the occasional cars that passed on the road. They all kept going.

During those hours, his mind dredged up the memory of every moment with Selena, revolving them like a kaleidoscope, an insoluble puzzle that hinted at being much larger and deeper than it appeared. What, in fact, had gone on with the Luteys' daughter in the forest? The idea of demons and witchcraft was absurd–but while the men in the mob were perhaps not paragons of intelligence, still, it took a great deal to induce otherwise peaceable citizens to burn a house, let alone one with someone in it. He remembered the Lutey woman's eerie words at the police station: *Those creatures was talking some language like snakes. And she was talking back.*

What "creatures"? Was it possible that Selena was involved with something as unpleasant as child abuse, that the "creatures" were men in disguise?"

And why had she pointedly not denied the charge of "witch"? *Not exactly. But not exactly not. Let's say they had some reason for thinking so.*

Or was it, after all, evidence of insanity: some *folie a deux* that Mrs. Lutey had fallen into?

And as for him, was he, as he had first suspected, the victim of some sinister game that manifested itself in enticing men to fall in love with her–including men like Icepick and Randolph–then abandoning them? Or–a worse thought, in a way–had she found Farrell so boring and inadequate after toying with him that she had paid him, in effect, for his services, then simply left to go on with her glossy, spoiled life? He could not believe that she was capable of such treachery: of telling him she wamted him too, of giving him a night of such unsparing passion, and then abandoning him as cruelly as if he were a doll she had outgrown.

The questions whirled round and round, defying every logical structure he tried to fit them into, exhausting him to near the point of madness. For the first time in his life he talked out loud to himself, and once, staggering drunk, hurled his glass across the room to burst against the wall.

"Is this what you meant when you said you'd *done* for me?" he shouted. "Be proud, bitch, it's working!"

But always, thinking was overwhelmed by the sheer raw despair of loving her, needing her, and not even knowing where she was. Her face was his first vision in the morning, his last at night, and he dreamed about her in between.

When the telephone rang one evening, he lunged for it as usual, then forced himself to slow, taking a long swallow of his fifth gin before picking it up.

"Howdy, stranger," said a female voice, and his heart leaped–only to sink instantly, leaving black bitterness, at the realization that the voice was Valerie's.

"Hey," he said without enthusiasm. In the pause that came, he struggled with the irrational anger that rose in the disappointment's wake.

"That's it?" she said, her voice gone cool. "Hey? I haven't heard from you in two weeks."

He closed his eyes briefly. "Val I don't know how to explain this, but now isn't a good time for us to talk."

"Is someone there?" The question was immediate and sharp, and he realized that he had heard it before.

"Yes," he said. In a very real way, it was true.

There came another, longer pause. He could sense her mounting fury as clearly as if it were shouted.

"So that's the way it is, huh," she said. "You come down here to get your wounds licked, then run around with somebody else. Does she know about me?"

He let the phone slide down so the mouthpiece was against his chest, and stared at a blank wall.

"Let me talk to her," the thin, angry voice demanded into his neck.

"I'm sorry, Val," he said gently, and hung up. The ringing began again in seconds. He ignored it, carrying his drink out onto the porch, and closing the door so the sound was only a distant muted buzzing. After a time, it stopped.

In the deepening evening sky, a flock of vultures circled knowingly, waiting for the end of a tiny paragraph in life's drama. The yellow oval of the dying moon hung over the hills to the west like a misshapen eye.

Two nights later, it was gone.

Soon after that, the dreams began.

He was traveling through a forest in darkness. The air was thick with mist, curling among the trees as if it possessed a sinuous life of its own. He did not like in the

276

least his surroundings, but was compelled to keep on putting one foot after the other, on the way to some destination he sensed but could not yet see. Tree limbs would suddenly appear out of the mist, twisted, gleaming with moisture, seeming to writhe like giant snakes. The night was absolutely, eerily still; even his own footsteps made no sound.

But worst by far was the sense that he was not alone: that some thing, or things, invisible and yet very real, were watching him with keen—and not benign—interest.

On and on he walked, his dread rising with every unwilling step, until at last he came into a natural amphitheatre at the base of a cliff. Here the mist parted, and though the sky remained inky black, the scene was precise and vivid. Stones taller than a man jutted up from the earth like ancient tombs. Terrified, but unable to resist, he moved forward to a flat horizontal slab, roughly the size of a coffin. Something lay on top of it. As he got close, he saw that the sides were covered with dark stains.

But it was the object on top that captured his attention. Now he could make out that it was a human figure, wrapped entirely in white gauze like a mummy. The belly was swollen grotesquely, as if it were pregnant. Moaning with fear, but unable to resist, he began to unwrap the mummified face. The sharp reek of mold and decay hit his nostrils as he peeled back the layers of gauze.

It was at this point, he would later remember—as the flesh of the face came bare—that some part of him began to struggle toward wakefulness: as if an instinct of self-preservation, rooted so deeply it overcame even sleep,

277

understood that he must not see what was about to be revealed. But while the struggle went on in his mind, his shaking fingers parted the last strands of the gauze:

To reveal his own face, white and doughy.

For a length of time he could not measure, all remained still. Then the belly began to heave—as if in labor contractions—except that the swelling moved, not down, but up. Slowly, in a loathsome undulating motion, it struggled through chest and throat, like the prey swallowed by a snake fighting its way back toward freedom. He watched with horror while the face, the pale cadaverous reflection of his own, distended until he thought it must burst.

Abruptly, it collapsed, and the eyelids flew open.

It was the instantaneous glimpse of what was struggling to emerge from those eyes that plunged him, howling, toward wakefulness.

For several seconds, he hung, caught between the two states. Then, with a sensation that was terrifying in itself, the part of him that had been present in the dream seemed sucked violently back into his body. The scream he had voiced with all his being was in fact trickling from his lips as a low moan. Seconds more passed while he struggled to regain control of his senses. During that time, he felt as if he were trapped in an invisible coffin, arms and legs pinned, an unseen weight crushing his chest.

But more, and far worse: that the presence that had threatened him in the dream had come back with him.

At last he was able to twist his head, and then, with a furious burst of effort, thrash his limbs. He sat up, panting. That he was wide awake now, there was no doubt.

But the sense of the presence remained. His panicked eyes searched the room. There were only the familiar shadows he had wakened to, peacefully, many times before.

Except–*there,* in the farthest comer, under the dresser: was that spot not blacker than the rest of the room? The source of the malignancy that surrounded him? He grabbed for the bedside lamp, nearly knocking it over in his haste, flicked it on, and aimed the beam at the corner.

There was nothing: only the familiar, dusty woodwork.

Trembling, he waited. Whatever it was, it seemed to have receded, if not disappeared, with the light. After a moment, he nerved himself to hurry across the room and switch on the overhead lamp.

Nothing again nothing, came a half-forgotten line of poetry in his mind, with its haunting hint of the nothing that was very much *something,* but something which–perhaps mercifully–could not be perceived. He shivered, suddenly and violently. Absurd though it might be in rational terms, he wanted to get the hell out of this room.

A glance at the clock told him it was a little after three. He did not have to work again until the day after tomorrow. A drink, then; perhaps several. Quickly, he pulled on jeans and sweatshirt, and with relief, hurried out. Switching on lights as he went, he took a glass of iced gin to the living room. There, he settled on the couch and began to ponder.

What deep, never-before-sensed part of his mind had manufactured such an unseen source of terror? In childhood, he had more than once come out of a nightmare trying to cry out; but nothing like that had happened for years, and never with anything approaching this intensity. He tried to remember what he had glimpsed in the mirror of his own mummified eyes, but he found it impossible to grasp. It had not been an expression or an image, but more like a sense of utter negation: an infinite blackness that seethed with evil intent.

With the wisdom that accompanies light, he decided the nightmare and the lingering terror were throwbacks to childhood: no doubt a product of his inner disturbance, a subconscious mechanism to release the unbearable tension within him.

No doubt, too, a Freudian would have a ball with the pregnancy motif.

But perhaps most bizarre of all had been the sensation of his dream consciousness returning to his body barely in time: as if it bad literally been some vast distance away, and had traveled back at unthinkable speed, to be present just in time for the return of wakefulness. There remained in him the distinct impression that if that part, whatever it was, had *not* made it back in time, the consequences would have been disastrous: as if the malignant presence that had awakened had tried to keep it there in the dream, and, failing, had come back with it.

Not just with it: *after* it.

And he could not quite banish the thought that whatever that presence was, it had not disappeared at all, but was only waiting for darkness to return.

Long into the night, he sat brooding on this bizarre intrusion into a life he had been, not so many weeks ago, on the verge of pronouncing hopelessly dull.

He awakened in the late morning, hung over and grainy. Sunlight filled the room. His fears of last night seemed preposterous.

And yet, he had not dared close his eyes until dawn. And as he went through his routines–shower, coffee, a meal, and later, a long run–he could not quite rid himself of the conviction that the presence he believed he had sensed–the black spot, as he was coming to think of it–was still very much with him, watching, waiting.

It was as if, during that instant when he had peered into his own eyes, he had somehow plunged into the waters of a dark sea, and in so doing, awakened a monster that dwelt there. Until that moment–as long as he stayed above the surface–he had been safe: the monster had been ignorant of his existence. But as soon as it spotted him, it had begun pursuit, and finally had risen out of its undersea lair to follow him from that world to this one.

As evening came on, he began to get the sense that there was a tiny black blur in the comer of one eye or the other. It was accompanied by the perception that something was creeping up on him. Several times, as he plowed dully through medical journals, he swiveled suddenly, his uneasy gaze searching the room; and absurd though he knew it was, reason caught up too late with instinct: a little later, he would repeat the action. A careful searching of his eyes in a mirror revealed nothing in the way of a scratch or particle trapped beneath the lid.

You are caving into stress, Farrell, he told himself sternly: not something that speaks well for a man in your profession. The truth is that either she will come back or she won't. There is nothing you can do about it, In the meantime, grow up, get her off your mind, and throw this other thing out with her. Briefly, he considered calling Val to apologize; but it was a conversation he simply could not face.

What he needed, he decided, was a real night's sleep.

He rummaged through his medicine drawer, considering and discarding several of the samples that pharmaceutical salesmen were forever showering on him, and finally settled on a mild sedative. He had never taken sleeping pills, or any other sorts of downers or uppers, and was determined not to let any habit gain the smallest foothold. Drinking was bad enough. But in his present state of agitation, he had only another restless night to look forward to; it was time to break the cycle. He washed down the pill with the rest of his drink, took a three minute shower, and fell, still damp, into bed.

It seemed to Farrell that he was standing at an open window, gazing out over a grassy field, eerily visible in spite of the moonless night sky. At the far edge, a dark fringe of trees might have been the end of the world. He sensed that he was waiting for something, and the stillness around him was absolute, as if even the creatures of the night were hushed in anticipation of what was to come.

Then, at the treeline, the leaves stirred and began to part. Something was coming unhurriedly but steadily toward him, making a dark furrow in the knee-high silvery grass. In his dream he leaned forward, gripping the windowsill, with the distinct feeling of a prisoner grasping the bars of his cell, panicked at the approaching fate he was helpless to escape. Whatever it was remained impossible to make out–there was only the sense of something darker than darkness, a defined but unperceivable negation–but from it emanated a cold black menace, a controlled fury of tremendous power, underlined by delight in the ripping destruction it was about to bring to him. The terror that clutched him was like an icy iron claw twisting in his bowels.

His gaze, perhaps understanding a truth that his mind did not, refused to look at the approaching blackness–as if it held an evil too awful for humans to confront, the deep, unimaginable secret at the heart of creation, beyond death or madness.

But he began to see the shapes that accompanied it: creatures that looked like a Bosch nightmare, hovering, flitting in agitation through the darkness, with eyes and mouths that seemed to be gaping pools of the same hungry blackness the central shape epitomized. They all burned with a terrible thirst for life, his life.

And infinitely worse, for the precious, unknowable inner part that made him *him*.

Nearer and nearer they came, until he could actually hear the rustling of the grass, and now a sensation began in his mind as of high-pitched, whispering, sibilant voices. From somewhere in the deep reaches of memory, words rose and echoed:

Those creatures was talking some language like snakes.

His mind issued the command to whirl and run, but his body refused to obey. His hair was on end, his mouth stretched wide in the rictus of a silent scream, his limbs locked in paralysis.

It was then that he remembered, in an instant of horrifying clarity, the pill he had taken. He understood then that the only thing that could save him, that had saved him last night, was not flight, but vigilance. But full consciousness refused to return, and as the blackness and the surrounding hungry shapes with their soft silent cries neared the house, he was finally aware that the real menace was not outside him at all: that the approaching horror was only a mirror of the black seed within him, which in his dream had crawled from his loins to his head in an evil parody of birth, and was now swelling and stirring in his eyes: writhing in insane deadly fury like a snake in his brain, striving to devour him from the inside out.

In dreamlike slow motion, with a willpower he had never imagined he possessed, Farrell dragged the window shut. Then he crouched, forcing himself to remain at the threshold of consciousness. Outside the thin wall, the silent voices whispered, and fluttering as of fat clumsy fingers seemed to brush at the glass. Faint shadows danced against the wall opposite, of reptilian limbs and long taloned fingers and elongated heads, flitting back and forth in growing agitation.

Again and again, sleep caught him and dragged him into its embrace, only to be swept aside by his panic at the increased franticness only inches away, at the evil squirming inside his skull, that would lie malignantly in wait until weakness had triumphed over him, then suddenly rear up, striving to overpower him. Again and again, he might have succumbed, but for the desperate pleadings of that threatened inner part of him—that *this,* above all other things, must not take place.

His only sense of the time that elapsed was that it was endless. But at last, he was aware that the whisperings and clawings had ceased, that the fury in his skull had subsided, that the light in the room had changed subtly from the blackness of night to the first cool tint of dawn.

Cheek against the floor, he wept hopelessly for the few moments before he gave in to sleep.

SIXTEEN

For perhaps the tenth time in the, past forty-eight hours, Gene Farrell picked up the phone, started to dial, stopped, and hung up again. But now his hand stayed on the receiver, while his stare remained fixed on the calendar hanging on his kitchen wall. It was October 9. As closely as he could figure it, the moon would be at its nadir tomorrow night.

He closed his eyes and inhaled deeply—then opened them and this time, dialed the number.

When Valerie answered, he said, "Hi," trying to put brightness and nonchalance into the word.

There was a perceptible pause before she said, 'Well." Her voice was flat and cool.

"How are you?" Farrell said, then added lamely, "Seems like we haven't talked in a while."

"Has your little girlfriend taken off?"

"Val—"

"Or was it girl*friends?*"

"I want to take you to dinner. Say, tonight."

"I haven't heard a peep from you in almost a month, and all of a sudden you want to take me to dinner. Come on, out with it: What are you after? Did you get beat up again? Or just looking to get laid?"

He had expected it to be bad, but not this bad. His eyes stayed on the calendar, at the date that seemed to be approaching like an express train, and be heard the note of pleading urgency in his own voice.

"Val, I need to talk to you. I'm sorry for the way I behaved, I've been very confused. I can explain, and I will, I promise. Now, can I please come see you tonight? I'll take you anyplace in the city. Please?"

There was another, longer pause, and he found himself praying to nothing: Please, I just need someone to spend these next couple nights with, I know it's wrong, I'll make it up to her somehow—

"Gene," she said. Her voice was kinder, and he was already breathing thanks when her next words stopped him. "I think you need professional help. You've gone from being a mature man to complete adolescence. You want what you can't have and don't want what you can have."

"Val, it's much more complicated than that. I know I've been acting like a fool, but some really strange things have happened, things I had no control over. I know I need help sorting it all out, and Val, I'm asking you for that help."

Again the pause; he waited, breath held, until his throat began to ache.

"Well, the answer for tonight is no. I'm going with a friend to Santa Cruz for a couple of days. A man friend, and that's *man,* not boy. After that, I'll start thinking about whether I want to see you again."

"Val, please break that date," he said. He tried to sound calm, but his voice cracked as he went on. "I know it's a lot to ask, but think about all we've meant to each other. I'm in trouble, serious trouble, and I need to be with you."

"If you're in trouble, see a lawyer. You seem to be getting into as lot of it these days, and I'm out of pity." The hard tone was back. "And don't pull that shit on me about all we've meant to each other. I invested three years of my life in you, everything from doing your laundry to sucking your cock, and you turned around and dropped me like a hot brick."

Miserable, Farrell closed his eyes. He had no words left. It was all too true.

"If I decide I want to see you, I'll let you know," she said. The telephone clicked.

Numbly, with automatic precision, he poured a stiff drink. His gaze caught the field outside, and he shivered. The golden October twilight had not yet given way to dark, but the memory of what had happened last month was fresh as a raw wound: the night when he had, as he had come to think of it, lain on his bedroom floor wrestling a demon, not just for his life, but for his soul.

He had spent the day after the sleeping pill disaster in town, shopping, eating lunch–anxious to be around people. But finally there was no place to go but home. He had sat on the porch, staring dully at the deserted road in front of the house.

What was happening? One ugly dream could be explained away as an anomaly, but two . . . And when had it become reality? He had no memory of its beginning; he had gone to sleep, and then found himself overlooking the field. His gaze moved to the right, across the silvery grass. The furrow was a distinct black line. It was undeniably there.

It must have been there before, he decided; he had just not noticed. In fact, that was probably what had triggered this madness: for some incomprehensible reason, perhaps having to do with his mental unrest over the past weeks, he had sleepwalked, seen the parted grass, and some atavistic facet of his consciousness had supplied images to become the focus of all his disturbance.

His eyes lifted to the east, to the little mountain range he had so many times watched the moon rise over.

That was when he realized that the past few nights had been moonless.

When the moon dies, poor love, all your questions will be answered.

And finally, the memories that had been lurking at the edges of his mind–the memories which, he realized, he had been actively trying to repress–surfaced.

The story of Lyle Randolph clawing at his own eyes before throwing himself into the chilly waters of San Francisco Bay. The tiny, not quite distinguishable image Farrell imagined he had seen in the pupils of the biker who had shattered all the mirrors in his house before making his final mad plunge off the mountain road.

He stood abruptly, angry at the panic rising within him, helpless to prevent it. *Imagined* was the operative term, he tried to assure himself. He was assimilating elements of experience–without regard to whether they were real or fantasy–into a subconscious scenario worthy of Poe.

He jumped off the porch, stalked around the corner of the house, and stood facing the furrow, sighting up to the dark wall of trees at its far end as if challenging whatever had lurked there, in his imagination, during. the past night.

But even as his mind reasoned with itself, his skin began to crawl with an electric sense of dreadful antici-pation. The sun had disappeared; the sky was turning the pale blue of evening. The grass swayed in a sudden breeze, and the leaves of the poplar trees rattled and whispered, a sinister sound that seemed to announce something coming. Unable to bear it, routed, he hurried back inside.

There he slammed and locked the door, checked the other doors and windows, and then forced himself to stop, breathe deeply, and think. This was, simply, insane. There was nothing there: he was acting like a child. He was distraught and exhausted.

He had never been religious; nor did he put much stock in psychiatry. But if it happened again, he decided grimly, it was time to talk to a shrink. Something buried deep within him was trying to work itself out–loneliness, despair, a sense of worthlessness for having been abandoned by the woman he loved and having aban-doned the woman who loved him, or all those things together with many more—and he was going to have to deal with the trouble before it made wreckage of his external life as well as the internal.

But nothing had happened that night, or any of the following ones. As he had waited in mounting terror for darkness, he had realized that the spots at the corners of his eyes, together with the accompanying sense of menace, were gone. Whatever that presence had been, whatever had risen from his own depths seeking to join it, it seemed to have vanished. At first suspicious, he had finally accepted the fact gratefully, and although he kept the lights on for the next few nights, his sleep was deep and peaceful. The aberration had been temporary, he had convinced himself, and was over with for good.

But then his conscious mind had reluctantly made the connection his subconscious forced on it. The phenomenon had taken place on the nights when the moon was at its nadir. What if, for some reason as inexplicable as the thing itself, it was limited to that time?

When the moon dies—

And what if it would happen again?

The thought was preposterous in the light of day, but all too easily recalled when he stared out the window at night. And as September had neared its end and the moon reached its fullness, then began to diminish as if a giant unseen knife were taking a slice from it each night, his resolution had dissolved, enough so that he yielded and made the call to Valerie: humiliated himself and, in effect, lied to her. He deserved all the scorn she had unleashed on him.

Still, it would have been worth it if she had said yes.

291

Nothing would happen, he assured himself for the ten-thousandth time. It was over. The moon had never had anything to do with it.

Nor had Selena.

Certainly.

There was one thing to be said for the madness, he thought grimly: for those few days, he had actually almost forgotten about her.

He finished the drink and poured another.

That night Gene Farrell dreamed that he was again walking, against his will, through the same dark, misty forest. And again, he had the sense of unseen presences around him, keeping pace with his reluctant footsteps.

As he came near the amphitheater, he began to hear a sound. At first it was so faint he could not identify it; it was only a high, thin, occasional voice on the wind. But gradually, he recognized it as weeping—and then, as that of a child. It rose, terrified, protesting—and was suddenly cut off by another voice, shattering the night with a shriek of insane laughter.

Filled with dread, he drew nearer and nearer. The great stones rising from the earth loomed like menacing sentinels guarding the secret he approached. Again he came to the altar where the mummified corpse had lain. But this time it was thrust violently aside, as if ripped from the earth by a giant hand, to reveal a spiraling staircase descending into absolute darkness.

It was from there that the voices emanated.

The unseen shapes that accompanied him paused, hovering at the stairway's entrance in evil anticipation.

Helplessly, he continued on, beginning his descent toward the hideous duet. What little light there was faded; the air became damp and clammy; and the walls, echoing with the mad laughter and hopeless weeping, came closer around him with each step.

At last he reached the place where the steps ended. Panting, he crouched and groped for the hole he knew was there, and slowly reached into it for what he must find.

With a shriek of triumph, something clamped down on his wrist. His fear surged like a bursting black ball; the sound trapped in his lungs tore free, a hopeless, desperate cry that was half scream, half roar. He threw himself backward, fighting the clinging, loathsome, reptilian grip that ferociously sought to drag him down. Slowly, his arm was pulled into the hole, then his head, then his shoulders, until only his thrashing legs remained, and he knew that he was about to come face to face with the unbearable *it*.

But once again, his terror overcame the bonds of sleep. There was the same jolting sensation of a distant part of him plunging back into his body. Again, his screams bubbled from his throat as choked moans.

The grip clinging so fiercely to his wrist was that of his other hand.

He sat upright, rage at his own weakness boiling over his fear. "I will not be jerked around by a goddamned fantasy!" he shouted, and immediately disproved it by grabbing his clothes and hurrying to the kitchen. There he resisted the urge to grab for the gin bottle–he was due at the hospital in the morning—and forced himself to comparative calm.

There was no more doubt as to whether it would happen again. It was as if the first night's dream was a set-up, a warning.

The second, when the moon was fully down—

By the time he stopped shaking, a plan had formed. Jon Kotzer, the colleague who was scheduled to work the evening, would be happy to trade off the night shift for the day. Farrell decided to call and ask him as soon as the hour was decent. There was safety in numbers, he thought unhappily. He could sleep through the morning and spend the night awake, alert—and in the company of other humans. Better to be a live coward than a raving mad hero.

He got a quilt and pillow, and with a light on in the background—ashamed, but unable to escape the sense of creeping shadows following him, barely glimpsed from the corners of his eyes—he stretched out once again on the couch, hoping for a few hours' rest.

Both the voices—the baby's weeping and the insane laughter—had been his own.

The ER was busy when Farrell arrived that evening. "Thanks for trading with me," he said to Kotzer.

"Are you kidding?" He glanced at Farrell curiously. "How come you wanted the night shift?"

"I felt the need of a little drama in my life."

"Anybody tell you you're not looking so hot?" Kotzer said, still watching him.

"I haven't been sleeping too well," Farrell mumbled.

"Yeah, well, heal thyself and all that. Bad for our image, when the doc looks like he's spent the night in an alley. You ought to get married, you know that? Settle you down."

"I'll keep that in mind."

Through the day, the sensation had never left him of being watched, followed; and as dusk came on, he had swiveled to glare at the half-glimpsed shadows enough times to awaken a burning pain in his neck. Another careful examination of his eyes had revealed no scratches or marks that could account for the phenomenon. He had even begun to imagine noises–the clank of a pan, or the thump of a book being moved–always behind him.

But as he had hoped, things improved at the hospital. He stayed busy, as the line of actually injured and merely paranoid flowed steadily through the doors, and he almost managed to forget his fears.

Then, a little after midnight, he was listening to an elderly black man's complaints about chest pains, when something–not a sound, but some interior signal unperceived by the senses–made him turn sharply to look behind. Straining as if to hear, he felt the too-familiar foreboding rising within him.

"My daddy died of a heart attack," the old man was saying. Farrell swiveled back, disoriented, having to think to remember what he was doing in this tiny tentlike cubicle, standing over a slumped man he had never seen before. "I never had no trouble till now, but it feel like it's jumping around in there, you know?" His eyes were yellowed, watery, frightened, and Farrell stared into them, feeling his own fear tighten a notch. He stood, managing to smile and pat the old man's shoulder reassuringly.

"You lie down and take it easy for a while, Mister Crenshaw," he said. "I think you're fine, but if you start to feel funny, just call a nurse, and I'll be right here. Okay?" The old man nodded doubtfully, and Farrell hurried out of the cubicle's claustrophobia, trying to breathe deeply, trying to make himself believe that the still-rising panic was only a result of subconscious expectation.

The emergency room had no windows. He strode down the hall, ignoring a question Janet Black was starting to ask him, and threw open the door of the first office he came to. For seconds, he stood without moving, his eyes searching the dark room, his fear crawling like a nest of insects beneath his skin. Then he took five steps to the window.

The evil blackness was advancing across the parking lot below, surrounded by the grotesque frolicking imps. Farrell closed his eyes, counted three, and opened them again.

They were still there. And closer.

Heart hammering, he spun around and trotted back down the hall to the ER.

"Mrs. Black," he said fighting to control his voice, "will you please come with me a minute?"

She looked surprised, but said nothing as she followed him. Only when he gestured her into the office did she give him a glance that might have expressed either disapproval or interest as to why he had summoned her to a darkened room.

"Will you look out the window," he said, keeping his back turned to it, "and tell me what you see?"

She glanced at him again, but went to the window. "The parking lot," she said after a moment. "Cars. Some trees." He inhaled, then turned.

The procession was within fifty yards of the building, the imps' dancing wilder than ever, the hungry hissing cries beginning to sound in his mind.

"Mrs. Black," he said unsteadily, "I am about to do something highly irregular. I am going to ask you to call in another physician to take over for me, immediately."

"But, Doctor," she began, amazement clear on her face. The expression changed to concern. "Are you sick?"

"I am much worse than sick," he said. "I can't explain, but I need somebody to cover the ER, right now, *stat!*"

Her voice followed him down the hall. Past the astonished faces of patients and staff he sprinted, dodging gurneys and meal carts, bursting through the doors into the cafeteria, to collide headlong with a nurse carrying a tray. Cottage cheese and silverware flew into the air, dishes clattered onto the floor, while the poor astounded woman slid backwards on her rump across the linoleum. Farrell ran on without slowing, through the kitchen, fending off steam tables and dishwashers as if they were tacklers, and finally raced out the door to the service road behind the building. Wild-eyed, panting, he paused to look up.

The blackness was directly ahead of him, the swarm of grotesque shapes advancing in a frenzy.

In what seemed like dreamlike slow motion, he turned and ran back, groping for the door handle while the hovering shapes swirled around his head, their hungry cries vibrating in his mind. Back through the kitchen, skidding through the spilled food in the cafeteria, distantly noting the annoyance on the face of an attendant with a mop, then down two flights of stairs until he was in a sub-basement. His frantic gaze found a supply closet. He threw himself through the door and slammed it.

But blackness instantly engulfed his mind like a talon of iron, ripping his consciousness away from light and warmth and life itself. Fast as thought, he flashed along an endless spiraling labyrinth of corridors. They were like the coils of ail immense dragon, and they were crammed with wraithlike beings, crushed in the twisting, endlessly tightening snares, shrieking out their hopelessness and agony. On and on he hurtled past, his own inner cries rising in frenzy, understanding that he was approaching the unendurable heart of evil.

For what might have been eternity, he screamed, thrashed, fought with undreamed of strength, hovering just on the threshold of being sucked forever into that raging black hunger, while the thousands and billions of tormented wraiths screamed with him in an insane cacaphony of despair.

When, exactly, it faded, he would never know. He returned to consciousness to find himself being gently shaken. He was on the floor, curled tightly into a ball. A janitor was kneeling beside him.

Farrell muttered thanks as the man helped him to his feet, hardly hearing the concerned questions that followed him as he stumbled to the stairs. Back on the main floor, he saw through a window the gray light of dawn breaking. He shuffled into a bathroom. With the light on full, his eyes in the mirror seemed normal.

But when he turned it off, allowing just enough in from the hall, he could see the tiny black images, as of something tightly coiled, in the pupils.

When he walked back into the ER, the place stopped. All personnel turned to him. Jon Kotzer put down a clipboard and stared, a combination of fatigue, annoyance, and concern on his unshaven face.

"There's some people want to talk to you, Gene."

Farrell nodded, knowing who they were: the chief of staff and the head administrator.

"I take it you got your drama," Kotzer said.

"All I wanted," he said dully.

"Are you okay?"

"No," Farrell said. "I'm not okay, Jon. Sorry you had to come back."

He nodded vaguely at the nurses and walked outside to his truck. There was no point in sticking around to be flayed by the bigwigs; he had no possibility of either explaining or atoning for his actions. He was finished in the emergency room or any other specialty that required capable handling of stress, and possibly as a physician altogether. He could imagine clearly the chief of staff's stern face:

"I think you'd better embark on a program of therapy, Gene, before we can discuss what future you

299

might have in medicine." As if there was any therapist who could touch this one. He laughed aloud, a short savage bark. A witch doctor, perhaps: a real shrink.

He drove slowly home, made a drink, and sat on the porch, regarding sardonically the golden autumn morning. If no one else could see the creatures, then the only explanation, in the eyes of the world, was that he was certifiably insane.

But that was a trifle compared to the problem itself.

It could come after him anywhere, and it was growing stronger. He shivered violently. There was no way he was going to survive a third assault.

He filled his glass again and leaned back wearily against the porch rail. By all indications, he would have a month's reprieve. First, he needed sleep. Then a visit to Elaine Ross to learn everything he could about Selena's past.

And then twenty-eight days to try to find a solution to this mystery that threatened his life, his sanity, and something he had never before imagined he possessed: his soul.

PART FOUR

October 1988

SEVENTEEN

In a tenth-floor apartment on Russian Hill, Gene Farrell stood with a Tanqueray in his hand and gazed out the tall windows over the northeast tip of San Francisco spread below him. It was like looking at a life-sized tourist map. The stalk of Coit Tower, golden in the late afternoon sunlight; the long diagonal strip of Columbus Avenue, running through North Beach; the Wharf, Ghirardelli Square, and the fleet of red cable cars bobbing up and down the steep hills–all were thronged with people who seemed happy. Charming, he thought, and turned to survey the room.

The decor was from the early part of the century, heavy and lush, with a carved mantel and marble-faced fireplace. The furniture was antique European, the carpet and drapes heavy and dark. There was a sort of funereal sense about it, and considering what he had learned about Charlotte Clermont, that was not altogether surprising.

He had called Elaine two days ago. "You ignored my advice and fell in love with her, didn't you," she said in

303

gentle accusation, when he finally came out and declared that he simply had to locate Selena.

You don't know the half of it, he thought. "You told me her grandmother was still alive."

"Oh, yes, very much so. She's younger than I am, dear, not a dinosaur."

"Would it be possible—would she see me?"

"What you mean is, would I arrange a meeting?"

"Well, yes."

There was a pause. "Charlotte isn't very social any more, and in particular, she's sensitive about anything to do with Selena. Is it really so terribly important?"

"'Terribly' is just the word," he said.

"How, exactly, do you think she could help?"

"I just thought—you know—Selena might have checked in with her. Given some indication where she was going."

"I doubt it. Unless I'm very much mistaken, they haven't spoken in years."

"Elaine," he said. "Please. It's the only chance I have."

"If she wants so badly not to be found, maybe you shouldn't be looking."

"It isn't a question of should or shouldn't. It's a question of *must*."

"I'm not sure I approve of this, Gene," she said sternly. "You're holding something back. Maybe it's time you told me what it is."

Farrell closed his eyes. "When this is all over with, I give you my word, I'll tell you right down to the last detail"—and added mentally, *if I'm still alive.*

Another pause. "All right, I'll see what I can do. But if I were you, I'd let Selena go and consider myself well rid of her. She's lovely, but perhaps you've come to see what I mean about her being bad luck."

"Yeah," he said quietly. "Perhaps I have."

Then he had waited in an agony of impatience until Elaine called back with the welcome news that Charlotte Clermont would receive him at her apartment. He left immediately for the city, booking a room at the Hyatt Regency, hardly noticing the parking attendant's face when he drove up in the battered Datsun truck. In his room, he put on his best Harris tweed coat and his only silk tie, and even made an effort to tame his unruly hair. For this, he was leaving as little as possible to chance.

It had taken him only a few minutes to check and confirm that both Lyle Randolph and Icepick had died in the dark of the moon.

Charlotte Clermont had greeted him at her apartment door, directed him toward a bar where glasses, ice, and several expensive bottles of liquor were set out, then left the room to finish a phone conversation. When she returned, he saw again that she was possessed of that rare quality that made some women ageless: a product of flawless skin, bone structure, and great care. Her hair was done up in a chignon, accentuating her hollowed cheeks and fine nose. Her makeup was confined to a trace of eyeshadow, her perfume a faint scent. It was clear that she took as much care with her body as with her grooming; she moved with a grace and litheness that reminded him, with a force that brought a thickness to his throat, of her granddaughter.

305

"Won't you sit?" she said, gesturing at a couch. Her voice was husky, her gaze level. Farrell obeyed, sinking into the deep cushion. She sat, too, and half-turned to face him, drawing up one leg beneath her. Her dress rose several inches above her knee. Confused, he looked away and sipped his drink.

"Elaine speaks very highly of you," Charlotte said. "She's a friend of your mother's?"

He nodded. "They went to college together."

"And you're here because of my granddaughter."

"Yes."

She tapped her fingers thoughtfully on the couch's back. The nails resembled long oval pearls.

"That was all Elaine told me," she said. "I agreed to meet you, but I'll be straight with you, Gene. That's not a part of my history I like to look back on, and I'm still not sure I'm prepared to discuss it. So why don't you start by telling me exactly what you want to know, and why."

"Fair enough," he said. "It's pretty simple. I sort of fell in love with Selena, Mrs. Clermont—"

"Charlotte."

"Charlotte. Then, just as we were—getting started, she disappeared. That was several weeks ago. I wondered if you might have heard anything from her, or have any notion of where she might be."

"The answer to that is simple, too: no. I've had virtually no contact with Selena since she was an infant. That might sound harsh, but the circumstances of her birth were so devastating, I just couldn't ever bring myself to deal with her."

"I can understand that."

306

"Can you? Can you understand what it felt like, to have spent a night smoking pot and drinking wine and screwing my boyfriend at the time–a man who masqueraded as a hippie to disguise his laziness–and then to come home to a ringing telephone and the news that my husband and my only child had died horribly? That if I had been there with them, as I should have been, it never would have happened? Can you grasp that?"

Farrell stared into her eyes, seeing a hint of twenty years of pain and guilt. "No, I guess not," he mumbled, lowering his gaze. "I'm sorry."

Her hand patted his knee. "I'm not trying to lay anything on you, as we used to say. Only to explain." Then she added, "Maybe to myself.

"Anyway, I'm afraid I can't help you find Selena. I heard, of course, what happened at the winery; I'm not sure she ought to be found. It's none of my concern any more, at least officially, but I can hardly believe that beautiful old house burned to the ground. I spent many happy years there, before I turned into such a horse's ass." Abruptly, she stood. "But what I *can* do is make you another drink. How about it?"

He handed her the glass, and found his eyes automatically following the tight swing of her hips as she walked to the bar.

"Mrs.–Charlotte–I didn't tell you quite everything about Selena and me."

She said nothing, only raised one eyebrow.

"You're going to think I'm crazy, and I don't blame you, but I'm going to tell you anyway: something's haunting me."

This time, she stopped, the Tanqueray bottle poised, and stared at him. "Haunting?"

"It's worse than that," he said, hearing the panic rise in his voice, marking him as a madman, but unable to stop it. He stood, moving toward her, his hands gesturing with a will of their own. "There are some sort of– creatures–and they're coming after me, and nobody can see them but me. Listen, I know how that sounds, I'm a doctor, for Christ's sake, I did my time in the psych wards. But whether I'm crazy or not doesn't matter, because it's happening, and it's going to happen again, and it's driving me over the edge."

His hands dropped to his sides. That's it, he thought dully. Your one outside chance, and you've blown it.

But she did not look frightened or alarmed. Instead, her face had gone thoughtful. "And what does that have to do with Selena?"

"I think she did it to me. I think she tried not to, but she did." Her eyebrow rose again, but she said nothing, and he kept talking, the words tumbling out. "And I have to figure out a way to stop it before it kills me. So I came to ask if there's anything you can tell me that might help me understand this."

She handed him the drink and said, "Come sit again."

This time, her knee was practically touching his, and her fingers on the couch back were so close to his neck he could almost feel the long nails pricking his skin. His spine tingled.

"I didn't tell you quite everything about Selena either," she said. "The truth is that when she was born, I had every intention of raising her, to try to make up for the parents she would never have, and the burden she would always bear. And, of course, to deal with my own guilt. She was a beautiful child, and no trouble; she hardly ever cried. She was really very solemn, as if she already knew what had happened.

"But within a few months, I couldn't continue. It's hard to explain. It seemed as though there was some sort of–energy, or presence–around her that was very disturbing. Something that guarded her, that meant harm to anyone who got close.

"'I never actually saw anything, although sometimes I thought I was about to. Perhaps I would have if I'd kept her. But it was impossible for me. I was alone–I'd come to my senses, and made a break with all the people I'd been hanging around with. It was just her and me, in a house I rented in Marin, and with no one else to lean on, and grieving for my husband and daughter, this extra–threat–whether it was real or imaginary, started to unbalance me.

"I hated to abandon her, but I had no choice. I got her the best professional child care I could, and then schools, and when I sold the winery, I left her the house and a trust fund that would keep her well off for the rest of her life. I would have done anything in the world for her–except be with her."

Outside, the afternoon had deepened into twilight, and the rich colors of drapes, carpets, and furniture had softened. The silence was intense; Farrell could hear the ticking of the antique clock on the mantel.

"So you see," Charlotte said, "I don't know whether you're crazy or not. But if you are, maybe I was too. And maybe we're not the only ones."

"What do you mean?" he said quickly.

She shrugged. "I'm sure I seem unfair in saying what I did about a baby. But afterward, nearly every time I heard anything about her while she was growing up—from one of the schools she was at, or through some other official channel, or just through the grapevine—it had to do with some kind of tragedy."

He was about to ask her to elaborate, when her fingernails brushed his neck. He shivered violently, whether in response or fear he could not tell, and stood.

"Thanks very much for your time," he said. "I think I'd better go."

She rose too, her hand reaching for his arm, stopping him. "You're a very attractive man," she said. "*I* wouldn't have run away from you."

He lowered his eyes. "You're very attractive, too," he mumbled.

She shrugged, half-smiling. "I hate to make a fool of myself, but I've long since abandoned pretense. I don't get much company. I wish you'd stay awhile."

He took her hand with his own. "Charlotte, I don't think I made myself quite clear," he said unsteadily. "I've got less than four weeks to get this figured out. If I don't, I'm a dead man." He watched her eyes change from soft to concerned. "Dead," he said again. He gave her hand a squeeze and let it go, turning toward the door.

"Wait," she said.

She went into another room. He waited uneasily, his eyes automatically searching the darkening corners of the apartment, until she returned with a small leather-bound diary. "It was my husband's. He kept it during the final months of his life. I started reading it soon after his death, but I couldn't bear it. I don't know if there's anything in here that will help, but take it."

He nodded dumb thanks, and they walked to the door. As he stepped into the hall, she said, "Gene. She was given her name because 'Selena' was written on the last page.

"But I could never believe it was my husband's handwriting. And there was no one else in the house until the doctor came."

He stared, first at the book, then at her.

"If there's anything I can do," she said, "call me." She kissed his cheek, and quietly closed the door.

The hotel room was plush, with a view of the Bay and a two hundred dollar per night price tag. There had seemed to him no point in hoarding money. He ordered a fifth of Tanqueray and a plate of hors d'oeuvres from room service, tipped the bellboy twenty dollars, made a drink, and sat with his feet propped up on the windowsill and Donald Clermont's diary in his lap. The Bay Bridge to Oakland was a stream of light. When he found himself wondering if he would ever cross it again, he abruptly opened the diary.

A little over two hours later, after staring at the panicked lines on the last page—*They dance as my daughter dies*—followed by the single scrawled word

311

Selena in an obviously different hand, he closed the book, leaned back, and rubbed his eyes. The food he had ordered was untouched, the ice in his drink long since melted.

Was it Aristotle who had said, "We must always prefer the probable impossible to the improbable possible?"

The conclusion was inescapable. If he had been more detached, he would have found it fascinating in its shattering of modem assurance that such a thing as a being from a different, spiritual plane of reality could exist; could become manifest in this one; and could even impregnate a woman. What were the consequences of that parentage for the child?

They think I'm a witch.

And are you?

Not exactly.

But not exactly not?

Something like that. Let's say they had some reason for thinking so.

But for him, those questions were academic. The only matter of real importance was, once this thing had started, was there any way to stop it?

About that, the diary gave no clue.

He stood, made a fresh drink, and paced. Finding Selena, it was clear, was out of the question—even if there was anything she could, or would, do to help. Any normal structure of protection—the law, psychiatry, even orthodox religion—would ridicule, openly or covertly, his story, besides being as helpless as he was. Try to find a clergyman with experience in such matters, or some sort of occultist? He had never had any contact with such people. He knew that the vast majority were at best ineffectual, and often outright frauds. How could he begin to winnow out the genuine article? He had a few short weeks.

There was only this: it had almost certainly happened to others. Had she not hinted that she understood all too well what must come? Didn't it seem clear that this was what had driven Icepick to soar off Trinity road, in a last wild attempt to flee? and Lyle Randolph to leap into the black waters of San Francisco Bay, after trying to claw out his own eyes?

Perhaps someone, somewhere in her past, had escaped.

His pacing intensified. It was only the slenderest of chances, and tracing her history would be difficult. The last few years were lost; no one but she knew where she had been.

But before that—

I don't know whether you're crazy or not. But if you are, maybe I was too. And maybe we're not the only ones. Nearly every time I heard something about her, it had to do with some kind of tragedy.

He pulled bits of paper out of his wallet, scattering them on the bed, fumbling for Charlotte's phone number, then waited impatiently as it rang four, five, six times. His eyes closed in relief when he heard her husky, "Hello?"

"It's me, Gene," he said. "Can I ask you one more question?"

"Of course."

"You said there were other tragedies. Can you remember any specifics—names, places, dates? Any clues at all?"

"Well," she said hesitantly. "There were two or three institutions, child care centers and schools, where I was told that people had quit suddenly while they were working with her, or that asked me to withdraw her, without any clear reason. And twice"—she paused— "someone died. Once a classmate, once a teacher. She wasn't at all directly connected, but she seemed to be— associated, at least in people's minds. This was all when she was very young. With the kind of money I was paying, I was able to find other schools for her without difficulty."

"But nothing after she was older?"

Another pause. "Once or twice, I heard remarks insinuating something of the kind. That more than one man she'd been seeing had some unfortunate accident."

"But you can't remember who they were?"

"Not off hand. You know the kind of thing: someone saying it to someone else at a party, just within your hearing. It was never anything Selena was directly in- volved with—just that bad luck that seemed to follow her. I never let myself dwell on it, and I'd managed to put it out of my mind."

Neither spoke for a moment. "I'm afraid that's not much help," she said.

"Can you think of anything else?" He tried to keep desperation out of his voice. "Anything at all?"

"Well—there was once when she left a school abruptly. The reason I remember is that it was the first

314

time *she* asked to leave, instead of the other way around. I think she was nine or ten. It was in Switzerland."

"What happened?" he said, gripping the phone.

"I'm not really sure. I got one of those stiff, formal letters from the headmistress, Frau Somebody, saying that Selena had asked to move to a different school in France, and did she have my permission. I cabled back, yes. I suppose I should have been more concerned—but mainly, I tried to see to it that she got what she wanted."

And stayed away from you, Farrell thought. "Do you remember the name of the place?"

"The school, yes: the LaTour Academy in Lausanne. I'm sure they're still there, they've been in existence at least a hundred years. I can't remember the name of the headmistress, though, and I didn't keep the letter. It would have been ten or twelve years ago, if that helps."

I'll let you know, he thought—or not. He said, "I'm sure it will. Thanks."

"Of course." Then: "Was that all you wanted?"

Farrell's gaze went to the window, to the bustling city he was almost certainly spending his last days in. Why not? he thought. Why not a night with this undoubtedly sensuous woman? It would probably be his last chance for that, too.

"No," he said, "that's not all. I finished your husband's diary, and I wanted to tell you you've been wrong about one thing: you couldn't have changed it one bit by being there that night. Nobody, nothing, could have helped them."

Quietly, he hung up, then turned to the phone book to call the airport and arrange passage to Lausanne.

EIGHTEEN

The train from Interlaken traveled with maddening slowness, and Farrell twisted impatiently in his seat, oblivious to the beauty of the little valley through which they climbed. A clear brook, glittering with the cold sparkle of autumn in the mountains, paralleled the track. Although the lower slopes remained green, snow began a few hundred yards up and thickened to a year-round white mass at the peaks. The air was so crisp it felt brittle.

The houses were like chalets in a fairy tale, precisely painted, the yards perfectly maintained. People moved briskly about their business, a no-nonsense attitude clear in their manner and faces, and Farrell remembered the growled comment of an Englishman with a cast in his eye who had struck up a conversation while they sipped beers in the Interlaken *bahnhof,* waiting for their respective trains:

"So you're bound for the heart of *Schwyzerdeutsch* country, eh? Coldest bloody people on earth. Nazi sympathizers during the war, you know."

316

At last the train stopped in Grindelwald. Farrell trudged up a hill and walked into the first hotel of any size, a huge old edifice that advertised the name Regina in letters a yard tall. Inside the elegant lobby, he suffered the contemptuous glances of the full-faced desk clerk at his haggard appearance and single piece of luggage, a leather garment bag beaten and stained from years of use. He had not anticipated this extra phase of his journey, and had not brought either enough clothes or a warm coat for the chilly mountain air.

He paid in advance, an outrageous rate for the in-between season, and was led by an unctuous Italian bellboy to a second-story room just large enough for a bed, a desk, and a sink. A single tiny window overlooked the hotel's expansive back lawn, swimming pool, and tennis courts, all shrouded in disuse with the approach of winter. Farrell realized that he should complain, but simply did not care enough. He gave the bellboy five American dollars and instructions to bring him ice, and went to stare vacantly out the window. There, he tried to force his exhausted brain to decide how to proceed.

He had found the LaTour Academy in Lausanne without trouble, but had been curtly informed that the headmistress at the time of Selena's tenure there, a Frau Holzmann, had retired. Learning her address had been more troublesome; the secretary with whom he dealt was cold, overbearing, and intractable.

But as he was about to surrender in discouragement, the new headmistress returned, and upon learning the reason he had invented for his visit—that Selena was suffering from severe emotional problems, and he was a psychiatrist trying to gather information on her background—invited him into her office. She was a French woman named Maillot, and she agreed—after examining Farrell's identification, and obviously being impressed both by the fact that he was a physician and that Selena's family was able to go to such expense—to check the records.

Selena's transfer out, at age ten, was verified; but Frau Holzmann, usually meticulous in her descriptions of such incidents, had stated only that the student expressed a strong wish to be elsewhere. Shortly after that she had retired, leaving both the academy and Lausanne. Like the secretary, Mme. Maillot was reluctant to divulge her address; but Farrell's obvious weariness and sincerity finally moved her.

"I'm afraid it won't do you much good," she had said, handing him a card with the Grindelwald address. "From what I understand, she doesn't receive visitors. *Bonne chance.*"

Then had come the endless train ride. During those hours, his sense of the absurdity of this mission, of the fact that in reality, he was only pacifying himself with the same sort of nonexistent hopes he had all too often seen dying patients clutch at—that his life was, in effect, over—had become like a razor in his mind, cutting the meaning out of everything he had ever done and been.

A tap came at the door, and the bellboy entered with a leather ice bucket. He lingered after Farrell's murmured thanks, and Farrell wondered what was on his mind: another tip? The offer of a woman? Or even of himself? He was young, eighteen or twenty, with jet black curly

318

hair, smooth olive skin, and sloe eyes that could have belonged to a faun. Farrell repeated the thanks firmly and closed the door.

From his bag, he took the liter of Glenlivet Scotch he had bought at the duty-free shop in Orly. He had discovered that three or four drinks would help him sleep for a few hours, before he awoke in fear that the dreams were about to begin again. But without the alcohol, be could not sleep at all, and he could not countenance the idea of stronger drugs, lest another nightmare find him helpless to defend himself. The long-term result was a haziness of mind, a grainy quality to his perception, the result of exhaustion coupled with being either slightly drunk or hung over virtually all the time.

How could he get this stern, elderly German Swiss woman, who received no visitors, to see him?

What good would it do him if she did?

He stretched out on the bed and closed his eyes, leaving the drink half-finished. The afternoon light in the room was gray and soothing. But even as sleep began to settle over him, a wary inner guardian warned it away. For minutes, the battle went on, his fatigued body and mind yearning to yield, but controlled by a vigilant sense of self-preservation that had known too much panic during the past weeks.

Wearily, he sat up. He could continue swallowing Scotch until it overpowered his defenses, catch two or three hours of restless slumber, then awaken half-drunk, disoriented, and facing a sleepless night; or he could go out and begin this probably rewardless task.

He rose, washed his face and brushed his teeth, and put on the tweed coat and tie that were his only pretense to respectability. Then he walked through the Regina's lobby onto the main street of Grindelwald, looking for Frau Holzmann's cottage.

He found it without trouble. Not wanting his business known at the hotel, he wandered into cafés and taverns until he found an English-speaking bartender who was less frosty than the others; and, with carefully casual questions, learned the approximate location. From there, it was a matter of following the main street past the last of the chalets, through a series of small meadows, and finally into a forest that grew increasingly dark and close as the little valley narrowed into a steep mountain canyon. Grindelwald, he thought: Grendel's Wood. Yes, the monster would have been at home here.

At last he came to it, perhaps a mile out of town: a small A-frame chalet of dark wood, immaculately kept like all the others, with a distinctly unwelcoming picket fence and gate. Alone in its clearing, surrounded by tall conifers, it seemed ludicrously like the old witch's gingerbread house in Hansel and Gretel.

He hesitated, trying to see into the windows. There were no lights and no signs of activity. Finally he braved the gate to knock on the door, half expecting a big St. Bernard to bound snarling from the back of the house. But nothing moved in the early evening stillness, made twilight by the tall thick trees. His knocks went unanswered.

So, what? Camp out on the doorstep until she returned? For all he knew, she might be out of town, or even out of the country. She could be gone for days, or forever. She could be dead. After twenty minutes of growing discomfort in the darkening woods, he started unhappily back down the path to town. He could only try again in the morning.

He had gone perhaps a half-mile when he saw a figure approaching. His heartbeat quickened. It was a woman, elderly but walking briskly, wearing a wool shawl and carrying a net market sack. When she got close, he could make out her clear eyes and stern, gaunt features.

"*Guten abend,*" she said firmly, without pausing in her stride.

"*Guten abend,*" he repeated, and stood helplessly, already intimidated, as she passed. Then he blurted out, "Excuse me, are you by chance Frau Holzmann?"

She turned, her face now wary, even hostile, and she stared back at him without answering. It occurred to him that she might not speak English; but as the former head of an international school, that was unlikely; and in any case, she would certainly have caught the name.

"Frau Holzmann?" he said again, projecting all the sincerity and politeness he possessed into his voice.

"And who are you?" she demanded. The words were clear, with only a trace of accent.

"My name is Gene Farrell," he said, and remembering his experience at the academy, added immediately, "I'm a doctor, a psychiatrist, from the United States. I have a patient named Selena Clermont–"

At the sound of the name, she recoiled visibly, her eyes widening, then instantly going hard again.

"She's having severe emotional problems," he continued quickly. "We don't know much about her background, she moved around a great deal, and I hope you wouldn't mind spending a few minutes talking with me–"

"I am retired," she interrupted brusquely. "I do not wish to discuss my former occupation, or students, with anyone. Kindly excuse me."

She started walking again, and he hurried after her, jumping in front of her to block her way.

"Please, it's extremely urgent, we're afraid for her life. Won't you help just for a few minutes?"

"Young man," she said evenly, "if you do not move immediately out of my way, I will call the police."

Farrell tried to detect a hint of softness in those glacial blue eyes. There was none. He stepped back. She brushed by him and strode on.

For seconds, he stood unmoving. Then he whirled and shouted after her:

"Okay, it's not *her* that's in trouble, it's me! I don't know what she did, but it's killing me! For Christ sake, won't you help?"

Frau Holzmann's stride might have faltered, or he might have imagined it. But she continued on, and soon was lost in the gloom of the forest.

He walked slowly back to the hotel, hardly aware of the near-freezing chill the evening was bringing.

In his room, he automatically reached for the bottle. The hotel's yard was dark now, the remaining twilight lost in the shadow of the huge mountain at whose foot the building stood. Nearby rose the giant mountain, the

322

Eiger. Grendel and the Ogre, he thought. It seemed grimly apropos.

Although he had eaten only a meager breakfast, he could not entertain the thought of food. It seemed superfluous, silly. Instead, he drank, thinking of nothing, letting his mind toy with absurd practicalities. No trains left the village until morning. The nearest airport of any size was Geneva. It would probably be forty-eight hours before he could reach home.

There, he could decide what to do with the remaining days of his life.

He was pouring his fourth Scotch, the bottle almost half empty, when a tap came at the door. Expecting the bellboy, he opened it, and stood stunned at the sight of the elderly woman, wrapped tightly in her shawl, her eyes, at last, giving evidence of a battle that conscience had won.

"I have always thought someone would come," she said. She turned and began her brisk stride down the hall. Farrell grabbed his coat, slammed the door, and trotted after her.

The front room of her cottage was precisely as he would have expected: an oval coffee table on which rested neat stacks of chaste publications, the European equivalents of *Sunset* and *Ladies' Home Journal;* an old pine cupboard displaying hand-painted plates; a couch and pair of overstuffed chairs. Floor, walls, and ceiling were all of wood. On the mantel above the huge stone fireplace, an elaborately carved cuckoo clock seemed almost like a parody, a finishing touch to the stock Swiss chalet. Every last article was precisely ordered and immaculate.

The rapid walk to the cottage through the chilly night, together with adrenaline, had made him forget both fatigue and the lethargy of alcohol. Frau Holzmann had not spoken at all, and had discouraged his attempts to start a conversation by shaking her head, leaving him seething with anxiety. Hardly pausing when they entered, she tossed her shawl on a chair and knelt to stoke the modest fire. Then she said, "Come," and led him through a door into a back room.

This was so different from the front his mouth opened. Bookshelves lined the walls floor to ceiling, stuffed with volumes, many of them old and leather-bound. An enormous wooden desk looked suspiciously like it had come from a school. On it were an old manual typewriter, a scattering of papers and notes, and a half dozen books. A couple were open, one to a page of what looked like alchemical symbols. He half-expected to see a skull, perhaps resting beside a guttered black candle. A large window overlooked the forest glade that served as the cottage's back yard, dark and forbidding, and Farrell shivered at its similarity to the field behind his house.

"Sit," she said, motioning him to a straight-backed wooden chair that looked, like the desk, to be a relic from an earlier era of education: as if it had been designed to keep students' attention from wavering. She sat on another, facing him, hands in her lap, spine erect; and for most of a minute, she said nothing, only studied his face. Her own was unreadable.

Then, exhaling, she said, "So. You have slept with her."

It was not a question. Farrell nodded.

"And now you feel you are in danger."

He nodded again.

"Very well. Let me make tea, and then we will talk."

In the few minutes that she was gone, he did his best to put his anxiety on hold. Automatically, he examined the contents of the bookshelves. Although the titles were in German, French, or Latin, it was clear that most were related to the occult.

Frau Holzmann returned with a silver tea service on a tray. He accepted a cup gratefully; even with the fire in the other room, the cottage was cold.

"Do you wonder at my books?" she said, gesturing at the collection.

"I've never seen any like them."

"Many are quite rare. I have invested much of the money my husband left me, and a great deal of effort, in acquiring them. Until a few years back, I dismissed all such thinking as idiocy, the lowest sort of superstition. Undoubtedly, most of it is."

"*Most?*"

She did not answer. Her eyes seemed softer now, as did her voice. "Ten me what has happened to you."

Haltingly, Farrell described his night with Selena and the resulting dreams.

"I can't fight it off again," he finished wearily.

"I suppose I am fortunate to be a woman," she murmured. "You are not the first man to have fallen into this trouble, I fear. She was very lovely, *ja*–even as a girl.

"Very well, I will tell you what I know. It is little enough. But it brought me to"– her hand swept the room, indicating the books and manuscript–"this."

Farrell poured another cup of the strong tea, and hunched forward, forcing his tired brain to listen and absorb.

"In Lausanne, there was a banker," she began. "His name was Steicher. He was very wealthy. He had sent two daughters through the academy, and maintained a close connection, donating money regularly. He kept a vacation home on Lac Leman, and when his daughters were in school, he made a practice of inviting one or another of their friends to spend some time there. After his daughters grew up, he continued this, always choosing girls who came from far away–who were boarders. These girls were always pretty. Nubile.

"This had been going on for some years before I came to take over the academy. I disliked the practice immediately. It was acceptable while his daughters were in school, but not afterward. I did not care for the man, either; he was smug, self-satisfied, the worse kind of German. His wife was a poor, frail creature he had brow-beaten almost into nonexistence. But there was nothing I could do–he gave too much money, was too influential, and I was a newcomer. Further, there had never been any evidence of wrongdoing, although at least two girls had left the school soon after vacationing with him and his wife. It is my belief that all of them were either bribed or frightened into silence.

"Then Selena arrived. She was nine years old, maturing early, and an extraordinary mixture of woman and child. I was there when Herr Steicher first saw her. He could not take his eyes off her, and his delight was apparent when he learned that she was not only from America, but an orphan. To no surprise, she was invited to the vacation home.

"She was a quiet child anyway. Of course it was natural that she would keep to herself upon first arriving at a strange school, but it soon became clear that this aloofness was deliberate. She would not allow others to become close to her, and her ways of maintaining this distance suggested very sophisticated. thinking. I had noted in her records that there had been dismissals from other schools earlier in her life, and I was prepared for rebelliousness. On the contrary, she was a model student, obedient and very bright—only cold. Later, I began to consolidate these impressions, and I believe I now understand her reasons for being as she was.

"She did not wish to go to Steicher's, but the invitation from such an influential man was more a command.

"Then when she came back, her quiet had hardened into anger, a silent fierce resentment. It was not the fury of a little girl, or even the sort one usually encounters from adults: more the deep-seated brooding of someone who has suffered an irreparable injury, a wrong that can never be put right. This change in her gave weight to my suspicions about the man, and I tried to get her to talk to me, but she would say nothing. Even back then, before I ever thought of any of this"—her hand again indicated the shelves of books—"she made me think of Milton's Satan, too proud to yield to the enormous injustice he believed he had suffered."

She was staring beyond him as if gazing into the past. Her hand groped for her empty teacup. Farrell rose quickly and filled it.

"And then?" he said, sitting.

She shrugged. "Steicher died." Her voice had gone flat and harsh. "Less than two weeks after they returned from the 'vacation.' He rushed out of his house late one night and apparently made a mad run through the city, At last he fell, or threw himself, under a train. His wife said he had been tormented by nightmares, increasing in intensity. They involved pursuit. And, yes," she added quietly, "although I did not realize this until later, it was the night when the moon was at its darkest."

For half a minute, neither spoke. Then he said, not believing it himself, "It could be coincidence."

She shook her head slowly. "It happened twice more that I know of. Both times, in the moon's dark. Both times, to men like Steicher, vile enough to debauch a little girl." Her gaze rose to meet his. "But, you see, these other men did not seduce her. She seduced them."

Farrell stood and walked to the window. "In other words, she'd learned what she could do, and she started hunting."

"That is the only conclusion I could come to. I had been watching her carefully, you see, and I alone made the connection between her and these men. No one else even noticed that there was contact, but I had seen her at social events with the community, talking with them. It was innocent enough on the surface, but I detected her flirting, with a sophistication far beyond her years—deliberately arousing their interest. Why she chose them in particular, I do not know. Perhaps she sensed, as children do, that ugly, hidden side to them.

"I have come to believe that this deadly power had followed her all her life, that it was the reason she had been forced to leave her earlier schools. That as a child, she had no control over it. Perhaps it preyed especially on those she cared for, and this was the cause of her aloofness.

"But she learned to hide such incidents, to dissociate herself from them if she could not prevent them. Then, after she was seduced by Steicher, she realized that, in some way we cannot understand, she could direct this evil to men."

"She didn't stop there," Farrell said. "When she got too old to interest the child molesters, she started after criminals."

"Yes? And why, then, did she choose a doctor, a seemingly pleasant man? Do you also hide evil secrets in your heart?"

"No," he said ruefully. "I'm not interesting enough to be evil. She tried to keep me away. I finally—more or less raped her."

"Raped her? Or were only firm?'"

He turned, surprised to hear such words from a woman he had automatically pegged as old and sexless. Her gaze was calm, direct, and he had a sudden vision of her in her youth, flaxen-haired and sapphire-eyed, but forced to conceal passion beneath the prim exterior demanded by the times—yet probably understanding much more about the ways of the sexes than he ever would.

"You do not seem like any rapist to me," she said.

329

He nodded, a silent gesture of thanks. "What happened finally?" he said. "Between you and Selena."

She gazed down into her teacup, lips compressed. "This is what is difficult for me to think about," she said. "It is why I did not at first wish to speak to you. Sometimes, in the light of day, I still think my mind must have played a trick on me, or that old age has destroyed my memory." She shook her head. "But the truth is, I know perfectly well what happened, and it fits with the other events: the deaths of those men—"

She paused, and Farrell said, "And with what's happening to me."

She nodded. When she continued, her voice was low. "I confronted her. I told her I had seen her with those men, that I knew what she was doing—only not how. I threatened to bring the matter to the police if she would not tell me. There might be no link established to their deaths, I said, but it would come out that she was a little harlot.

"Those were the words I used; little harlot. It is to my undying shame that I did what people so often do: when a child is misused, blame the child. It was I who should never have allowed her to go with Steicher to begin with.

"So. She became furious. 'Very well,' she said. 'If you wish to know, I will show you.'"

Frau Holzmann had hunched into herself, hands clasping her teacup in her lap. "Suddenly, I was aware that there was something else in the room with us. What it was—if it was one being or many—I do not know. I never saw anything." Her gaze rose, an element of pleading in it, a request not to be dismissed as insane. "But I assure

330

you, Herr Doktor, I felt it. Not only the presence itself, which terrified me almost into paralysis. Something began biting me, tearing at my skin. It was like having the flesh ripped off my bones with red-hot pincers."

She was shaking, and he went to her, placing a comforting hand on her shoulder. Her hand covered his. After a moment, she began again.

"How long it lasted, I do not know. Seconds, perhaps minutes. I know I screamed. It was late afternoon in my office; I had deliberately waited for a time when no one else would be there. I remember thinking that this torment could go on forever—until I died.

"But it stopped. When I recovered my senses, I was crouched and cowering in a corner. I of course stared in horror at my arms, expecting them to be ruined. But my skin was unbroken, unbruised. Selena watched me, very calm, very controlled—not at all like a child.

"She then told me that she had no intention of explaining anything to me. She did not want any longer to stay at the academy, and demanded that I arrange an immediate transfer to a school in Aix-en-Provence. Further, I had best not breathe a word of what had happened.

"I arranged the transfer next morning. Within a few weeks, she was gone. I submitted a resignation soon after, and at the end of the year, bought this house and began to accumulate my library. Until this moment, I have kept my promise not to speak of her.

"For long, I feared that she would appear someday to take further revenge for my hasty words and harsh treatment. But I have come to believe that she is, in the main, innocent—the victim of a terrible curse—and that she only used such power as she showed me in order to protect herself.

"That, and—after she learned what she was capable of—to destroy men such as Steicher."

She released Farrell's hand. He returned to his chair.

"There's reason to believe," he said, "that her father was—not human."

Frau Holzmonn nodded. "I had suspected something of the sort."

"I read her grandfather's diary. He seemed to believe that he'd been seduced by a demon, or spirit. He ran into it at a pagan ruin in France—did something crazy, like signed his name in blood. And then it attacked his daughter."

"Yes. In ancient times, such a thing was held to be not uncommon. Many figures in history—Alexander, Nero, Attila, even Luther—were said to have been the products of such unions. Of course, this was almost certainly slander by their enemies.

"But who can say? When a person who is ignorant of such things begins to tamper with them, the consequences may be far beyond what he has bargained for. This is in the nature of evil: to seduce the unwary, until they have gone too far."

Farrell swiveled and scanned the many shelves of books. "You've read them all?"

"Yes."

"Is there anything that gives you any idea as to what a man in my situation might do?"

She sighed. "Most of what is in them is, to a greater or lesser degree, absurd. There is, I think, no help there. If it were in the nature of possession, or a curse, there might be the possibility of exorcism, or of some other means to lift it. But I suspect that in truth, it is not. It is more like an evil reversal of nature: she has impregnated you, spiritually rather than physically. When the child comes forth–"

He shivered, remembering his dreams. "Why hasn't it happened yet?" he said, rising from the chair. "Why have I lasted as long as I have? It's almost like whatever it is is deliberately trying to drag it out."

"I think you are, comparatively speaking, an innocent. That gives you a sort of resistance to this evil seed. Perhaps the doom of the others was speeded by the darkness in their hearts. Imagine how your own madness would swell if it was compounded by constant awareness of the evil acts you had committed–and must soon pay for."

"But I *did* commit an evil act. Maybe I didn't exactly rape her, but she tried to stop me. I mean, thanks for trying to let me off the hook, but it was my fault."

"Yes? And after I told you of what happened to me, do you think she could *not* have stopped you if she had wished?"

Farrell stared at her, stunned.

"You see," Frau Holzmann said quietly, "she used you. What her reasons were, I cannot know. But there is no doubt that what she did, she did deliberately; and unless you are hiding an evil you have not told me about, then she can only have sold you in order to gain something for herself."

He slumped again into his chair.

"Do you know the myth of Selena and Endymion?" Frau Holzmann said. "She was a moon goddess who fell in love with a handsome young shepherd. She cast a spell on him so that he would sleep forever, belonging always to her. Many myths are metaphors for deeper truths. In casting that spell, she as well as killed him, did she not?"

"But she did it out of love," he said helplessly.

Frau Holzmann shrugged, "What does that matter to him?" She paused, letting the words sink in. "You have asked me for advice. Only one possibility occurs, to me: she must die before you do."

Slowly, he raised his head. "You mean kill her?"

"A terrible thought, I know. Perhaps it would not even succeed. But those who profess to know about such things hold that demonic forces are ultimately mercenary, without loyalty: prepared, even eager, to turn on those who have controlled. them. It may be that her blood would satisfy them, and they would no longer torment you."

He tried to imagine pointing a gun at her, pulling the trigger as he gazed into her lovely eyes: watching them dim, then go out, forever. Or holding her, struggling, by the throat, crushing it with all his strength while her features grew distorted and pale, and at last her thrashing stopped.

He shook his head. "Even if I could find her," he said softly, "I could never do it."

"Then," said Frau Holzmann, "she has murdered you."

NINETEEN

He bought the gun in Reno, in a secondhand store near the railroad yards, on an early November afternoon heavy with incipient rain. The man behind the counter had the bloodshot eyes and purple nose of a drinker, and watched Farrell as if he remembered him and still held a grudge about something that had never happened. Farrell pretended to be interested in the entire row of weapons on display, and moved slowly back and forth along the glass counter a couple of times. But he had seen immediately the one he wanted: the one that would do. It was a Smith & Wesson .41 magnum with a six-inch barrel, and looked clean and relatively new.

"Hardly been fired," the storekeeper agreed. "Fella'd just bought it when he got laid off. It ain't your best concealed weapon, but it sure packs a punch." Farrell hefted it and spun the cylinder, allowed himself to look grudgingly satisfied, and signed a statement swearing that he was not convicted of or under indictment for a felony and did not intend to use the weapon to commit a crime. He laid four one-hundred-dollar bills on the counter, and received the pistol and thirty-three dollars change.

"Good piece to have around the house for protection," the storekeeper said, watching him. "Guy can't be too careful these days."

"I know what you mean," Farrell said, and pushed past the jingling doorbell out into the street.

He drove slowly through the seedy part of the old cow town, parallel to the tracks, past the cheap hotels and taverns and pawnshops that thrived most when everything else was going under. The thin layer of asphalt paving had worn off in places and his wheels rumbled on brick. Three men with matted hair, dirty jeans, and bedrolls over their shoulders were crossing the street ahead. One stepped aggressively in front of the truck, but jumped out of the way when Farrell did not swerve. He glanced at the man as he passed, and saw a vacant, weathered face, a mouth cracked in a leer that showed stumps of brown teeth. Look in their eyes, he thought, the answer was the same: nobody home, come back next lifetime.

Had it always been like that, or was he only now beginning to notice?

He chose a bar for no particular reason and parked in front. As he stepped out, a beat-up, early-seventies vintage Chrysler of faded green turned the corner and passed slowly by, muffler clattering on the pavement, while the several Mexicans inside looked him over. A block down, a fat, middle-aged woman in red stretch pants was crossing the street, carrying a Frisbee. The air was strangely warm, wet, and sultry, the sky a leaden gray. He pushed open the bar's heavy scarred door.

The place had the look of one of the old railroad taverns where the pensioners drank up their checks while their women hugged glasses of gin and quarreled. It reeked of smoke. The row of faces at the bar swung automatically to size him up, faces lined and drawn with drink and weather and rough living. Hairlines carried the mark of hats, hard or cowboy, military or railroad, the men had worn all their lives. When their narrowed. eyes registered him, the interest in them went out as quickly as it had sprung up, and the conversations–querulous, drunken voices arguing endlessly about things that had long ago lost any importance for anyone–began again. Against one wall, an emaciated man slumped snoring. Beer from an overturned bottle dripped on his knee. Farrell ordered a Wild Turkey on the rocks and took it to a table in the corner.

As the moon had peaked and then dwindled, he had begun, with clinical detachment, to plan out the mechanics of the coming event with the same sort of methodical foresight he had brought to the practice of medicine. The shotgun, he decided, would be awkward and unreliable for his purposes. He could not envision putting the barrel in his mouth and trying to fire it with his toe. California law was full of strictures on handgun purchases which he had not the time or patience to deal with, so he had decided to make the few-hour drive to Nevada.

It had also been something to do besides wait.

The drunk against the wall reared up abruptly and slammed his fist on his table, making the overturned bottle jump.

"Fuck a bunch of child support," he croaked, and swiveled to glare around the room before letting his head sink back onto his arms.

Farrell stared into his glass, the amber miniscus like a lens that magnified and distorted the human wreckage around him: people once clean and strong and full of hope become fading drunks, eyeing each other blearily over rotgut liquor in a seamy bar. It was a forgotten, improbable room in hell, where they could hide and never have to fight again, where the only change they would ever know was diminishment, where they could succumb to the wonderful relief of admitting, once and for all, defeat.

He had never dreamed he would one day join them.

Across the room, a rotund man wearing a salmon-colored leisure suit that looked like it had come from a bargain basement fifteen years before and not left his body since, ambled to the jukebox and thrust a quarter in the slot. The strains of a country song began to thread their way through the harsh, hacking voices. Farrell could not name it, but he had heard it before: another chapter in the endless saga of broken love.

Whatever faint hope he might have had that it was not going to happen–that he would be spared–had vanished. The disturbances had begun already: the moving objects, the sense of unseen presences. And the dreams. There had been a kaleidoscope of images over the past nights, each sufficing to bring him awake

339

sweating and trying to cry out. He would hear the sound of something dragging, slowly and heavily, across the floor toward him, and thrash his way to consciousness, only to find his room empty of anything tangible but thick with the familiar menace.

Empty until last night, when a shadowy shape had leaned over the bed, laying its clawlike, tendoned hand on his shoulder, and the grip had remained while he struggled into wakefulness. There was no one there, but his bathrobe was lying in a crumpled pile on the floor beside him, where he knew he had not left it.

In his exhaustion, the distinction between dream and reality, sleep and waking, had grown blurred. One night, he had raised his head from uneasy slumber on his couch to see several small grotesque figures outside his porch window, and had leaped to his feet and run screaming down the hall—only to realize, minutes later, that they were children, trick-or-treating on Halloween.

And finally, the moon had disappeared.

If his figuring was correct, he had two nights left.

He stood, unnoticed in the sodden raucousness of the bar, and left as quietly as he had come.

Outside, the rain had started, a light warm drizzle that was a relief from the sullen, unyielding clouds. He put the truck in gear and eased out into traffic. At the first liquor store he saw, he stopped and bought a bottle of whiskey. A sporting-goods store sold him a box of shells.

As the afternoon waned, he was on Interstate 80, climbing out of the Nevada desert onto Donner Pass.

The mist deepened as he reached the mountains and he savored it as if it were a blanket of protection, isolating him from the traffic around him: from harm. It lent a surreal sense to the expanses of dense forest and clean granite he saw when the clouds parted. The summer had been long and dry. It was good to see rain once more. In the high mountains, there would probably be snow.

He found the turnoff without trouble, an exit road a little way past Truckee. A few miles farther along, he pulled into a campground that gave access to the Desolation Wilderness, where he had roamed more than once during his college days. The name was fitting. Only a few other vehicles were parked at the trailhead. At this time of year, on a weekday, it was unlikely that he would encounter anyone. He wanted to make certain that the pistol worked.

He put it and the whiskey in a rucksack, wrapped in a sweatshirt so they would not clank together. Then he started up the trail into the mist-shrouded forest. The air was colder at this altitude, and the backs of his hands began to get numb from the faint fine drizzle. He thrust them in his pockets and quickened his pace. There was nothing like freezing rain to work the chill in deep. Broken jack timber surrounded him, the dead barkless limbs glistening gray. Dry, they would be the color of bone.

It was just twilight when he arrived at the place he remembered; a rocky promontory jutting out over a canyon whose floor lay a steep several hundred feet below. He had camped here in the past, and chose it now because it was a good mile off the main trail; the sound of the gunfire, especially shrouded by the close clouds, was unlikely to attract attention. He spread his gear at the rock's outer edge.

Then he loaded the pistol with six fat rounds, pushing them in one at a time, taking a grim satisfaction in the weapon's precise metallic locks and clicks. He faced the canyon and sighted on a stump outlined clearly against the darkening sky. The pistol's feel was heavy and unfamiliar. He lowered it, breathed deeply, and raised it again with both hands. Slowly, he squeezed.

The whump jarred his shoulders and pounded his ears. A fist-sized chunk exploded out of the stump, clattering like a frightened rodent down the stony cliffside.

So: the gun worked, and it had not blown up in his face.

He touched off three more rounds, gauging the error of the sights; compensating a little high and to the right, blasting the stump to a honeycomb. It was a final absurd vanity. He had always been a good shot.

On the fourth—the last but one—he turned to a tree only a few yards away. Jaw tight, he spent thirty seconds imagining Selena Clermont's face before pulling the trigger. It dissolved into shattering bark.

When the muffled echoes had died in the canyon's void, he turned the cylinder so the final round was in the next position back from firing, so it could not go off accidentally if dropped. Then he heaved the box of shells far down into the deadfall, and as it crashed through the brittle branches, he thought about how death was often seen as a solution, but it was not. It was only an ending;

and after what he had seen that night cowering in the hospital closet, he could not even be certain of that.

He found dry wood and made a small fire. Then he wrapped his jacket tight around himself and sat, gazing down into the now-dark canyon, the whiskey bottle held between his legs.

In the weeks since his return from Switzerland, he had thought a great deal about all that Frau Holzmann had told him. Most of it, at this point, was academic. Only one matter of importance remained: her conviction that Selena had betrayed him—somehow sold him off for her own purpose. At first, the thought had maddened him, and he had refused to accept it. The thin thread that kept him from cracking completely had been the belief that she had cared for him, and whatever her reasons for leaving, they had not involved indifference to his fate.

But as the days passed, and he began to awaken in the aftermath of struggling nightmares, the hard reality had sunk in. There was, simply, no other explanation.

Until that acceptance, he had not blamed Selena even for killing him; would have forgiven her with his last breath. He would have done anything to have again a moment like the one that came back most frequently to his memory, when, after one of the times they had made love, he had held her face in his hands and stared into her eyes. Something had passed between them—some mysterious communication, a knowledge of each other so intimate and profound that his whole being seemed to swell with light. But it was precisely that which was now his greatest agony. His love had turned to hatred, not for the horror. she had brought on him, not even for taking his life, but for deliberately having used him.

Yes, he thought, he could pull the trigger now. But he would never have the chance. He would spend his last minutes alone, and it was his own brain that would take the bullet.

The embers of the fire had burned low. He rose, stiff and cold, and stamped them out carefully. He took his last drink of whiskey, and heaved the bottle over the cliff to join the bullets.

Then he shouldered the rucksack and started home, steeling himself against panic from the shapes he sensed accompanying him: promising him, with whispering sibilant voices he heard only in his mind, that this time they would have their way.

TWENTY

For the third month, Gene Farrell found himself walking, in the not-time of dreams, to the now familiar amphitheater. Again, the unseen presences accompanied his unwilling steps through the dark misty woods. But this time, he sensed them gloating, as if they knew that the final act in this ghostly drama was soon to come. As before, he descended through the upright stones to the glade's dark center. There, with mounting dread, he waited.

He became aware that the sky had turned into a vast hemispherical mirror, suffusing a strange somber light. No matter where he looked, he could see only his own reflected face, and he understood that he must go close and peer into it.

This was the moment when his waking self began to struggle for supremacy, but whatever held him kept its grip firm. Groaning with fear, he moved forward a slow step at a time, watching the images of his face grow huge all around him.

Then he leaned close and stared into his own eyes, magnified immeasurably by the dream mirror, and there, at last, he began to see the shape of what he had given birth to, crawling eagerly forward from his infinite reflections.

Rooted with horror, he stood helpless, lost among his own images, no longer able to distinguish his true self from them. He could not tell whether the creature was crawling into or out of him. He not only did not know how to save himself, but what to save.

When he finally came awake, thrashing and sobbing, there was the same lurching sense of that straying part of him plunging back into his body at the last instant. Gradually, he came to the awareness of his surroundings. He was on his front porch, fully clothed. Most of the lights in the house were on. Trembling, he got up, hurried to the kitchen, and started a pot of coffee.

He had stayed awake that evening, remaining outside, stretching his last full night on earth–trying to understand as much as he could of the life he had lived before it ended. But at some unknown point, sleep had come and taken him with both force and stealth.

He did not remember even feeling drowsy.

He stepped into the bathroom to splash water on his face, avoiding the mirror. But it drew him irresistibly, and on his way out the door, he turned back and leaned slowly forward.

This time, not even light could banish the tiny twin images in his eyes, wriggling with their obscene menace.

With shaking hands, he hung a towel over the mirror, and for the hundredth time, went to check that the pistol, with its single bullet, was where he had left it.

Then he poured a cup of coffee and waited for dawn of his last day.

TWENTY-ONE

He entered the field at sundown, with a canteen of water and the pistol, and sat cross-legged in the center. The evening was exquisitely clear. As the hours passed, he watched the western sky turn from gold to a deepening blue to a velvety shade somewhere between black and purple. The stars glittered like hard, cold jewels: presences he had come to think of as the only witnesses to his execution.

Inside the house, in a box marked "To Be Opened On My Death" were letters to his mother and father, and to Valerie. They said nothing about his reasons, only tried to explain how much each one had meant to him. Writing them had been oddly satisfying. He knew that he should have seen them or at least called—heard their voices once more—but he had not trusted himself to speak.

His exhaustion was forgotten in mounting adrenaline: ironically, he felt more alive than he could ever remember. His mind resisted the temptation to wander to the thousand things he was leaving behind—the emotion of love, the taste of the cool clear water he sipped, sunlight—and remained fixed on the moment when he would first see the furrow parting the grass. He touched the revolver's cold smooth barrel. He was determined to bear it as long as he could.

Time passed. The stars revolved in their eternal rounds. When his watch told him it was close to midnight, he stood, his straining eyes scanning the treeline, his heart beginning to pound.

At last, he detected movement at the field's edge.

His grip tightened on the gun. Hot blood rushed to his face. For seconds, it was all he could do to keep from turning and fleeing in panicked, weeping abandon. But he waited, feet slightly apart, hands at his sides.

Then he realized that it was not the expected black menace approaching, but a human being.

Stunned, he watched Selena cross the field. She wore a long white gown, skirt held in one hand, as if she were a girl in Victorian England out to gather flowers in a meadow. When she was ten feet away from him, she stopped.

Farrell realized distantly that the night had gone absolutely still. The air he breathed was cool and heavy with the scent of grass. Her face was composed, her eyes unreadable.

"Did you come to watch?" he finally said. His voice was harsh but soft, an eerie half-whisper.

She neither moved nor spoke.

"You sold me out," he said, in the same ghostly tone.

Her head might have moved in a nod or shrug.

"*Why did you come here?!*"

Slowly, her hand rose to point at the pistol. Her face was pale in the starlight, serious as a child's. Somewhere in the forest beyond, an owl hooted, a sudden, alarmed sound.

"All right," he whispered.

As in a dream, he performed the motions he had envisioned: thumbing back the hammer, aiming, and slowly, carefully, exerting the tiny pressure of his finger that would burst her lovely face into a mass of bloody tissue.

Then his hand dropped, and he whirled and threw the gun as far as he could. Panting, fists clenched, he faced her, and amazement swelled to overcome his rage and terror. She was smiling.

"I had to know," she said.

Then her fingers touched her lips in an odd motion, almost as if she were blowing him a kiss, and she turned away from him to the treeline. Farrell's gaze followed, and adrenaline surged like an electric jolt through his blood as he saw the parting grass and accompanying swirl of shapes. This time they were coming hard and fast.

Selena began to walk toward them.

Farrell lunged, reaching to stop her, but again, that ripping talon tore into his consciousness. This time he seemed to rise swiftly into the air, watching the scene below: his own body writhing on the ground, her white figure moving toward the oncoming shapes—and that black malignancy at their center.

And as he stared, finally helpless to keep his gaze away from it, he seemed to see an unending pageant of nightmare taking place within its dark vortex. Mounted armies rode slaughtering into cities and built pyramids of skulls to a gaunt, sly-faced idol. Fire burst from the mouth and eyes of a giant stone statue, while screaming children were cast into the inferno of its belly. Priests wearing plumes and copper stood atop pyramids and tore the hearts from living victims, holding them aloft for the roaring crowds below to see.

Behind it all danced a towering dark figure with a necklace of shrieking heads, its eyes pools of black raging hunger, moving among men and women of all races and times, talons slicing, dismembering, creating an endless river of bright blood that cascaded into the night, while the infinite hordes of shadowy creatures that followed howling in its wake descended to drink.

Into the center of that maelstrom Selena strode, and then the blackness inside him burst like a vast wave, crushing his senses and sweeping him away.

He awoke to the sound of birdsong. The graying sky in the east heralded dawn. For seconds he lay unmoving, stiff and cold, his face wet with dew, not comprehending where he was or what had happened.

Then it came back, and he scrabbled on his knees to the still white shape lying in the field. He gripped her wrist and put his ear to her breast, but knew, even as he acted, that it was useless.

He rocked back on his heels and crouched motion-less, too numb for grief, while the world around him opened into sunny vibrant life. Then his gaze caught an object in the grass a few feet away. Slowly, he picked it up.

It was a small silver vial that might have held perfume. A moment passed before he realized that what in fact was in it was congealing blood.

EPILOGUE

It was spring, and the south of France was in bloom. Lavender, hyacinth, and evergreens filled the evening with fragrance. The fields were covered with blossoms of every color and description. The forest was lush and green, bursting with new life; trees lifted their red-tipped branches like fingers in supplication to the sky.

Gene Farrell made his way unhurriedly through the woods, stopping now and then to listen to the trill of a nightingale, or just to drink in the sweet scent of the air. Though the forest was unfamiliar and the path hard to find, he felt no fear.

Since the previous autumn, his nights had been unthreatened by menace.

But he did not need the mirrors that no longer held terror for him to know that the man who looked back now was different: harder, older beyond measure; a man who rarely laughed.

A man who had been touched by evil.

The coroner's verdict had been death by massive stroke. There had been no trial or inquest. Farrell had said nothing about their meeting the previous evening: only that he had come out in the morning and found her in the field, dead. It was not that he was trying to protect himself, but that he had not wanted anyone else to know what had happened. It belonged to them alone.

What had kept him from suicide or outright insanity was his conviction that in that last instant before that black horror claimed her, he saw something silvery and shimmering, like a spirit of light, flit from her as quick as thought and flash away into the night.

During the months that had passed since then, he had come to understand that what she had taken from him was innocence, of the deepest and most profound kind. It had to do with his underlying conviction, never challenged because he had never known it existed, that things would always go his way; that he would always get what he wanted; that life would be essentially benign, if not to others, then to him.

In short, she had murdered him after all—or rather, that young man he had been. But in doing so, she had given birth to another self that was infinitely wiser, if also harder. And in that birth, she had sacrificed her life, as her own mother had sacrificed hers. Perhaps the second death had been, on some scale of justice hidden from human eyes, an atonement for the first.

What he would never know was whether she had done it more out of love for him or hatred of herself.

In some ways, he despised that younger, innocent—and ignorant—man. But there had been a beauty to him too: a goodness, a freshness, a yearning to improve the world around him, that was gone forever. Like the

354

memory of Selena herself, it continued to haunt him. What happened to those billions upon billions of past selves, remnants like shed skins of all existences since time's beginning, sloughed off from deaths not necessarily physical, still connected tenuously to the living and wandering like ghosts through the foggy labyrinths of memory, experience, lingering emotions?

What did you do when one of them touched your shoulder and assured you wordlessly that the only important matter of your life had come and gone?

All he was sure of, finally, was that she had been his other half: demonic and deadly, yes, but also vibrant, mysterious, alive in a way that reduced what he was left with to mere existence. He had found her and lost her in a bitterly brief time, and there was only one hope, faint and absurd, that he would ever find anything like her again—if only for a night, even at a price he could imagine all too well.

He stepped to the edge of a cliff and gazed down at the countryside below. Perhaps a half-mile farther, in the bottom of a canyon, the slender silver band of a river gleamed in the twilight. Above it stood a ruin that looked like a church or abbey. Directly beneath him, a few hundred yards up the cliffside from the crumbling stone arches, was a sheltered glade with upright stones that looked like rough pillars, forming a sort of natural amphitheater.

His fingers felt for the knife in his pocket—the knife he would use to offer his own blood to the dark goddess—and his eyes rose up to the moonless indigo evening sky. Then he began picking his way down the cliffside to the temple.

He would have been sure that this was the place he was searching for, even if he had not recognized it from Donald Clermont's description.

He had seen it before in dreams.

ACKNOWLEDGMENTS

Re-releasing these novels has only been possible with great support and expertise on many levels.

Next, After Lucifer owes a particular debt to three classic stories of the supernatural: "Canon Alberic's Scrap-Book" and "Count Magnus" by M. R. James, and "The Book" by Margaret Irwin.

On a more personal level, the major pillars of this undertaking consist of a Gang of Three:

As always, my wife, Kim, has been my mainstay, both for her technical skills and for keeping me relatively sane.

Jason Neal is the genius behind everything from the website and Facebook pages to cover design.

Prof. Lisa Simon has added indispensable advice on editing, content, and shaping the overall process.

We've managed to have a pretty good time together along the way.

My family—who never knew quite what to expect from me, but it definitely wasn't this—have been rock solid, with special thanks to my brother and his wife, Drs. Dan and Barbara McMahon.

Jennifer Rudolph Walsh, at William Morris Endeavor Entertainment, has been my guardian angel for more than a decade. Also at WME, Britton Schey launched the ebooks with swift competence; Claudia Ballard and Eric Zohn retrieved the rights for these new publications; and other colleagues have tirelessly promoted my work.

My terrific editors at HarperCollins, Carl Lennertz and Dan Conaway, along with their colleagues, gave me major support through critical years.

Going back in time to when the books first came out:

Prof. Ted Ahern, of Boston College, kindly provided all Latin translations.

Tom Dunne and Michael Carlisle were the editor and agent who made it happen.

Heartfelt thanks to all of you, and to the many other friends who helped along the way.

NEXT, AFTER LUCIFER

Ancient evil awakens in a rural French village, in the form of a Templar knight who was burned at the stake in the 14th century for practicing black magic. Now it's the 1980s, and his undead spirit, bent on possession of a human body, invades the lives of a wealthy American couple renting a nearby villa. A genuinely frightening story–not recommended for children.

"A well-turned tale of supernatural terror in which lurks one of the best–or worst–monstrous creations to come along in a month of Black Sabbaths." (Houston Chronicle, 1987)

ADVERSARY

A sequel to *Next, After Lucifer,* with the evil Templar, Guilhem de Courdeval, surfacing in San Francisco. He poses as a spiritual teacher and gathers disciples, using a seductive philosophy that quickly fulfills their desires and solves their problems. At first, it all seems innocent—until they realize that his true goal is to turn them into servants of evil, and they're in too deep to back out.

"A storyteller of exceptional depth . . . The story blends black magic and mystery within a tight plot. One of the real delights, though, is his talent for describing people and places in few words but rich detail." (Evening News, Norwich, England, 1989)

CAST ANGELS DOWN TO HELL

Baby Selena, conceived and born under sinister circumstances, grows up into a beauty–but she remains shadowed by eerie mystery. The only men she'll take as lovers are loathsome criminals and scum–and they all soon die, raving mad suicides. Still, no one suspects her hellish secret: she's part demon child, cursed to be followed by nightmarish "companions" that feast on the souls of the men she beds. Her human side hates what she's forced to do, and so far she's thwarted the companions by giving them only the rotten meat of corrupt souls. But now they're demanding a goodhearted young doctor who's smitten by her–and her strength to fight them off is exhausted.

"A stylish semisequel to *Next, After Lucifer* (1987) and *Adversary* (1988)... Supple, moody prose lends an aura of ancient mystery to the story . . . it's his best yet–a haunting work." (Publishers Weekly, 1990)